The Cradle Above the Abyss

By Anthony A. Policastro

FIRST EDITION

ISBN – 0615336779
EAN-13 – 978-0-615-33677-0

December 2009

Cover design by
Gary Val Tenuta
GVT Grafix
GVTgrafix@aol.com

This book is dedicated to the memory of
William and Theresa Policastro

Acknowledgments

It is with pleasure that I thank Trudie Martineau and Daphne Finnikin for their editing and copy editing services.

Anthony Samuel Policastro, founder of the Outer Banks Publishing Group, and the website The Writers Edge, with whom I've consulted and whose knowledge of the publishing industry is without bounds.

Finally, I would like to thank Loretta, my wife, life-long friend and companion for being my constant and loyal reader and for encouraging me to finish the book.

Part I—New York City

Chapter 1 - The Cradle

"The cradle rocks above an abyss, and common sense tells us that our existence is but a brief crack of light between two eternities of darkness," echoed in his mind, as he sat in the courtroom reviewing his notes, conferring with a phalanx of junior prosecutors, and thinking, intently and strategically, about the case before him. He wished he had never read Vladimir Nabokov's book *Speak Memory* because the catchphrase about the blasted abyss and eternal darkness was now forever locked in his memory. It was beginning to infringe on his mind at a time when he needed to concentrate and apply all his gray matter to the case.

Till just recently, the facts of the Tate-Bradshaw case, which was bound to become one of the most significant and highly visible cases of the twenty-first century, hardly fazed John Cole. As the lead prosecutor for the State of New York, Cole knew he could argue just about any case that crossed his desk, including the Tate-Bradshaw case. After four years in the military, two tours of duty in Vietnam, four years at the University of Tennessee, and two more years at Harvard Law School, Cole was a successful and confident lawyer. Now, however, during the last week of trial preparation, something had gone terribly wrong.

Search and destroy were two key words by which he lived his life. In the early days of Vietnam, it was search and destroy the enemy, and later, in law school, it was search and, above all, seek the truth. Even, honor the truth until death do you part. In time, however, Cole had come to realize regretfully that "truth and honor" could be just as evasive and destructive in a court of law as the enemy was in Vietnam.

If he wasn't a celebrity already, he could be one. In fact, he thought that the case that was about to begin almost certainly would make him one. Having his face plastered all over the morning paper and on the evening news wasn't all that bad. Secretly, he actually enjoyed the attention he was getting from the press, the bantering of attorneys before the judge and the jury, and the haggling over semantics. Whenever he negotiated a plea bargain, he often took a hard stance. His colleagues often thought he gloated somewhat especially during the negotiation of the plea-bargaining phase of a trial, when the defendant finally recapitulates, admits to his criminal and evil behavior and then, ironically and sheepishly, begs for a more lenient sentence or for his life. Cole lived for this moment—the moment of truth, turning the audacious, triumphant murderer into the sniveling wretch that he is before the eyes of the jury and, for a matter of fact, the whole world.

Eventually one gets used to the constant hounding of the reporters and the photographers, making the necessary adjustments to one's life. He certainly had. But, for Jenny Bradshaw and Robert Tate—two college students accused of killing their baby boy just minutes after he was born and then leaving the body in a dumpster in back of a dilapidated hotel along interstate highway twenty-five—the publicity of the case would be notoriously damaging. It would ruin their lives and the reputation and honor of their families. In their case, the truth, being potentially disastrous, could easily betray and send them up the river, lock them up in the penitentiary for life, or, worse, inject them with a serum for an early death. Search and destroy . . . search and destroy . . . seek truth and honor . . . search . . . the cradle rocks above an abyss, and common sense tells us . . . simple truths to live by. But, Cole couldn't get the damn phrase out of his mind. It seemed to him as if it had a will of its own that was growing ferociously, and like a malignant cancer, it was destroying everything it touched.

Chapter 2 - The Courtroom

The morning session was a disaster for the prosecution and had befuddled Joseph Valentino, a junior prosecutor and a recent graduate of New York University. Leo Albert, a recent graduate of Penn State, felt like crawling under the table. And, Samantha Stone of Boston College felt utterly chagrined, but with a sensibility of understanding. They had all arrived early as Cole had instructed them, each carrying a carton containing folders stuffed with documents and evidence. Entering courtroom 17A, on the seventeenth floor of the newly modernized state building, Joe, Leo, and Samantha quickly uncovered their cartons of evidence and began sifting through the material, searching for whatever they thought was necessary for the morning session.

Samantha's slender frame could hardly contain the beating of her heart. Although this was her first real case, she appeared quite confident and eager to accept the challenge. She even liked Cole and thought he was handsome and brilliant and a great mentor. In fact, she thought the last four weeks were particularly exciting, working late at the office with Cole, researching past cases, and writing briefs and arguments. She was a whiz at writing briefs and arguments.

Leo Albert slumped down into the chair next to Samantha and smiled thinly. His wiry frame and dangerously weak eyes—from the many hours of studying and reading at home and in the law library—cleverly hid a mind that was both inquisitive and brilliant. Joe Valentino took out a handkerchief and wiped the sweat from his babylike, oval face as he sat down at the prosecutor's table to review the papers that would eventually convict Jenny Bradshaw and Robert Tate.

Shortly afterward a large man with a chest that resembled the round, wooden barrels of the old Brotherhood winery arrived. He had long legs that looked awkward and funny in contrast to his round barrel chest. His dark, bushy eyebrows raised almost imperceptibly on his forehead as his eyes fell upon Samantha. He was the county sheriff. His gun dangled dangerously at his side. Then, Barry Wilson, attorney for the defense, entered the courtroom, followed by the stenographer, the administrator of court services, and the jury of twelve plus two.

When Cole arrived, he stood in the back and bristled at the sight of the courtroom. He thought it looked unusually strange, cold, and hostile this morning, especially in the cold light of day, which was flooding the room through six floor-to-ceiling windows. The vertical blinds had been adjusted so the maximum amount of light would pass through the thin vertical lines. The gallery had filled quickly with the press. Jenny's mother and father, Howard and Patricia Bradshaw, sat quietly up front, in the first row, apparently under great stress and in agony. Alongside the Bradshaws sat the Tates, Charles and Miriam. Charles, a retired businessman, looked straight ahead, while Miriam, Robert's mother, sat with her head lowered and her hands covering her face.

The court stenographer, a smartly dressed woman of middle age, adjusted the pince-nez on the bridge of her nose and then looked up and scanned the crowded courtroom. The judge's bench, which sat directly ahead and across the room from where Cole was standing, appeared majestic and overwhelming in a cold sort of way. The judge, for one thing, had the distinguished honor of being seated on a raised platform, several feet above the floor and above all other heads, forming the highest point in the courtroom. To the right of the judge's bench was a grease board and the sidebar, where counselors, jurors, witnesses, and experts could confer with the judge privately and off the record. The jurors took their seats facing the window and in the path of direct sunlight. Facing the judge's bench, a lectern became a line of demarcation splitting the room into two equal parts—to the left was the table for the prosecution and to the right was the table for the defense.

"Well, I see everyone made it bright and early," Cole said, as he approached the table for the prosecution, and smiled halfheartedly. Samantha eagerly returned Cole's smile as he took his seat at the center of the table. Cole recognized the look on Samantha's face as one belonging to schoolgirls whom had become fascinated with their teachers and professors. Her look worried him and he thought that he would have to find a way to let her down easily without ruffling any feathers. Undoubtedly, in a short time, this brilliant graduate law student would become a brilliant attorney, and he didn't want to stand in her way or distract her from what was really important: her career and the law.

Just then, Jenny Bradshaw and Robert Tate were led into the courtroom through a door located to the right of the judge's bench. They were following a guard not like sheep following a beloved shepherd who would sacrifice his life for the love of his sheep, but more like sheep being led to a slaughterhouse. Jenny smiled and nodded sadly to her mother and father in the front row of the gallery, and Robert waved quickly to his parents before sitting down stiffly. They were so frightened that they hardly appeared human in their movements.

The sheriff suddenly stood up, rising with an air of imperial formality and importance before the jurors, the audience, and the press. He straightened his backbone and announced in a loud, firm voice: "All rise for The Honorable Judge William T. Henry."

Judge William T. Henry, a spry man of medium height and build, entered the courtroom from a side door and quickly ascended the few steps leading to the elevated plateau from where he would judge and rule on those who came before him with a hard and merciless hand. Upon reaching his leathered throne, he swiftly sat down and took a moment to gaze at the faces of the wretches before him.

Looking down at the court through a pair of wire-rimmed spectacles, Judge Henry first asked the counselor for the defense if he was ready to make an opening statement. Wilson stood up and announced that he was indeed ready. Then, Judge Henry turned to Cole and asked the same question. Cole, however, made no rely. He sat there, vacantly, staring into space, as if he was on some other planet, miles and, perhaps, light years away from the rest of the world. He looked as if his mind was preoccupied and absorbed in some strange and horrible thought or idea. Samantha nudged his arm nervously and stealthily under the table with her elbow, and whispered, "Cole! Cole! The judge is speaking to you! Don't you hear him?"

Samantha scowled and glanced at Joseph and Leo apprehensively, wondering why Cole was acting so strangely this morning. She thought he was up to something, but she couldn't figure out exactly what it could be.

Cole jumped out of his chair while simultaneously groping for his papers and notes. He approached the lectern awkwardly and went through a whole ritual of pantomime. He nervously adjusted the knot of his tie and carefully checked the sleeves and cuffs of his shirt and jacket. He huskily cleared his throat, and stared suspiciously at his papers and notes, which he had placed neatly on the lectern under the reading lamp. Irritably squinting and rubbing his eyes, he turned his head toward the windows, looking directly into the burning sunlight of the morning. Languidly, he sipped cool water from his glass. His mouth had gone dry, so that he couldn't even spit. Conspicuously turning to the jurors, he examined their bored faces, first quickly and then more closely, one by one, with a sensibility of reverence. Finally, when all this was over, Cole looked up at Judge Henry and said, "Yes, Judge, the prosecution is ready to make an opening statement in the case of the State of New York vs. Jenny Bradshaw and Robert Tate." Then, stepping out from behind the lectern, Cole stood before the jury, resting his hand on the railing and occasionally waving it nonchalantly as he spoke.

"Good morning, your honor, and ladies and gentlemen of the jury. In the case of the State of New York versus Jennifer Bradshaw and Robert Tate, it is the intention of the prosecution to show that Jenny Bradshaw and Robert Tate are guilty of first-degree murder. I will show how Jenny and Robert had rented a room in a dilapidated hotel along interstate highway twenty-five, where Jenny gave birth to a beautiful, healthy baby boy. I will also show that minutes after giving birth Jenny and Robert Tate murdered the baby by holding it up by its arms and shaking it fiercely and deliberately, until they shook the life right out of it. And then, to be certain they had finished the gruesome job, they hit the child over the head with a blunt object, fracturing its skull into a million tiny pieces. In an effort to hide their horrible deed and save the good name of their families, they wrapped the little body in a brown paper bag and threw it into a dumpster behind the hotel, praying desperately that it would be lost in the refuse of society and humanity. Afterward, they checked out of the hotel and returned to their respective college campuses as if nothing had ever happened."

Samantha, Leo, and Joe watched Cole thoughtfully and attentively as he outlined the prosecution's case for the judge and the jury. Everything was going as well as could be expected. All our hard work was finally paying off, thought Samantha with a glow of satisfaction. Even Leo and Joe, who had argued and debated vehemently about the evidence and how it ought to be presented to the court, no small matter, sat as if they were in a trance listening to the words spoken from a god that dwells on Mount Olympus. For the moment, Cole's mind and tongue appeared as if they were perfectly connected. She heard him clearly articulate what he intended to prove in the minds of the jurors.

Cole glided along in the courtroom like a surfer racing before a great wave that was about to crash down and crush him or a skier flying downhill on a snowy mountain before an avalanche.

Samantha was hardly prepared for what happened next. She never would have expected it in a million years, she would say later.

Cole continued. "Furthermore, without any reasonable doubt, I intend to show through the evidence presented here today and in the next few weeks that . . . that . . . that . . ." And then it happened, suddenly, an unexpected slap across the face or on the side of the head at a time you had least expected it. Cole stopped abruptly in the middle of a sentence, losing both his train of thought and his poise. He scowled. Something was intruding into his thoughts. Something he didn't want to think about. The jury looked on in silence, waiting for Cole's next statement. He paused for a moment and walked back to the lectern to take a sip of water from the glass he had left there. Quietly, the jury and the judge waited, watching every movement and facial expression of the renowned lawyer. Finally, Cole started again. "The evidence will show that . . . that . . ." And then it happened again, and he stopped in the middle of his sentence.

Facing the jury, Cole looked over their heads and squinted at the window and the sunlight bursting through the lines formed by the vertical blinds. For a moment, he thought he saw an image surrounded by a blinding light. He couldn't make it out. One minute the image resembled a horse, and then the next minute, it looked like a buffalo. Then, he saw an eagle miraculously transform itself into a Beast. The Beast was climbing out of a hole in the ground—or was it a dungeon? Thinking that his mind was playing some kind of horrible trick on him, he tried to clear his head, but the words, which he desperately wanted to forget, kept coming back. Then, strangely and uncontrollably, the words just seemed to flow out of his mouth as he said aloud, "The cradle rocks above an abyss, and common sense tells us that our existence is but a brief crack of light between two eternities of darkness. . . ."

The jury was stunned and couldn't believe what they were hearing from the mouth of the handsome and renowned lawyer. Some of them thought this had to be a joke. In fact, some of them began to laugh, while others appeared perplexed and confused by the sudden interruption in the argument.

"Where the hell did that come from?" Leo said, turning to Joe and Samantha. He searched his scribbled notes and outline to see if he had inadvertently missed something.

"What did he say? What did he say? What is he talking about? The cradle rocks above an abyss? He never mentioned that before!" said Samantha, never taking her eyes off of Cole, who seemed to be swaying at the lectern like a thin, flexible reed blowing in the wind.

"I don't know," Joe said, as rivulets of sweat cascaded down the side of his face, forming large blotchy spots on his clean, white collar. Taking a handkerchief from his back pocket, he wiped away a river of sweat from the nape of his neck. "Wait! Wait! Shut up! Shut up! He knows what he's doing!" Despite his words of confidence, Joe was already having second thoughts about Cole. Something was definitely wrong. And, the judge wouldn't wait forever. Just then, as if the judge had read Joe Valentino's mind, he heard a loud roar coming from the bench.

"Counselor, we're waiting," Judge Henry said, tapping the bench with the tips of his fingers. He looked at his Rolex and then, again, at Cole. "The court is waiting! Now, if I'm not mistaken, you were saying something about a cradle rocking above an abyss? Is that correct? Would you care to elaborate, counselor? Where on earth are you taking us with this line of argument?" The judge was genuinely puzzled, as he contemplated the meaning of Cole's strange behavior in court and his last few words.

In the meantime, Cole's face had turned sickly pale before the court. As if transformed by some magical words of ancient times, he suddenly appeared haggard and weary. His blue eyes glazed over with the pallor of ancient dust, and the light, which was once clear and brilliant, faded and disappeared. With horribly cold and dull eyes, he now looked upon the court.

Cole believed that he was losing control of his most valuable possession—that which had brought him to the pinnacle of his career as a prosecutor and would eventually take him the rest of the way to the top, to the Senate, perhaps even to the presidency. He thought he was losing his mind. Now, he feared that he would lose it all, everything he had worked for. If he had more time to think about it, he would have felt bitter, even absurd, but at the moment all he could feel was a sense of chaos and confusion and darkness. Leaning against the lectern, he shuffled the papers in his moist and sweaty hands, so he could stall for time. He needed time, he thought. Yes! Time! That was it! He needed time to think and search for his next line of argument in the case! He needed to forget! Yes, that was it, too! He needed to forget!

He then said, "Excuse me, judge, and ladies and gentlemen of the jury, something had suddenly occurred to me and I'm sorry for the interruption. What I had meant to say was that I am prepared to present to the jury, today, and in the weeks to come, irrefutable evidence and testimony. Expert witnesses, Dr. Michael Lewis of Saint Sinai Hospital of New York City and Dr. Samuel Barnes, a coroner and forensic scientist for the State of New York, will explain and demonstrate exactly how the child . . . how the child . . .." And then as a glittering ray of sunlight caught the corner of his eye, he said softly and pitifully, "Search and destroy . . . search and destroy the enemy . . ." Cole looked around the courtroom alarmingly before lowering his arms to his sides in a sign of resignation and befuddlement.

By now Joseph Valentino was drenched in his own stinking sweat and Samantha Stone was shaking her head from side to side in complete empathy and commiseration with Cole. Leo started to pack up his things and if Cole had turned around at that moment and had seen him, he would have thought that Leo resembled a cowering dog running away with his tail between his legs. But at the moment, Cole was staring at the light passing through the windows of the courtroom.

"Counselor, will you please step forward and come to the sidebar," Judge Henry said, sternly.

Looking more like the nutty-professor than a highly paid lawyer, Cole stumbled around the lectern and approached the sidebar with trembling steps, weak knees, and an air of clumsy absentmindedness. Leaning forward and craning his neck to get a closer look at Cole, Judge Henry said roughly, "Counselor, are you feeling all right? Is anything wrong with you? You look awfully pale and disoriented, if I say so myself. I think you should ask for a recess so you might pull yourself together. Would you like a recess to collect yourself?"

"I'm fine, judge. Really, I'm fine." Cole thought about what he was saying and how silly it must sound to Judge Henry, and to the jury, and to his student colleagues sitting at the table behind him. He knew he was anything but well.

"From what I've heard this morning in your opening statement, counselor, I'd say you need professional help." And then, the judge added softly, almost imperceptibly, "John! What's wrong with you? What's happening to you? You're jumping around from one subject to another like a nervous law clerk that doesn't know what the hell he's talking about. I simply don't understand you. You're not making any sense. I'll ask you politely just one more time—Are you feeling all right?"

"Yes," Cole said firmly. "I'm fine, but I think I'll take that recess, now. I could use the time to review my notes with my team members."

Judge Henry looked at Cole inquisitively for a moment, and then he turned to the court and said loudly and clearly in a strong voice, "The court will take a ten-minute break." In another moment, the judge quickly disappeared from the bench.

As Cole joined his team of prosecutors back at the table, Samantha asked urgently, "John, what's wrong? What is going on here?"

Cole collapsed into a chair at the head of the table, lowering his chin and resting it on his chest. He looked around the table and saw three young, vibrant faces eagerly staring back at him. Bitterly, he thought they resembled the lions and tigers of the wilderness, waiting for an opportunity to attack and devour their prey. He knew deep inside that all they really wanted was to usurp his authority and take over his case. Just out of law school, and already they think they have the mentality and wherewithal to argue a case before the Supreme Court. Well, they may get their chance sooner than they had expected.

"Nothing. Nothing," he said. "We're just taking a break. I'm afraid I botched the opening statement." He paused and then with renewed concentration and strength he gathered his papers, stood up, and walked out of the majestic courtroom.

Chapter 3 - Lunch

Two hours later, Cole had finished the opening statement for the prosecution, and Judge Henry recessed the court for a one-hour lunch. Wearily, Cole and his team of young prosecutors—Valentino, Stone, and Albert—returned to their offices on the twenty-seventh floor, where lunch, a large platter of assorted sandwiches, had been ordered earlier by Cole's secretary and neatly laid out on the conference table in his office.

Cole's office was the second largest on the twenty-seventh floor in the state building, surpassed only by the office of State Attorney General Randy Scott. A huge rectangular room, it was beautifully decorated in deep, rich, dark colors of mahogany, purple, green, and burgundy. An old, ornamental oak partition, exquisitely decorated by hand and consisting of wood carvings of raised images, faces, bodies, letters, and symbols of the Ming Dynasty, stood just inside the threshold of the entrance and blocked the view of those who wished to look in. In an alcove in one corner of the room, a small table and counter supported a small electric drip Mr. Coffee Machine, an elegant sugar bowl, and a glass container holding wooden stirrers. Beneath the counter, a cabinet concealed neatly stacked packets of coffee, an assortment of thick, brassy, mugs, and fragile cups and saucers. Adjacent to the alcove and on the same side of the room, two huge, double-hung windows, draped in rich, velvety material, stood as sentries, guarding litigation papers and legal briefs. Two King Edward wing chairs, covered in fine English leather the color of burgundy, sat equidistant between the two sentry windows and flanked a leather sofa, also made from the same rich material. Directly in front of the sofa, an antique colonial coffee table provided readers with a choice of several law magazines and papers scattered across the top. Together, the sofa, the two wing chairs, and the coffee table created an area where victims and lawyers were invited to discuss their case conveniently and comfortably in an atmosphere of intimacy and cordiality. Across from the intimacy of the sitting area, a long, highly-polished conference table of rich, hardwood oak occupied the entire length of the opposite wall. Twelve high-back leather swivel chairs were pulled neatly and squarely to the table. At the far end of the room, in front of another tall sentry window, Cole's desk sat quietly and majestically. His desk was like any other desk, and was cluttered with the usual things—a phone, several stacks of papers, an "in" and an "out" box, and a desk calendar. From his desk, Cole could easily have swiveled his chair around to face his workstation and IBM computer where he could immediately have begun typing letters and documents. To the right of Cole's desk were two doors, the first led to a private laboratory and the second to the new law library and study room.

As Cole entered his office and sat at his desk, he saw the platter of sandwiches on the conference table and remembered his luncheon appointment with Gina Anderson, his fiancée. He frowned. Samantha Stone, Joseph Valentino, and Leo Albert followed Cole into the office. Joseph was hungry, so he immediately seized several ham sandwiches from the platter and went over to the sofa, where his huge body flopped into the chair with a sigh of relief and began eating. Samantha and Leo each took a sandwich and sat at the conference table, studiously reviewing notes they had made during Cole's disastrous and embarrassing opening statement.

Carla Jones, Cole's secretary, and Randy Scott, the attorney general, silently entered the office, and suddenly were overwhelmed by the feeling of doom and helplessness pervading the air. Scott felt as if he had just entered a funeral for an old, beloved friend. Mrs. Jones quietly crossed the office and placed a file containing a stack of litigation papers neatly on his desk. Cole looked up and saw Carla smile and for a moment he felt good and warm again. He was grateful to her because her presence brought him back from some dark and chaotic place, a place that he had come to loathe and fear. Then Carla turned and quietly disappeared behind the Ming Dynasty partition.

However, Attorney General Scott, a very distinguished looking man in his late fifties and of medium height and built, lingered behind and stood back at the far end of the conference table. An old navy commander, Scott recognized a ship listing in the wind and heading towards the rocks when he saw one.

"Well, Cole," he said calmly, yet with an edge of sharpness and command, "how did it go in court this morning?"

"I've had better days," Cole said painfully, and looking up, added, "We made an opening statement—nothing more." He knew he could have been more accurate in his description to Scott. He could have said, perhaps, that he botched it, or blew it in court. But, instead, he kept silent because he had more important things to think about. Yet, what could be more important than the case? Wasn't that what he lived for? Nevertheless, when these things are eventually discovered, won't they turn him into a mutineer in the eyes of the old navy commander? He thought that if Scott knew what he was planning to do, he'd have him drawn and quartered, or hung from the tallest yardarm he could find, just like they did to Billy Budd.

Then Cole said more emphatically, "You know, Randy, cases are never won simply on the prosecution's opening statement. The real test of a lawyer's mettle is determined by how well he or she can articulate what truly happened and identify how a person's rights have been violated under the law. Of course, a prosecutor's ability to present the evidence and question the witnesses during the examination and cross-examination period, under the intense pressure and scrutiny of the judge, the jury, the press and the public, is crucial. This represents the body of the case, and it is here, where an inexperienced lawyer usually loses the case. If you don't crack up or go insane, and if you can persuade the jury to see your side of the story, you could become one hell of a lawyer." Scott knew that Cole was saying this primarily for the benefit of Stone, Albert, and Valentino.

"You're absolutely right, John. I couldn't have said it better myself. And, I'm sure your sermon isn't lost on deaf ears." Scott nodded towards the hungry lions at the table.

Cole studied them, thinking that he had been just like them not too long ago. When he first graduated from Harvard Law School, he was hungry and he wanted to make a name for himself in the same way these young lawyers now wished to do if given the chance. Now, however, everything has changed, he thought. Somehow, the table had been reversed on him. Now, he felt as if he was the animal again being hunted down and killed rather than being the hunter. It was a feeling he disliked and loathed. It often reminded him of Vietnam, and that was something he wanted to forget. But wasn't New York City a jungle? He thought it was and he knew that there were plenty of miscreants roaming the streets of the city that he could hunt down and prosecute. Perhaps, he never really got over Vietnam. Perhaps, he only thought he did. Then, the sound of Scott's voice brought him back to the present. "I hired you because you're one hell of a lawyer and I know I'll never come to regret it," Scott said boastfully as he sat down at the conference table and reached for a turkey and lettuce sandwich on a soft, croissant roll.

"If you saw me in court this morning, Randy, I'm sure you'd have an entirely different opinion of me, right now. I'm ashamed to say it, but to tell you the truth, it was a debacle." Cole turned away from Scott's burning eyes, and stared out the window. "Ask them," said Cole dejectedly, and then, turning to Stone, "Samantha, am I right? Tell him!"

"It wasn't that bad, Cole—I think you're exaggerating a bit." Stone guardedly and involuntarily looked up at the two men facing each other—one her beloved mentor whom she respected and admired, and the other, a truculent, no-nonsense attorney general who could be excruciatingly hard and unforgiving.

"Well, anyway, Randy, I'm glad you're here," said Cole, recognizing Stone's uneasiness and wishing to alleviate it. "I have an important announcement to make, and I want you all to hear this." Cole sat up in his chair and looking Randy Scott, the attorney general, straight in his eyes, he fired a torpedo right at the navy commander's submarine. He said, "I've decided to step down as lead prosecutor on the Tate-Bradshaw case."

There was a strange, deafening silence in the room that lasted a few seconds, as the meaning of Cole's words registered in their minds. This was something they had not expected from their beloved and mighty mentor. Then, the clamoring began and it appeared as if all hell had broken lose and the fallen angels had escaped the boundaries of hell and were now rioting before the gates of heaven and God, Himself.

"What?" Valentino shouted loudly and nervously. Then he choked and coughed as a piece of croissant lodged itself in his throat. His face was turning red and blue from lack of oxygen.

Cole looked at Valentino and thought he resembled a large frog that had eaten too many mosquitoes and was about to vomit. Under other circumstances, he would have thought Valentino was funny and he would have had a good laugh, but Cole didn't exactly feel like laughing. He knew he was putting them on a spot, and he wouldn't be at all surprised if the old navy commander fired him. Of course, Cole knew he was a celebrity in the eyes of the public and if he were fired, the press would have a field day reporting the story. It would make the headlines of all the major newspapers nationwide.

"But you can't quit the case, now, John," Samantha Stone said, seriously. For a moment, she thought she was dreaming, she was really at home sleeping and this was all a terrible nightmare. But then she knew it wasn't a dream. It was for real. Cole was backing out on them, deserting the ship during a significant and dangerous mission. At first, she felt outraged and hurt and thought Cole was a coward, and then a moment later, she felt a pang of sorrow and sympathy. She tried to reason with him. "You're the lead prosecutor, Cole. You've spent hours on this case, preparing briefs and outlining the strategy that we ought to follow. You can't just abandon us now!"

"Oh, my God!" said Leo Albert, making the sign of the cross. "We're doomed." Leo had never been a particularly religion person. In fact, he only went to church on religious holidays like Christmas and Easter. But, now, he felt an uncontrollable need to pray to the Almighty Father and ask for help and comfort.

From across the conference table, Randy Scott could not conceal the frown and disappointment on his face. He felt as if Cole had betrayed him and had abandoned ship during a storm like Joseph Conrad's Lord Jim. Alarmed and annoyed, Scott blurted out, "What are you talking about, John? No one knows the case better than you do. You can't step down. You're only kidding, right? Please, tell me you're only kidding."

As he pulled his heavy frame out of the sofa and walked over to the desk, Valentino echoed melodramatically, "You are kidding, right?"

Maneuvering around the conference table like a commander moving on the bridge of a ship with absolute authority and power, Scott crossed the room and stood before his recalcitrant officer. He thought that if Cole had been under his command in the military during the war, he would have had him thrown into the brig and court-martialed. "You know, John, we could lose this case without you. Robert Tate and Jennifer Bradshaw could walk free . . .free!" Scott's face was now turning red. His eyes bored into Cole like a drill bite boring into wood. He said, "Especially with Barry Wilson, defending them. You know he's a damn good defender. If anyone could get them off, he's the one who could do it."

"I know," Cole said, thoughtfully. "I know. And, don't think I haven't thought about that or that my decision to leave this case isn't eating me up inside." He stood up and walked around the desk to address the young lawyers. "But, stop for a moment and just listen to me. Better yet, just listen to yourselves. You sound like a bunch of kindergartners. I can't believe what I'm hearing. You sound to me as if you don't have any confidence in yourselves or in your ability to prosecute this case. It's clearly evident to me that you think too highly of the defense. And, that's a mistake on your part. Now I know that you're just out of law school and this is your first real case, and you never argued a case like this in law school, let alone before a real judge like Judge Henry. But anything is possible, if you would only set your mind to it. I'm confident that you could win this case. All you need is to have confidence in yourselves." Then Cole reiterated a line he had blurted out in the courtroom earlier that morning during his disastrous opening statement. "The last piece of advice I could give you now that might help and lead you in the right direction is this: search for the truth in everything you do. You mustn't be afraid of the truth—no matter whatever it is or wherever it leads you. I too have to face the truth. Here, read this."

Cole took a crumbled piece of paper from the pocket of his suit jacket and handed it to Randy Scott, who read it silently, and then passed it along to Valentino, Albert, and Stone. They saw a message handwritten in big, twisted, deformed, and convoluted lettering that resembled the handwriting of a child's. It said simply, "John. Come home. Black Hawk needs you. Come quickly for the cradle rocks above an abyss." The signature read, "Corporal Salvatore Buccanon."

"I received this letter last week. At the time we were all pretty busy preparing for this case, so I never mentioned it to any of you. I convinced myself that there was nothing I could do about it. Although, what I really wanted to do was to tear up the piece of paper and just throw it away. However, the more I thought about it, the more I felt uneasy and guilty. Yeah, I was losing sleep at night, but that wasn't the worst part of it. What really bothered me and what really crawled under my skin was the Nabokov phrase you heard me blurt out in court this morning." Cole turned away, walked to the window, and looked down at the traffic and the office workers heading to their favorite restaurants for lunch. "I just can't seem to shake my head free of those damn words. It's funny, though, I don't even know what they mean. Oh, I know the literary meaning, of course, but I don't know what they mean for me or why this is even happening to me." Cole turned away from the window and forced a smile.

"Who's Corporal Salvatore Buccanon?" Stone asked. "And, what is he talking about—the cradle rocks above an abyss? If you ask me, he sounds pretty sick and frightening."

Scott asked condescendingly, "Is he a friend of yours, Cole?"

"No! Yes!" said Cole sharply. "I mean no. He's not a friend of mine. We were friends once, a long time ago. We grew up together in Nashville—that's all. We also served together in Vietnam, back in sixty-eight. I have a picture of the platoon on the wall, here. You may have seen it." Indicating the picture, he said sadly, "It's a picture of our platoon, before we got shot up. Sal's there—he's in the front row, second from the left, standing next to me. Black Hawk's the tall, big fellow in the back, the Indian. He's the one wearing the Indian headdress, the war bonnet."

"John, I don't know what Corporal Buccanon and Black Hawk mean to you or what they want from you, but I do know one thing—you can't walk out on us now," said Samantha Stone. But, deep inside of her, she realized that Cole had already made up his mind. He was being spirited away from her and this case by two Marine Corps buddies. One looked like a drug-crazy hippie and the other a stand-in for a John Wayne movie. She wanted to cry but succeeded in holding back the tears. There'll be plenty of time to cry later, she thought, after she wins the case.

"How can I make you understand that underneath this suit, this tie and jacket, I'm basically a marine—a grunt, and that marines live by a code of honor, Samantha?" Cole knew it would be difficult if not impossible to get them to understand his position. Except for Scott, the others weren't even born when the Vietnam War was raging and destroying the young and old alike. Nevertheless, he continued his explanation. "When in the jungle or on the beach, marines learn very quickly that if you want to survive, you have to pull together as a group and look out for each other. If you don't, you're as good as dead. I don't know how many times I had to wake my guys up in the middle of the night and send them out into the jungle to look for Company M, or Company L, because they got themselves in trouble and they needed help. We never hesitated or shrank from our duty. We went out there, knowing very well that some of us would not be returning, but we went out there, nevertheless, because we're marines, and there's a code of honor, a pledge, a bond between us, that's greater than life and greater than death."

"And what about the pledge you made to the people of the State of New York when you accepted this job?" asked Scott vehemently. "Have you forgotten about them?"

"No, I haven't forgotten," said Cole hopelessly and sorrowfully. "But, I can't turn my back on Black Hawk either. If he needs me, I have to go. I really have no choice and that's part of what I've been struggling with this past week."

Cole walked over to his desk and punched in the last four digits of his phone number, followed by an access code and said, "I received this message on my voice mail, this morning. I want you to hear this."

Immediately, the room filled with the sound of a soft, female voice, announcing a series of messages. "Message number one . . ." John advanced the recording until he found the message he wanted. Annoyingly, the soft voice continued, "Message number ten, from an external phone, received today, May 21, at 6:45 AM." A loud male voice, harsh and raspy, burst through the speaker, "John, this is Sal—ah, Corporal Buccanon. I didn't know if you had received my letter, so I took the liberty of calling your folks at home to get your phone number. I hope you don't mind. Anyway, you've got to come home right away. I have some bad news about Black Hawk—a letter—he needs you. Call me when you get home!"

And then, Corporal Buccanon's voice was suddenly interrupted by the sound of the operator's voice as she announced the time remaining for the call. "You now have fifteen seconds to conclude your message or you may deposit another fifty cents, please."

"John, I'll have to talk fast. All I have to say is come home right away. Black Hawk needs you badly, and we have to act quickly— for the cradle rocks above an abyss." The eerie message ended, the harsh, raspy voice disappeared, and the sound of the speaker went dead.

Cole walked around the desk, again, and stood in front of Stone, Albert, and Valentino. He said ardently, "Okay, so now you know why I have to leave you and why I'm depending on you to finish and win this case for us. If it's any consolation, you should take comfort in knowing that I should be back in a week or two." Of course, Cole wasn't exactly sure this was true. He had absolutely no idea how long this crazy adventure with Corporal Buccanon and Black Hawk would take to complete: one week, two weeks, a month, six months, or even a year. There was no way of knowing. He paused, now searching their young and inexperienced faces for a sign of understanding, and then added, "Don't let me down. You have the facts. We've discussed them over and over again for the past month or more, and you know our strategy and the proper method of presenting the facts in court. You know what to do. Just go out and do it. And now, I have a luncheon appointment with Gina, and I'm running terribly late already." He glanced at his wristwatch and started for the door.

"You can't leave us now!" Stone shouted, standing up and dropping her arms at her side in a flare of melodrama.

"I just want to know one thing, Cole," Randy Scott shouted as Cole walked across the room and was about to disappear behind the Ming Dynasty partition.

Cole stopped and turned, silently.

"What power does Black Hawk have on you, Cole? It's more than a pledge or some cockamamie code of honor."

And then Cole smiled halfheartedly, waved with one swift movement of the hand and disappeared behind the partition.

"What is it, Cole?" Scott shouted long after Cole had gone. "What is it? I want to know! I want to know! Tell me! Tell me!"

Chapter 4 - The Taxi Ride Across Town

Cole took the elevator down to the first floor of the state court building and walked hurriedly across the crowded lobby and through the huge glass and steel framed doors. He hailed a yellow taxicab, jumped in, and gave the driver an address.

Leaning back against the leather seat, Cole peered out the side window of the taxi to view the pedestrians milling along the crowded streets, before the high fashion and specialty shops of New York City. He remembered the day he had graduated from Harvard Law School and how proud his mother and father had felt that day. They had driven to the north end of Boston that evening and dined out in one of those fancy and extremely expensive Italian restaurants along one of the many narrow streets. He remembered sitting there in the restaurant on that memorable night and thinking he'd come a long way for a country boy from Tennessee who went off to Vietnam and nearly got himself killed, along with his best friend and his whole platoon.

He sighed, and the taxi driver looked back over the front seat and said, "Are you okay, buddy?" Now he wished he could forget all of it, everything that had ever happened. If he had the opportunity to do it over again and change the course of history, he surely would not hesitate. But he also knew it was useless to try to change one's fate. Everything happens for a purpose, he told himself, trying to ease his conscience. He realized he couldn't change the past, nor could he change what he had become—a paranoid, merciless, prosecuting attorney. Cole would often shrug and smile when other attorneys and judges would stop him in the hallway or on the street or in a restaurant and praise his keen insight into the law or his relentless determination and high conviction rate. However, when he looked into the mirror each morning, he scowled and loathed himself.

Cole came back to himself and while he was looking out the window, he realized the taxicab was heading north on Eighth Avenue in the direction of the Plaza Suite and Central Park. He closed his eyes, and suddenly, as if summoned from the depths of his soul, he heard Nabokov's words echo in his mind: "The cradle rocks above an abyss . . . the cradle rocks above an abyss . . . and common sense tells us." And then, as if in contrast to Nabokov's words, he heard the military catch words: "Search and destroy . . . search and destroy . . . search and destroy." When Cole next looked out the window of the taxi, he saw a crowd of pedestrians milling about as if they were in a movie, walking in slow motion. Cole bolted upright when he thought he recognized someone in the crowd. It's Black Hawk, he said to himself. How could it be?

"Pull over!" Cole shouted to the driver of the taxi. He stepped out of the cab and shouted, "Black Hawk! Black Hawk!" Black Hawk turned and his eyes were red and teary. He was naked from his waist up and on his head he was wearing a faded war bonnet. Around his neck and shoulders a heavy chain pulled and tugged at him, bending his neck downward towards the ground as he walked. Cole saw a figure leading Black Hawk away as if he was a prisoner. He didn't recognize the figure leading Black Hawk. The man was large and hairy, resembling a monster with huge flaring nostrils, and large black eyes. For hands and feet, the creature— that's what he looked like to Cole—had paws and talons. Then the creature turned and looked back at Cole, and for a moment, Cole felt a chill—as cold and damp as the dirt covering a grave—run up and down his spine. The creature bellowed, making a wild roaring sound, reminding Cole of thunder from an approaching storm. The reverberation pierced and nearly shattered his eardrums. Cole placed his hands over his ears, but with little effect.

"Hey, come back! Come back!" shouted the taxi-driver, as Cole started after the fleeing figures. "What about my cab fare?"

Cole wove his way through the milling crowd in chase of the fleeing figures. Black Hawk! Black Hawk! I have to stop them! I

have to stop them before it's too late! Cole didn't know why he
had to stop them or what he would do if he actually caught up
with them. For some reason, that didn't seem to matter to him
now. In fact, Cole noticed his body appeared to be acting
involuntarily and contradictory to what his mind was telling him.
While his body was running recklessly forward on its own
volition, his mind was telling him something else—Turn around!
Turn around! Fool! For a moment, Cole thought he was dreaming,
but, the very next moment, when he collided with a caterer
wheeling several trays of hot and cold food for a business
luncheon across town, Cole knew he wasn't dreaming. He felt a
sharp pain in his leg shoot up to his thigh as he slashed his knee
on the corner of the rolling cart the caterer, a young woman, was
wheeling to a van parked at the curb. Sprawling to the ground,
Cole felt his blood, warm and gooey, dripping down his leg and
soaking his trousers. He got up and started running again. So
intent was he on catching up with Black Hawk and the Beast that
he never bothered to look up, and therefore, never saw the eagle
flying overhead, following them. But he felt it and thought he
heard the majestic bird's wings cutting the air like a helicopter.
Whoop . . . whoop . . . whoop! Then strangely, Cole thought of the
Red Sea, which Moses had parted by raising his staff over his
head and creating a path for the Israelites to make their escape
before the onslaught of the chariots and charioteers of the
Pharaoh of Egypt. He didn't know why he had this idea, but then
he scowled as he saw the crowd milling the street instinctively
separate and create a pathway or escape route for Black Hawk
and the Beast. Was it possible that the Beast, leading Black
Hawk, perhaps, to his death, was as powerful as Moses? Cole
didn't know.

He pushed his way through the crowd, which refused to give
him an inch of space, and gradually he became aware that
something was changing. Then, looking closer, he saw their eyes
and their yellow complexion. For a moment, he felt a pain in the
hollowness of his stomach, and he thought of Vietnam. Yes!
These people were Vietnamese! He turned a corner and now it
was dark as midnight and he was walking through a village in
North Vietnam. He felt a sense of déjà vu because he had been
here before, in this very village. Now, he suddenly realized he was

carrying an M-16 rifle, and he had the idea that he was an anachronistic time traveler since he was still wearing his business suit; the same suit he had worn in court that morning. But where the hell did the rifle come from?

Large drops of water began to pelt his face as he made his way through what appeared to be a village. He could hear the voices of women and children and soldiers shouting, although he couldn't make out what they were saying. Cole knew that whatever it was, it wasn't good. The voices seemed to be crying and wailing hysterically. The rain increased in intensity, cutting into his face as he followed the figures of Black Hawk and the Beast. He couldn't see them now, but he knew they were there. The rain had turned into a monsoon and Cole was completely drenched from head to foot. Then, he heard a soldier shouting, "Fire in the hole!" and Cole ran to the end of the village, where he saw American and North and South Vietnamese soldiers standing around a hole in the ground. They were shielding their faces from a terribly hot flame that shot up from out of the ground and licked the dark sky. The blazing fire lit up the faces of the soldiers, creating grotesquely distorted masks.

Cole could hardly subdue the tremors in his arms and legs and the feeling of despair and sickness when he saw the Beast and Black Hawk emerge from the fiery hole in the ground, which was roaring and belching flames like a furnace. Still constrained by his chains, Black Hawk followed the Beast with a bowed head.

The soldiers who had been standing motionless and silent started shouting and firing their rifles at the Beast. But the bullets seemed to pass through him without doing any damage. The same bullets that passed through the Beast, however, went on to find other targets: other flesh, human flesh. Without the capacity to discriminate, the deadly bullets found their targets in the soldiers standing around the hole in the ground and the blazing fire. One by one, they began to drop and finally their guns became silent. In the prevailing chaos, Cole saw what was happening and he stepped forward and shouted, "Stop it! Stop it! Don't you see you're only killing yourselves! You fools!" Cole saw the bodies of the fallen soldiers lying twisted on the ground. He realized that the blood oozing from their wounds was mixing with the rain and being soaked up by the earth.

How much blood has the earth soaked up, since the beginning of man? Since the beginning of time, even? Probably, enough blood to fill an ocean, Cole thought. No amount of blood could quench its desire and thirst.

Then, Cole saw the Beast coming for him, and he could not move. His legs felt as if they had turned to lead. Laughing and howling like a wolf ready to pounce and devour his prey in the wilderness, the Beast approached Cole, and swiftly, without warning, stabbed him in the chest up to the hilt with a short dagger. Cole was stunned, and when he looked at the dagger protruding from his chest he saw a pool of warm blood spreading and soaking his white shirt. He felt absolute shock and terror. He fell to the wet ground, but managed to look up and see the Beast standing over him and Black Hawk behind him weeping.

"Ha! Ha! Ha!" bellowed the grotesque figure. "You can't stop me, Captain Cole! Before long, I will have you and Corporal Buccanon in chains along with Black Hawk! Ha! Ha! Ha!" Then the Beast reached down and slid a chain around Cole's neck and shoulders. It was old, heavy and cold.

Cole struggled to free himself but he could not break loose from his chains. Then the Beast tugged hard at the chain and nearly pulled him up to his feet. "Get up! Captain Cole! Get Up and follow me!" the Beast said.

Cole felt the tug at his shoulder and neck, but all he wanted to do now was close his eyes and die. He could feel his lifeblood leaving his body. In a moment, he would be dead, he thought, and then there would be nothing but the darkness of the abyss.

"Get Up! Get Up!" He heard it again. But this time, the voice sounded different and when he opened his eyes, he realized he was back in the taxicab. The driver, a Vietnamese immigrant, was shaking him gently on the shoulder, and saying, "Get Up! Get up! Sir, you have arrived at your destination—The Plaza Suite." Cole shook himself, sat up and looked out the window. Yes, indeed he was sitting in a cab in front of the Plaza Suite and across from Central Park. He wanted to believe it had all been a dream, just a bad dream, but deep inside, considering everything that had happened this past week, he knew it was much more. He felt as if he was caught up in something that would only get worse. Cole paid the driver, stepped out of the taxicab, and reluctantly entered the Plaza Suite Hotel, dreading his luncheon appointment with Gina Anderson.

Chapter 5 - Gina Anderson

Gina Anderson, Cole's fiancée for the last five years, had realized that something was wrong earlier in the week when Cole had begun to act strangely and absent-mindedly. She noticed how, in the middle of a conversation, his mind would suddenly drift away and then he'd become flummoxed. She knew then, intuitively, that he wasn't listening to a single word she was saying. She'd become furious whenever this happened, wanting to cry out and stamp her feet. On a few occasions, she had turned to Cole vehemently and said, "John, I swear, you haven't heard a word I've said all evening. What's wrong with you, darling? You seem to be preoccupied with something. What is it?"

"Nothing," Cole had said nervously. But, he was lying. He was afraid to tell her the truth, because he thought she would think that he was losing his mind. She would never understand the commitment one makes to a fellow marine, a commitment that might make the difference between life and death.

"Is it another woman?" she had asked bluntly as her dark, cold eyes bored into his skull.

"No," Cole said honestly, shrugging his shoulders. "I was just thinking." And, Cole decided that that was all he would say on the subject, at least for now. He realized that eventually he would have to come clean and tell the truth, that it might ruin his political opportunities, and he might even lose Gina in the bargain. But as he reflected on his situation, he thought perhaps that wasn't so bad an idea as it first appeared.

Gina now looked at her watch for the tenth time and scowled. "He's late again," she thought. "How would it look for the next Governor of New York State to be late showing up for a meeting with the President of the United States or with the Secretary of State? Not very good at all, I'm afraid."

She recalled how several years ago when Cole was prosecuting a serial killer who had terrified the people of Brooklyn, the Bronx, and Queens he arrived late for one of Ella Morrow's fabulous fundraising events at the Waldorf-Astoria. Rachel Hughes, one of Gina Anderson's childhood friends who inherited millions from her father's steel business and art collection, made the disparaging remark that Cole was irresponsible and that he would never amount to anything in the world.

Although Ella graciously and elegantly shrugged off Rachel's disparaging comment and dismissed it with a wave of the hand and a mild laugh, she had never forgotten the incident, and on many other occasions when they were together she never neglected to mention it to Gina. Ella even went so far one day during a luncheon as to insinuate that Gina was wasting her time with Cole and that he had succeeded in lowering her expectations. Ella often said, "Don't sell yourself short, Gina! Aim for the stars, my dear! And, don't settle for anything less than the heavens!"

Gina looked at her wristwatch again and then thought angrily, "I do hope I'm not wasting my time with him. He absolutely does have the right qualities of character and discipline of mind to take him to the top. And, besides, Daddy likes him, too."

Cole entered the restaurant and walking briskly and anxiously, he made his way through the crowd and then turned in the direction of the elegant table where Gina Anderson was waiting and wondering if, indeed, she should have taken the advice of her dear friend Ella Morrow.

As Cole approached the table, he knew from past experience that Gina had arrived approximately twenty minutes earlier and though she looked calm and placid on the outside, beneath the surface she was boiling over like a kettle of tea that sat too long on the fire.

He also knew that he had something very difficult to tell her that she probably would not understand, taking what he had to say personally. Cole flinched as he thought how at times Gina could be so unreasonably obstinate and cruel-hearted. Admittedly, she was a brat who had been spoiled devotedly and lovingly for the past twenty-seven years by her parents, the Honorable Senator James Anderson and his wife, Martha. Gina had always been accustomed to getting her own way, especially in matters of finance and the heart. She had the Senator and every man who dared to venture into her warm waters wrapped around her finger. This was almost guaranteed due to her family's wealth and political connections, but perhaps more so on account of her elegance and beauty. Her long legs and voluptuous breasts often caught one by surprise. But these were easily surpassed by her soft, white complexion, and her flaming black hair and dark eyes.

"Sorry, I'm late, darling," Cole said anxiously, as he slid into the chair opposite Gina, and smiled. "Court ran longer than I had expected and the traffic on the Avenue was absolutely terrible. You'd think the President was in town." He searched her white, powdered face quickly but carefully, scanning for a clue that would tell him what kind of mood she was in this afternoon. He was hardly surprised when he saw a mask and two sharklike eyes staring back at him coldly.

He shuddered and for a moment he had a vision of the great white shark that menaced and ate several of the inhabitants and summer visitors of Martha's Vineyard in the movie *Jaws*. He remembered how Richard Dreyfus, playing the part of an oceanographer and marine biologist, went down into the murky depths of the ocean in a cage to shoot it with a flimsy spear gun. He had never forgotten the look on Dreyfus's face when the shark had attacked him and bent the cage as if it was made of tin foil and straw. When Dreyfus came face to face with the shark and looked into its black eyes, he nearly died of fright.

"Well. It's about time," Gina said, looking up from the menu and frowning at him. "I've been waiting at least twenty minutes for you. You're becoming irresponsible, John."

"The Tate-Bradshaw case went to trial today, darling, and you know what that means—opening statements, numerous delays, and butterflies in the tummy. I was lucky to get out when I did. Randy nearly had a fit, and you should have seen him raving and yelling in front of Samantha, Leo, and Joseph. And now I'll probably be late for the afternoon session."

"If this kind of behavior keeps up, I don't know what father will think," Gina said. "You know, father is planning a dinner party next week and a few of the most important and powerful people in New York politics will be there, don't you? And, if you show up late, like you did this afternoon, I'm afraid you're not going to make a very good impression on them, darling. And, you might ruin any chance there is for becoming the next governor of New York State."

"The governor?" Cole said, surprised. "Oh, darling, are there no bounds to your ambition?"

"No. I'm afraid not, and why should there be? I've always been a precocious child, and now that I'm an adult I'm certainly not going to change. Not for you or for anyone! You can ask Daddy, if you don't believe me."

Cole did believe her, and that was the problem. It made him nervous whenever he thought about Gina and her damn ambition. She reminded him of a character from a play he read back in high school: Macbeth. But, it wasn't Macbeth who turned his blood cold so much as Lady Macbeth, who pushed and encouraged her husband to commit regicide. "Hail, King that shall be!" Shakespeare wrote, and Cole shuddered at the thought. He could not help but imagine that Gina was the quintessential Lady Macbeth, and in the words of Shakespeare, he often thought of her as "my dearest partner of greatness." Was there nothing Gina wouldn't do for her husband, so he might become the next governor of New York State? Or, perhaps, she was looking beyond state politics and had her eye on the presidency of the United States? Cole was convinced that she would stop at nothing to get her way.

Gina swiftly scanned the restaurant for the waiter, who was standing attentively at another table across the room, taking an order from a group of Chinese businessmen.

"Next Saturday evening could certainly be very important to your career, darling. Father's invited just about everyone from Albany and the City—Governor Thompson and his wife Dorothy, Mayor Hadley and his wife Cora. He also invited Police Commissioner Santoro, the entire city council, including the objectionably petulant Mr. Sebastian. And he just had to invite the Governor of New Jersey and her husband, and a few others— politicians, sports commentators, and businessmen."

While Gina rattled on about the details of her father's upcoming dinner party, Cole reclined in his chair, tuned out the nauseating sound of her voice, and desperately attempted to find meaning in the recurring phrase "The cradle rocks above an abyss . . . the cradle rocks above an abyss. . . ."

"Johnny! Johnny! Look at me! Look at me!" Gina furiously tapped the table with her little hand, trying to get his attention. "I swear, Johnny, you're not listening to me. What's wrong with you? I'm beginning to think that you should see a doctor. I'm sure Mother could recommend one."

"No. No. It's not necessary," said Cole absent-mindedly, and then he looked into her black eyes again. "Continue, darling. Please, continue. I was listening to you, honestly. I was just distracted for a moment by a thought." Cole had no doubt that the "thought" he had mentioned so insouciantly had come to posses him and turn his life upside down, creating a shambles of his relationships both at work and in his private life. He understood the truth of the matter: he had lost his power of concentration. No longer could he focus on the Tate-Bradshaw case. After weeks of preparation, he thought he missed something crucial—some important piece of evidence that might sway the jury. And that wasn't all that he lost. From the moment he had received Corporal Buccanon's phone call, his appetite, which was usually hearty and robust, had diminished considerably. For weeks now, he had skipped breakfast and lunch, surviving on leftover scraps of pizza and ginger ale. Moreover, he couldn't sleep, and night after night he'd wake up at two o'clock in the morning to stare at the digital clock on the table next to his bed.

"As I was saying, then, I'll expect you at three or four at the very latest. I do hope to get to Southampton before the governor and his wife."

Just then the waiter walked over and stood attentively at the head of the table. "Would Madam and the gentleman like to start the afternoon with a cocktail?" he said merrily.

"Yes, bring me a whiskey sour."

"Nothing for me, thank you," said Cole. As the waiter retreated, he looked up into Gina's dark, cold staring eyes and said, "Darling, I know that for the past week or more I've been behaving absolutely dreadfully. I've been a little absent-minded the past few days, but believe me I have an explanation." He paused and took a deep breath. "Last Monday, I received a letter from someone back home whom I hadn't heard from for ten or more years. He used to be a friend of mine. His name is Salvatore Buccanon, and we grew up and served in Vietnam together."

Groping for a glass on the table before him, Cole paused momentarily and took a sip of ice-cold water. After clearing his throat, he continued. "You can imagine how surprised I was when I first received his letter. Salvatore Buccanon, a corporal in the marines, said that Black Hawk, a friend of ours, was in trouble and he needed our help. Black Hawk lives in Wolf Creek, South Dakota. Last night, Corporal Buccanon left a similar message on my answering machine."

Cole paused again, and searched Gina's countenance for some sign of compassion. He saw none, and that disappointed him. She was as cold as a dead mackerel. He then said softly and tenderly, "I'm sorry, Gina, but I've decided to return to Tennessee and meet up with Corporal Buccanon and then head over to South Dakota to see what this is all about."

"What?" Gina asked in astonishment. "You don't honestly mean that! You can't leave now! Are you crazy? Do you know what you're giving up? You're giving up an opportunity of a lifetime. Some of the most influential people in New York politics will be at father's dinner party and when they discover that you've gone off on some cockamamie adventure, they'll think you're foolish. Is it the case? Is the case too much for you, darling?"

"No. It has absolutely nothing to do with the case," Cole said quietly, and deeply regretting having told her. If he had left town without telling anyone, as he had originally planned, he would not be sitting her now listening to a plethora of disparaging remarks from his fiancée.

"Then why are you leaving?" she snapped. Her face writhed in disbelief. "Is it because of your silly friendship with Corporal Buccanon or this Black Hawk?"

"It's more than just a friendship, darling, you don't understand." Cole struggled to maintain a solemn and steady demeanor, despite Gina's petulant and vituperative condemnation. He continued, "We're marines. We had all served in the marines together, and we've all been through some pretty rough times, seen some terrible things, and survived a hellish war. That does something to you inside. You have no idea what it was like out there in Vietnam and even if I could explain it to you or describe it, you couldn't possibly understand. I've known Corporal Buccanon all my life, and Black Hawk, well, if it wasn't for him. . . ."

"Why? Why couldn't I understand?" Gina whined, pursing her lips and twisting her long slender fingers into a ball.

Cole flinched awkwardly and then reached across the table, held her twisted fingers and began caressing them warmly. He said, "Darling, you're so young and naive in the matters of war. I don't expect you to understand what I'm talking about. But all I can say is that I just cannot turn my back on Corporal Black Hawk. I just can't."

"How long will you be away?" Gina asked.

"For as long as it takes."

That's all Gina Anderson needed to hear. She quickly withdrew her hand from Cole's embrace, and said testily, "You're right, I don't understand you. But, I can see clearly now that Ella Morrow was right when she said to watch out for you. I've been wasting my time with you, Johnny. You're totally irresponsible. Now how shall I explain this to father and the governor?"

"I'm sure you'll think of something," Cole said.

Gina Anderson wanted to cry, but with supreme effort she held back her tears. She knew that crying in public, especially before Cole, her betrayer, was unthinkable. Her status and position in society forbade it. And then, just as the waiter approached the table with her whisky sour, Gina stood up abruptly, and shouted, "Do you want to know something, Johnny? You might have gone to Harvard and you might live and work here in New York City, but in your heart, you're nothing more than a country hick." She threw her twisted napkin down onto the table.

"Your drink, Madam," announced the waiter.

"Give it to *him*," she said scornfully and loudly, nodding her head toward Cole, who sat wishing she had not made a scene in public.

"I'm sorry, darling," said Cole with a sense of finality.

"If you change your mind, Johnny, you know where I can be reached," Gina said sharply and turning melodramatically she pushed the waiter out of her way with one stiff arm and marched across the entire length of the restaurant, disappearing through a huge archway.

Cole signed the bill and thanked the waiter, slipping a few dollars into his sweaty palms. Then, feeling like a man who had been exposed in the commission of some devious crime, Cole left the restaurant, smiling at the patrons halfheartedly, as he passed by their tables.

While the junior prosecutors huddled around Cole's desk across town, listening to Corporal Buccanon's message for the nth time and arguing the instability of the messenger's state of mind, Cole stood languidly on the steps of the Plaza Suite Hotel gazing vacantly at the entrance to Central Park. Walking past the Plaza, tourists were startled and frightened by Cole's eerie face and burning eyes. Here, they saw a well-dressed man who might have it in his mind to do something horrible or unimaginable. After all, they thought, anything could happen in New York City.

But Cole was not contemplating anything horrible. On the contrary, he was thinking about Nashville and the farm where he grew up with his parents. He wondered just how much they had changed since the last time he saw them some fifteen years ago. And then, while staring at the treetops swaying in the afternoon breeze, he heard the haunting words echoing again, "The cradle rocks above an abyss, and common sense tells us that our existence is but a brief crack of light between two eternities of darkness."

Part II - Nashville

Chapter 6 - Leaving New York City

Leaving New York City and the Tate-Bradshaw case behind and returning home to the family estate in Nashville, Tennessee, was not an easy thing for Cole to do. He had never been one to abandon his friends nor a sinking ship; that is, not until all the women and children and the last passenger, the last crewman, the last man aboard, had been successfully and safely evacuated. But now, he felt like Lord Jim, standing on the deck of the Patina in the China Sea, looking down into the hull of the ship at the tide of crushed humanity. Cole remembered how the human cargo reminded him of sardines packed tightly in a tin container and how their wailing and prayers only added to the chaos and pandemonium of the scene. The Patina was sinking and in the eye of his mind, he saw Lord Jim leaning against the railing of the ship, looking down into the hull and then at the lifeboats being lowered into the water. He saw Lord Jim struggling awkwardly and miserably with his human fears, and while one voice in his head said, "Jump! Abandon Ship! Save yourself, fool!" another voice said, "You're an officer. Abandon ship now and you'll be court-martialed and forever labeled a coward." Standing on the brink of the precipice, before the eternal darkness of an abyss, the moment of truth had finally arrived for him. And at that moment, Cole recalled, Lord Jim had decided to save himself. He leaped into the lifeboat, never once giving the human cargo a second thought until it was too late; too late for the human cargo and too late for his soul.

As an officer in the marines, Cole had never given up on a soldier who had been trapped, wounded, or left dying in a rice paddy or jungle. Later, as a highly paid prosecutor for the State of New York, he had never walked out of a case once it had begun. But now, Cole had to make a choice. He had to choose between Black Hawk and the Tate-Bradshaw case, and between his own personal honor as an officer of the Marine Corps and Gina Anderson and everything she and her father represented and what they had to offer, including marriage and a bright future in New York politics. There was never any question in Cole's mind, however, concerning what he had to do. Cole knew that he really didn't have a choice. There was only one thing a reasonable man in his situation could do, and that was to live his life and even die, if necessary, according to the code of honor. That's how he had survived in Vietnam and got through the war, that's how Black Hawk had come to save Cole's life on that fateful day long ago. And that's why he could never forget or turn his back on Black Hawk, or even Corporal Buccanon, who despises him, or any other marine.

After the luncheon with Gina Anderson, which had ended in disappointment and frustration, Cole reluctantly returned to his condominium on the West Side where he began to set his affairs in order and pack for the long overdue trip home. In the evening hours after supper, Cole sat down at his desk in the study and penned two letters. One was addressed to Randy Scott, the attorney general for the state of New York, and began, "If you are reading this letter, Randy, then I am dead. And possibly, Black Hawk and Corporal Buccanon are dead, too. Needless to say, everything I have tried to accomplish in my life has been for nothing." Cole went on to explain in detail why he had been compelled to leave on such short notice. As a former naval officer, Cole believed that Randy would understand and perhaps even condone his actions. But Gina Anderson was different and would not be so forgiving. Therefore, he labored over her letter till late into the evening, scribbling several drafts before he felt absolutely confident that his letter precisely expressed his feelings and was completely truthful and honest about the uncertainty of his future. When the letters were done, he carefully sealed them inside separate envelopes and then placed the envelopes squarely on the center of his desk, so they would be easily noticed.

He sat back in his chair as if in a trance. Mixed emotions floated to the surface of his mind and toyed with him. First he felt as if he was playing the part of an unfaithful lover in some hackneyed drama, writing a Dear John letter to his fiancée. Then he felt as if he was a seer tormented by his own blindness. It was one o'clock in the morning by the time Cole crawled into bed.

Early Saturday morning he checked his apartment one last time before locking up. Stealthily, he took the elevator down to the garage where he neatly stowed his soft-covered black leather valise in the trunk of his BMW.

Quietly and gently, Cole pulled his BMW out from the underground garage and started down Seventh Avenue. He drove several blocks before turning into the Lincoln Tunnel at 34th Street. Once on the Jersey side, Cole headed south, taking the New Jersey Turnpike, Route 95, toward Washington, DC. Two hours later, he crossed the Delaware Memorial Bridge. At the summit of the bridge, he scanned the sky overhead and saw the Pleiades wane as the sun appeared brilliantly in the east over the gently rolling hills of the garden state. Thirty minutes later he had entered Maryland and was making great time.

It was nine o'clock when Cole approached Columbia, Maryland, and Washington DC, and the traffic came to a near standstill for miles. His BMW crawling along the highway, he scowled at the overweight drivers as they drank their coffee and ate their Dunkin' Donuts. Some drivers were already on their cell phones calling the office or their wives. Cole saw the turnoff for the beltway, Route 495, that circles Washington DC, and caught a glimpse of the traffic, standing motionless, bumper to bumper, or crawling like a snail. It took another thirty minutes to drive through Washington DC. Upon entering Arlington, Virginia, Cole jumped onto Route 66, heading west.

By noontime, he felt hungry, so he stopped for something to eat at a restaurant in Front Royal, on the scenic Skyline Drive, running through the beautiful Blue Ridge Mountains in the Shenandoah Valley and National Park. Afterwards, Cole followed Route 66 West and then, later, picked up Route 81, heading southwest. By dusk, Cole had made it to the border of Tennessee and there he stopped at the Day's Inn in Bristol for the night.

That evening Cole dined at the café adjoining the motel and then retired to his room for a quick shower and rest. As he bathed, the local news report captured his attention. Emerging from the bath in his robe, Cole turned to the television screen and saw a reporter interviewing Randy Scott, General Attorney for the State of New York. Flanked by Samantha Stone, Leo Albert, and Joseph Valentino, Scott had been stopped in the hallway by a reporter and a television cameraman, as he was leaving the court. Cole listened attentively as Scott answered several questions about the case. When the reporter asked about Cole's withdrawal from the case, and if Scott thought his withdrawal might jeopardize the prosecution, Scott shrugged his shoulders and announced that Cole's retirement was strictly personal business.

"And, are you taking over the case, now that Cole has withdrawn?" asked the reporter as the crowd pushed against him.

"Yes. As a matter of fact, I am," said Scott. "I'm personally taking over the prosecution, and I will be assisted by Samantha Stone, Leo Albert, and Joseph Valentino." Then, the reporter turned to Samantha Stone, and the lights of the camera flashed into her dilating eyes. She looked harried and exhausted. The reporter tried to ask her a question, but Stone pushed her way past him as if he were the carrier of a rare disease.

Turning off the television, Cole climbed into bed. He slept fitfully, tossing and turning, thinking about his motives. In fact, he was starting to doubt himself. He thought that he should return to New York and fulfill his responsibility to Scott and the State. It wasn't fair leaving them holding the bag, as I did. Samantha looked absolutely petrified this evening on the news. And Leo, and Joseph, what are they thinking? Cole wondered. Do I really want to get involved with Corporal Buccanon again? He's unstable and a menace to society, and there's no telling what he'll do once he gets started. He's like hell on wheels with his Harley. Then Cole thought about Black Hawk who had saved his life in Vietnam and felt if there was anything he could do for the marine, he would do it.

Cole finally dozed off into a heavy slumber and a fitful dream that he could not remember when he woke up in the morning.

Meanwhile, outside in the parking lot, where his BMW stood sentinel, a black raven with black-ruby eyes had lighted upon his car and began to shriek wildly and demonically.

Early the next morning, the black raven was gone. And after hungrily devouring a hearty breakfast of bacon and eggs, home fries, grits, orange juice, and coffee, Cole climbed into his BMW and drove deeper into his home state of Tennessee, following Route 81 West to Knoxville and then picking up Route 40 West to Nashville.

"It feels good to be going home again," Cole thought. He saw the bustling city of Knoxville give way to the rich and fertile farmland of the south. He saw acres of yellow corn and wheat, and rows and rows of pure white cotton balls, and the large leaves of the tobacco plant growing abundantly under the warm and penetrating sun. He saw cows and horses grazing leisurely in the fields behind the white wooden fences, red barns and towering silos. He saw John Deere and American Harvester tractors plowing and turning the soil of the good earth, and he saw orchards of bountiful fruit trees of every kind. He breathed deeply and felt the good air fill his lungs. Perhaps for the first time in twenty-five years, he actually felt alive again, as if a heavy burden had been lifted from his shoulders. He felt like a boy again, coming home to his family after school or after plowing a tract of land in the north field, his shirt drenched in the sweat of his labor. Once again, he felt as if he belonged to the earth in a very profound and mystical way. And, it made him feel good.

Cole remembered reading somewhere in the business section of *The New York Times* or *Southern Living* that Nashville had become a cultural center of education, commerce and manufacturing in the south. Now he saw for himself the plants and businesses that had sprung up like wildflowers across the region. He saw printing and publishing companies, meat packaging and coffee roasting companies, and mills for the production of flour, feed, lumber, cotton, and textile. They were flourishing. In short, the economy was burgeoning and growing in leaps and bounds. As a result of the new opportunities in the south, Cole wasn't surprised that more and more people were finding jobs and relocating their families to the Nashville area.

Approximately twelve miles east of Nashville and just outside of Lebanon, Cole drove past a familiar sign that read, The Hermitage. A national shrine and the home of President Andrew Jackson, the site made Cole feel a queer shiver run up his spine. He recalled that during a school trip to The Heritage he and Buccanon had stood before the tomb of President Andrew and made a pledge to follow in his military footsteps. The gardens surrounding the former president's mansion were elegant and beautiful. Cole didn't know it then, as a high school senior, that his decision to follow in the military footprints of President Andrew Jackson would change his life forever.

Cole finally reached Nashville and drove through a small but growing industrial area of foundries and limestone quarries. He recalled reading how, in addition to the Grand Ole Opry, Nashville had made a name for itself in confectionery, fertilizer, mattresses, feather pillows, cloth and paper bags, clothing, shirts, rayon and cellophane, shoes, hardwood floors, building materials, furniture, stoves, furnaces, and airplanes. As for an educational center, there were Vanderbilt University and George Peabody College for Teachers. Nashville also had one of the few homes for Confederate soldiers in the south, a Confederate Cemetery, and a National Cemetery.

In the heart of Nashville Cole stopped momentarily to view the magnificent Greek design of the state capitol building, completed in 1859, which contained the Tomb of James K. Polk, the eleventh President of the United States. Opposite the state building, Cole gazed upon the War Memorial Building, built in 1925, and Centennial Park where a replica of the famous Pantheon at Athens stands. While viewing the Pantheon through the window of his car, Cole scowled as he uttered the words, "Forward Achians." At one time, these words held a special meaning for him, connecting him to the past, to the writings of Homer, to his epic poem *The Illiad*, and the Achian warriors who fearlessly marched forward into battle and into the blackness of the abyss. Cole abandoned the phrase years ago, after the disastrous ambush. Now, he thought grimly, gloomily that the phrase "Forward Achians," once an absurd password and a rallying call for the troops, had ironically become a statement of grief and sorrow.

Cole's family estate, located on the southwest side of town, ran along the Cumberland River and consisted of approximately one hundred and forty acres of pristine farm and woodlands. While three-quarters of the land was dedicated to growing crops, specifically corn and wheat, one quarter was held aside to feed a herd of 200 cattle. The farm also supported twelve horses, and dozens of chickens, roosters, pigs, and milking cows. The topography of the land for the most part was relatively flat, with hills and knolls rolling gently in only one or two spots near the river. On the other side of the river, the land ran flat again for about two hundred feet before leading to a copse of woods.

As Cole carefully turned his metallic blue BMW into the long, tree-lined driveway of the family estate, he saw in the corner of his left eye the familiar sight of a scarecrow hanging and lurching from a post and crossbeam he had helped his father build years ago. With straw protruding from its blue denim shirt and jeans, the body of the scarecrow looked abnormally bulky and heavy. The head was made from a white linen shirt stuffed with straw and tied in the back, shaped like an overripe, oblong grape. Black eyes and a grinning mouth were awkwardly drawn onto the linen shirt. Cole's attention was then drawn to something that was perched on the right shoulder of the scarecrow. It was a large, black raven and he thought he saw it plucking viciously and ardently at the eyes of the scarecrow. Turning his head to get a better glimpse of the bird, Cole suddenly felt the car swaying under him, so he quickly faced forward again and glanced into his rearview mirror. He saw the grotesque raven devouring the eyes of the scarecrow, and then he heard its terrifying shriek. One wonders just what Cole would have done had he seen the raven flying high overhead following his car as he motored along the countryside. Never once had he bothered to look up into the sky. If he had, he would have seen the mad raven and its flight of wicked determination. And, he would have thought that it was possessed by an evil intelligence. In fact, the raven's behavior clearly showed that it had little or no fear of the human form. Hell No! Within seconds, the spectacle was over and Cole forgot about the raven as his ancestral farmhouse and the barn came into view and he realized that he was indeed home.

Chapter 7 – On The Farm

As the BMW came slowly to a stop between the farmhouse and the barn, Cole turned off the engine and just sat there in the car, taking in the scene and thinking. He was astonished that after fifteen years nothing had changed. Everything looked the same to him—the trees, the land, and the fields of corn and wheat. From where he was sitting, he saw the cattle and the horses grazing in the pasture. He saw a rooster chasing several chickens across the yard and into the barn. He heard the pigs and piglets grunting happily in their pen. He saw the clear, rushing water of the Cumberland River, the white colonial house, the garage, the red barn and silo, the stables, and the henhouse. It all came back to Cole, and it seemed as if the land was imbued with a quality of eternal power and beauty; it was fresh, green, and eternal like a rock, like the universe.

Then, suddenly, Cole's mother, a short and slender woman in her midsixties, with short brown hair and sparkling emerald-green eyes, came running out of the house, shouting, volubly, joyfully, "Johnny! Johnny!" Cole saw his mother and realized sadly and dishearteningly that something had, indeed, changed. The woman running toward him, once a lovely, strong, and vibrant woman who had carried him, fed him, and loved him had grown older. With no little effort, he hid his anguish and pain. Sooner or later, he thought, nature will betray us as it does to all living things.

Theresa swiftly crossed the driveway and waited patiently for her son to climb out from his car. Cole could not help but smile and thank the Almighty that this sweet, elderly woman was still as agile and as strong as ever.

As Cole stepped out of the car, Theresa grabbed him in a bear hug around the shoulders, kissed him, and then buried her face in his chest, desperately wanting to hide the tears in her eyes. It was a miracle, she thought, it really was a miracle. God had finally answered her prayers—Johnny was home again and that's all that mattered. For years now, Theresa had been convinced she had lost her only son to the big city, where the jungle was made not of overgrown trees and brush, as in Vietnam, but of concrete walls as in the city of New York. She knew her son had been enamored with the judiciary system and had unavoidably spent numerous hours in court, in judge's chambers, and in his office reading complaints, litigation, legal briefs, and law books. Rarely did her son have time for anything else.

"Why didn't you call and let us know you were coming?" Theresa said elatedly, joyfully, wiping away the tears from her eyes with a little white handkerchief she pulled from her sleeve. "Wait till your father sees you."

"I would've called but I didn't want to worry you," said Cole, and smiled brightly. He remembered how his mother would insist that he call her whenever he went out and arrived at his destination. He remembered making such phone calls from the Buccanons' house whenever he had visited Salvatore or Susan. He was eight or nine years old then. Now, he embraced his mother and kissed her again and held her in his arms for a moment or two, and said, "You don't know how I've missed you. I should've come home sooner."

"You're here with us now—that's all that matters," Theresa said cheerfully, and then, remembering her girlfriend and neighbor, she said enthusiastically, "Johnny! What a coincidence! Look here! It's Susan! She's been visiting with me, darling. You remember Susan don't you?"

Susan Buccanon, Corporal Salvatore Buccanon's sister, had stopped by the Coles' to visit with Theresa for the day. When Cole drove up to the farmhouse, she had followed his mother out onto the porch and into the barnyard. He had a mental picture of

Susan. He remembered her as being moderately tall, with long slender arms and legs. When he last saw her, Susan was strikingly beautiful, with pale, blue eyes and light blond hair smartly cut, shoulder-length, and styled. But now, the woman standing a few feet behind Theresa looked plain and jaded. He thought she looked more like a homespun country girl than a ravishing and sophisticated debutante who left her home state of Tennessee to become a member of the jet set in California.

Cole looked at her and smiled warmly, "Of course, I remember Susan, Mother. We practically grew up together right here on this farm."

With an awkward shyness, Susan stepped forward and held out her small, slender hand. Cole noticed an imperceptible hesitation on her part – a moment of pause – as if she was trying to decide whether she should kiss Cole or simply shake his hand. She decided that a handshake would be less intimidating and less complicating.

"Hello, Johnny," Susan said and then she grabbed his hand firmly, confidently, and shook it. "How are you?"

"Hello, Susan," said Cole, looking into her pale, blue eyes and sensing an uneasiness, as if a certain fear was swimming beneath the surface. "It's been a long time."

"Yes, it has," said Susan, thoughtfully, her confidence slowly returning after the shock of seeing Cole after fifteen years. Susan was never one who might be easily flustered by meeting old boyfriends. But, she had never thought she would be standing in front of Cole again—not in a million years.

Now, turning to Theresa and taking her hand, Susan smiled warmly and said, "Well, Theresa, I'm sure you and Johnny have a lot to talk about. So I'll just be running along. I'll call you in the morning—if you don't mind. Good-bye." Then, she turned to Cole and extended her hand. "Good-bye, Johnny. I'm glad you've come home. I hope you'll stay awhile."

Now it was Cole who was speechless and flustered from the shock of seeing Susan after so long a separation. His mouth had suddenly become dry, and he groped for words. For the first time in years, the articulate prosecutor who always had something to say felt like an idiot. He followed her to the car, held open the door of her Explorer, and watched her climb in. She rolled down the window.

"We have a lot to talk about, Susan. Why don't you and Sal come by this evening for dinner?" Cole said, grinning boyishly and losing himself in her deep blue eyes. Cole knew that he was there for one purpose only and that to meet up with Salvatore and resolve this business concerning Black Hawk. But he found himself captivated by Susan once again, and he knew that if he didn't ask her to dinner, he might come to regret it perhaps for the rest of his life. Besides, it would give him a chance to get reacquainted with her, he thought. Not that it might lead to anything, because that had ended years ago, right after they had both graduated from high school and went their separate ways. Seeing her now, however, stirred up old and deep emotions, which he thought were better left undisturbed.

"Sure, why not . . . I'd like that," Susan said with a smile, and then she started the Explorer and pulled away.

Just as Susan had turned onto the main road leading to town, Cole's father, William, came racing in from the north field. He had been surveying the farm and going over some details with Jake Snow, the farm administrator and manager, when he heard the roar of the engine and saw the BMW turn into the driveway. Recognizing the BMW from the description of the car Cole had given him over the phone, William had dropped everything, clambered into his pickup truck with Jake Snow, and sped back to the farmhouse. Cole and his mother saw the truck racing along the open field like a bat flying out of hell, jouncing up and down and then coming to an abrupt stop in the middle of the barnyard.

"Why, I'll be damn. It's really you!" William said excitedly, climbing out of the truck. "Call Dr. Meinhard, Mother, I think the pills he gave me last week are affecting my vision." He hugged Cole and slapped him heartily on the back with his big, thick working hands. Jake Snow did the same. "What's a big New York State prosecutor like you doing in these neck of the woods? I think the boy's lost, Mother." More seriously, he asked, "How long has it been, son? Fifteen years?"

"Fifteen years, Dad. That's how I reckon it." Cole and his father embraced again.

"How's New York?" asked Jake.

"Busy and crazy as always." Cole smiled and he looked at Jake and remembered the first time he saw him. He was a young man with a wife and a growing family back then, and he showed up on the farm one day in the summer of '64 looking for work. The wife and children were sitting in the car. There was always something to be done around the farmstead, so William gave the young man a temporary job. In short time, Jake proved that he could handle just about anything from repairing old, dilapidated tractors, fences, and barns to tending to the livestock, plowing the land, and harvesting crops. One week later, William hired Jake as a regular and within a year's time, he was managing the farm on his own.

"I can't believe it," said Theresa vibrantly. "You have no idea how wonderful it is just to see you again. There's so much I have to tell you. But, we'll plenty of time to talk later, after dinner. Tonight, I'm going to cook your favorite meal, son."

"Where's your things? Let's bring them in the house," William said, and then he smiled again feeling just as proud as a rooster in a henhouse.

While Theresa prepared dinner for the family, Cole unpacked the car and hauled his luggage into the center hall. From there, he carried them up a narrow staircase to a small room in the back of the house.

He opened the door to his room slowly and apprehensively, not knowing what to expect, and paused for a moment or two at the threshold before entering. As he entered the room of his childhood, it seemed to Cole that he had stepped into a time warp. He felt he had traveled back in time, to the tender age of nine or ten. And yes, it was just as he had remembered it. From where he stood he could see the worn, battered, double-hung window that looked out directly over the barnyard and open fields and woods. To the left, he saw at least fifty acres of yellow corn, to the right another fifty of wheat, and beyond that, the woods, dense and green. The window was open but the air in the room felt stale and hot. Diaphanous curtains, white and frayed, with a slightly faded floral design, hung from a small curtain rod, stopping six inches from the floor. The shade underneath the curtain had also faded and curled at the edges. The twin-size bed, lying cozily against the adjacent wall, was covered with a brown quilt bedspread, and looked warmly inviting. The dresser, made of fine oak wood, had four drawers and had been shoved into a corner. Across from the bed, there was a small wooden desk with three drawers and stacked on top of the desk was a dictionary, a thesaurus, and a reading lamp. School pennants and diplomas from Nashville High, the University of Tennessee, and Harvard Law School proudly decorated the walls. Above the dresser, Cole saw three photographs. They were attached to the wall and had been very carefully arranged. One was a picture of Susan and Cole at their high school prom. It was one of those quick-shot pictures taken by the official school photographer while everyone waited impatiently in a queue for their moment in front of the camera. Susan was wearing a navy blue chiffon gown, and stood stiffly, erectly, like a cardboard figure, while Cole, wearing a black tuxedo and cummerbund—his first—slouched comically to one side. The second photograph was a picture of Cole on his graduation day. William had shoved the camera into Jake Snow's trembling hand and ordered him to take the picture. It was a group shot of Cole flanked by his mother and father. Cole was in cap and gown. The third photograph on the wall was a picture of Cole and Salvatore Buccanon posing nonchalantly before a bus that was to take them to Camp Pendleton where they would be inducted into the Marine Corps. Buccanon was smiling grandly and looked as if he was going to a picnic, while Cole looked seriously distressed and grim.

Hearing his mother's voice emanating from the kitchen on the first floor, Cole suddenly jumped and woke up from his trance. He listened quietly for a moment. Then it came to him: his mother was standing at the kitchen window and speaking to his father who was walking toward his pickup truck and reminding him not to forget the sour cream at the grocer's. Wearily and absent-mindedly, Cole threw his luggage in the corner of the room next to the small closet and collapsed on the bed.

Once a week, whether or not it was needed, Theresa would change the bedding, sweep the floor, and dust and polish the furniture. But, lately, however, Theresa had noticed that Susan always managed to stop by just at the right time—whenever there was heavy work and cleaning to be done. She knew it wasn't coincidence. After Betty's death in 1977 from cancer – she was a heavy smoker - Theresa had unofficially adopted Susan, treating her as if she were her own daughter.

Chapter 8 - Father McFarland

Cole heard a commotion at the front door, hurried footsteps, low conversation, and a few words. "I'm so glad you could make it. You're just in time, please come in. Oh, you shouldn't have." He woke up slowly and for a moment had forgotten where he was. He looked around the room and when he saw the pictures, diplomas, and pennants hanging on the walls, the window, the curtains, and his desk and lamp, it all came back to him—he was in Nashville. He was home.

Cole sighed heavily and swung his legs over the side of the bed, placing his feet firmly on the floor as if to test the reality of his environment. He got up and went to the bathroom, and looked at his face in the mirror. The face that looked back at him was worn and tired. He shook his head and splashed cold water on his brow. Then, he washed his face and combed his hair. For dinner, he dressed casually wearing jeans, loafers, and a light blue polo shirt. When he looked at himself in the mirror again, he thought he looked quite collegian. Then he went downstairs to join the others.

Theresa and Susan were preoccupied setting the table with a fine white linen cloth, his mother's finest and oldest china, silverware that was passed down from one generation to the next, goblets from Manchester, England, and long-stem wine glasses from the San Bernardino Valley in California. It looked like a holiday—Christmas. The atmosphere in the house was festive and merry.

Theresa moved gracefully between the rooms, back and forth, from the kitchen to the dining room, and then back again, inspecting the silverware, checking the roast beef, folding a napkin, and feeling the firmness of the corn. She held a glass up to the light and then dried a water stain from its rim; she had cut, boiled and mashed potatoes, and steamed French-cut string beans. She removed the biscuits from the oven and tossed the salad, the tomatoes, the cucumbers, and celery. She mixed the gravy and the natural juices, and chattered incessantly and pleasantly with Susan, who followed Theresa's every move.

William was slouching at the end of the table and struggling to extract a cork from a thin, narrow, long-necked bottle of Chardonnay.

As Cole quietly stepped into the dining room, everyone stopped what they were doing and looked at him for a moment as though he was a stranger. And then, without hesitating or missing a beat of the rhythm of life, they resumed their activities.

"Have a seat, darling, dinner will be ready in a minute," Theresa said as she stepped into the kitchen. She returned shortly with a large roast of beef on a serving platter and placed it in the center of the table.

Pop! The sound echoed as the cork came loose from the narrow, long-necked bottle of Chardonnay and ricocheted off the ceiling.

William looked up at the ceiling, saw the mark left by the cork, and winced. Then, with the dexterity of a maitre d', he poured the wine, filling to the rim the glasses around the table. As he counted the places, he realized that someone was missing, and bellowed loudly in a harsh and rowdy voice, "Where's Father McFarland? He's late!"

As if Providence had answered William's question, Cole heard a car pull into the driveway and come to a stop just outside their back door. A minute later, Father McFarland, a huge, bulky man, with a wild crop of curly red hair and a face as round and freckled as a spotted hot air balloon, entered the dining room. The pastor of St. Patrick's parish greeted everyone cheerfully and enthusiastically. His emerald green eyes glistened as he studied the faces around the table. When he saw Cole, whom he hadn't seen for fifteen years standing at the sideboard, he embraced him in a bear hug and muttered, "God Bless you, Son. God Bless. It's been a long time, by God, and I daresay you're looking as fit as a fiddle." The formal salutations over, Father McFarland stepped to one side of the table and sat down ponderously in a slender chair that groaned and squeaked under the bulk of his weight. Despite his ordinary attire—black trousers and black shirt with a white collar—he evinced a kingliness and grandiosity that could not have been matched by the Archbishop of Canterbury or the King of England. Susan slipped into the chair next to Father McFarland and across from Cole, and Theresa and William sat at opposite ends of the table.

After everyone had taken a seat at the table, Theresa turned to Father McFarland and said, "Father, would you be so kind as to say a little prayer or to pronounce a blessing before we begin." As was his wont in these situations, Father McFarland closed his eyes tightly, meditated for a few moments, gargled his throat with a sip of red wine, and then uttered something totally incomprehensible and unrecognizable, at the end of which he said loudly and gloriously, "Amen."

William frowned and decided to pour himself another glass of wine as Father McFarland took center stage to expound vigorously and furiously his political leanings and inclinations toward the present administration in Washington, DC.

Cole appeared content to just sit back and listen quietly. From across the table, he watched Susan. He was amazed how she appeared to be listening so attentively to every word spoken by Father McFarland. It was as if her life hinged on his approbation. She smiled and blushed like a schoolgirl whenever he finished telling one of his lurid stories about a senator or a congressman on Capitol Hill who had had an affair with this young intern or that campaign worker. However, beneath her smiling face and clear, blue eyes, Cole sensed an undefined sadness and melancholy and he wondered what might be its source. Was it the unexpected twists and turns of life? Was it because life somehow never turned out exactly the way one had planned it? Everyone knew, he thought, that the best laid-out plans could be destroyed in the wink of an eye. Years of hard and calculating work shot to hell in less than a minute—like a pheasant, flying south during hunting season. A hunter raises his gun, takes aim and fires, and in a few seconds it's all over for the pheasant. Walk into an ambush or step on an antipersonnel land mine in the jungle and you'll find yourself lying somewhere without an arm or a leg, or a face, all in a matter of seconds. Your whole life could be changed permanently in those few seconds.

As his father poured another glass of wine and handed it to Cole, the words that had haunted him for the past several months returned. From deep within the recesses of his mind, he heard a voice repeating, "The cradle rocks above an abyss . . . the cradle rocks above an abyss and common sense tells us. . . ." Suddenly he thought about Black Hawk and wondered what this was all about—the unexpected letter from the past, the strange phone call from Corporal Buccanon. Where was Corporal Buccanon, by the way? Why didn't he come to dinner with Susan as he had planned?

Cole stroked his chin thoughtfully as Father McFarland said in a condescending tone, "Sal was sitting at the bar at General Lee's Bar and Grill. I saw him as I was passing by the establishment. I had stopped to admire the stain glass of the front window, which Lee had imported from Italy, when I looked in and saw him sitting there alone at the bar and he was drinking.

"I would have recognized him anywhere. He had poor T-bone tied up to a bumper out front, and he was barking at everyone who sauntered by. I stood there for a couple of minutes and I swear! Oh, please forgive me Lord!" Father McFarland raised his eyes to heaven penitently and made the sign of the cross. "That's a vicious dog, he has there. Not at all like Roscoe. Now, Roscoe was a dog! Kind and gentle and friendly as they come. Man's best friend, if you know what I mean. He was dependable and loyal. I felt really bad when old lady Hanley's car tagged that dog. Its hindquarters were fractured in several places, and Henry had to shoot it dead—right there in the middle of the road in front of the boy who was red-eyed and wailing and had to be no more than ten years old at the time. My, my, and the boy moped around for days after that," and then after a pause, "Roscoe was a fine dog, a good, fine dog. God rest his canine soul."

Cole glanced casually and uneasily at Susan and from the corner of his eye, he saw her sitting quietly, stoically at the table, one hand dangling limply at her side and the other suspended in midair over her plate. Her head was bent forward and her eyes stared vacantly into space, seeing but not seeing, and her ears heard the spoken words, hearing but not hearing. He saw his mother unconsciously purse her lips and roll her eyes upward toward heaven. She nodded her head, feeling nothing but sympathy for Susan and the heart-wrenching pain she had to be suffering because of her inebriated and senseless imbecile of a brother.

Father McFarland continued. "I wouldn't be surprised, my dear,"—now speaking directly to Susan—"if Salvatore ends up spending the night in the tank again."

"That's a shame, a real shame," William said pityingly. "If he continues to follow this path of destruction, he'll eventually kill himself. Just think what it might have done to Henry and Betty if they were still alive." Then turning to Father McFarland, he said, "Why don't you speak to him? You're a priest! Can't you persuade him to stop drinking like the devil?"

Indignant, Father McFarland said, "I'll have you know, William, I've spoken to the lad on more than one occasion concerning his liberal habits and the destructive nature of whisky. But there's a stubborn streak that runs in him . . . "

"Where did he get it from? Certainly not from Henry or Betty," Theresa said reflectively. Then she looked at Susan and said with heartfelt sympathy, "I feel sorry for you, my dear. I feel sorry for you because you're the one who has to put up with him. I didn't see this stubborn, mean streak in him until after he came home from the war. Unfortunately, your brother had changed when he went to Vietnam. He became a monster, a bully, a drunk, a cheat, and a womanizer. And after Betty and Henry died, I'm sure there was very little you could do to rein in the animal he had become."

"Surely, you're exaggerating, Mother?" Cole reproached her, though he had an idea his mother wasn't exaggerating. He knew just how Corporal Buccanon had changed once he had arrived at Vietnam and was exposed to marijuana, alcohol, and death. Now Cole wanted to change the subject and spare Susan the pain she might be feeling from hearing any more of these harsh words about her brother.

"I'm not exaggerating," Theresa said as she turned to Cole. She crinkled up her nose and added, "He's despicable. He's filthy. He never bathes," and to Susan, "I don't know how you can stand the smell. He wears the same leather jacket, jeans, and boots for days. And the way he comes racing through the countryside on his motorcycle, you'd think he was racing in the Indy Five Hundred. The noise scares me half to death."

"He's really not all that bad," said Susan courageously. "I know he's changed, but a lot of people who had been through the war had changed. He's not the only one." Cole knew that Susan was referring to him and was suggesting that he, too, had changed and not necessarily for the better. She glanced at him from across the table and then lowered her eyes.

"Sal's a hard worker, I'd have to say that for the lad," William said as he reached for the bowl of mashed potatoes, scooped out three big spoonfuls, and plopped it on his dish. "Every morning, bright and early, I can hear the tractor out in the field, a low humming sound in the distance. I know it's him. The other day when I was down at the eastern end of the field, I got a glimpse of him on his tractor. The sun was high in the sky and I could see the heat waves shimmering above the field. I felt as though I was out in a desert and looking at a mirage." Then he said sadly, "He looked so forlorn and forsaken out under the hot sun. Poor lad . . ."

"The boy was never forsaken, William! You know that as well as anyone," said Theresa firmly. Then, turning to Father McFarland, "You know, Father, there were a lot of folks in this town that cared for Salvatore. He had friends here, but when he returned to Nashville after the war with those horrible tattoos all over his arms and started to take up drinking and fighting in public places, people around here just gave up on him."

"He's blessed to have Susan and good Christian friends like all of you to watch after him," Father McFarland said as he reached for another succulent slice of roast beef. "He's blessed."

"He may be blessed all right, but Sam Watson, the owner of the Colorado Cafe, wasn't blessed last Saturday evening when Salvatore showed up and got into a fist fight with some roughnecks from Memphis. They wrecked the place, and by the time the sheriff arrived, it looked as though a twister had passed through it. The damage had to be in the thousands."

Susan looked around the table slowly, and in defense of Sal's past transgressions and savage behavior, she said unapologetically, "I don't expect any of you to understand this, but I love my brother Sal."

It appeared to Cole as if Susan was on the verge of tears, and he didn't want to see her cry, not again. Too many people have shed tears already. Weren't we drowning in tears? Wasn't the world drowning in an ocean of tears? And, he thought, this is the legacy of war, families sitting around the dining room table crying over the dead and the living dead, which no one seems to mention at the beginning of a conflict. He now understood that the men and women who had survived the war weren't necessarily lucky because they would have to carry, perhaps for years to come, their guilt and the horrors of war with them to their grave.

Susan was holding back her tears now despite the tremor in her voice. "Even with all his faults, beneath his roughneck exterior, there's a person living deeply inside of him who has the capacity for doing good things." Then she turned to Cole for a sign of assurance. "Am I right, Johnny? You know Sal better than anyone here. You and he were in Nam together. Tell them! Tell them that he's a good person!" She was almost pleading now.

Cole immediately recognized Susan's plea as a desperate call for succor. He knew that she could not possibly have known the hatred he felt in his heart toward Sal—how they had grown apart after the ambush.

She was, therefore, surprised when he responded like a lawyer, sounding cold and stolid. "I don't think I can honestly answer that, Susan, without first speaking to him. Yes, we grew up together, and we went to war and fought together, and bled and cried together, but I've learned that people change over time, some for the better and others for the worse. I know that during the war Sal changed, as I have, as well as a million other guys. After the ambush, we drifted apart—if you know what I mean. Oh, I saw him a few times in the hospital in Japan, but for the most part I lost track of him right after that, right after we were released. When I got home from the war, I went on to law school, as you know. When Sal got home, I was already at Cambridge. I don't know Sal anymore, Susan, not like I used to. I'm not sure what he's like now. But, if you're asking for my opinion, after listening to what everyone has said here this evening, I'd say that he had a monkey on his back when he left Nam and he probably is still carrying that monkey around with him today. Perhaps, he's still fighting the war."

Father McFarland made the sign of the cross, and then helped himself to another ear of corn and some fluffy, golden-brown biscuits with a butter-flaked crust. When he had finished he said, "Well, if the poor lad is still fighting the war, he ought to get some kind of professional help. The VA, for instance, can arrange for individual and group therapy sessions for veterans who are still suffering from stress and post-traumatic syndrome. And, if, for some reason, he doesn't want to go through the VA, he can always seek out professional help on his own. If Sal needs someone to talk to, tell him to drop by—anytime. My door's always open."

"Thank you, Father McFarland," Susan said awkwardly, and she was genuinely touched by Father McFarland's offer. "I'll mention it to Sal."

"And, when we go to bed tonight, let us remember to pray for Sal and for all the veterans who are still suffering and living the horrors of war, past, present, and future. The Lord has given us an awesome power, children. A power that too often is neglected by the very people who need it most. It is the power of prayer! Let us use it! Here on earth, most people fail to pray. And those who do pray often do so without knowing how to pray properly. Many of them pray only when they want something from the Lord. Let us pray now, dear brothers and sisters, for our brother Sal. Father, we pray for our brother Salvatore. We pray for his salvation and redemption." And then after a long pause, Father McFarland added as if it was merely an afterthought, "Amen!

Chapter 9 - After Dinner

After dinner, Cole led Susan—as he had done so many years ago and so many times before—to the verandah, where they sat in rattan wicker chairs and watched the sun drop indolently behind the distant trees. They chatted, cheerfully and uninhibitedly, as old friends often do upon meeting one another after a long separation. After watching Susan all night from across the dining room table, it seemed to Cole that her maternal instincts had finally taken over her persona. This was evident in her strong defense of her brother Salvatore, he thought. It seemed to him at least that Susan had finally found a way to reconcile the inner forces that had driven her in opposite directions and evidently ruined her life. Now, she appeared to be somewhat happier than she was before, as if her desire for new experiences and adventures—to see new places and make new friends—had been spent. It had run its course, and now, he thought sadly, she looked like a woman who had given up and resigned from life. There was no doubt in his mind that she had returned home to her family—what was left of it—to old familiar friends, to the farm, and to Nashville. Cole realized that Susan had done something he thought he could never do: come home again.

He had lived in the city for too long ever to return home for good. Whenever he was overwhelmed by the urge to pack it in and call it quits, he'd remember reading Thomas Wolfe's books *Look Homeward Angel* and *You Can't Go Home Again*, and the urge would quietly subside. He was often comforted by the idea that he could look back whenever he wanted to but he could never go home again. Susan, however, had, indeed, come home and he found that he admired her for it. Despite the passing years and the frayed edges, he thought that she was still a ravishingly beautiful woman. Yes, she looked worn out and tired, but Cole knew that the broken dreams of one's youth had a way of turning life upside down and inside out. And in its place, it could easily create a life you never would had imagined was possible.

Cole was admiring her slender figure, and her clean, natural, complexion, and her moist lips when he thought he heard the sound of a raven cawing and flying overhead. He looked up and turned around as if to follow the sound, but he saw nothing extraordinary. He wondered if it was the same black bird that had attacked the scarecrow when he first drove up to the farm. He remembered how it ruthlessly plucked at the eyes and how that had sickened his stomach. Then he dismissed the idea, thinking that it was nothing but his active imagination, and said to Susan "You know I think you're absolutely beautiful."

Susan accepted his flattering words graciously, and responded with a reserve and timid smile. It occurred to Cole that she was playing it smart, keeping her emotions safely locked up in a secret room in her heart.

Cole continued, "The other day, while I was preparing for a case, I stopped and thought about you. I thought about us, and how we used to have fun. If I remember correctly, you used to love horseback riding, fishing, and hiking."

"I still do. Some things never die."

Cole thought that perhaps she might be referring to something more intimate than horseback riding or fishing. He wanted to believe that she was alluding to the love they once felt for each other, love that somehow was lost or pushed aside as they were growing up, and replaced by adult ambitions that simply drove them apart and prevented their feelings from fully blossoming. If some things never die, he thought, then, perhaps, she might still be in love with me. He wasn't sure, and he was afraid to ask. So, he followed a safer train of thought.

"I remembered how we used to go into town on the weekends and catch a picture show, and how on Saturday mornings, I'd come riding by on my bicycle and we'd go riding together to the stadium to watch the football games."

"Yes, I remember," said Susan.

"And the senior prom! Do you remember our senior prom? You were absolutely the loveliest girl at the prom. I still have our picture hanging on the wall in my room."

"I know."

"It all came back to me—rather suddenly and unexpectedly. I hadn't given it much thought for a long time. But, I'm glad I'm thinking about it now. We really had a great time here growing up together."

"Yes, didn't we?" Susan said, reluctantly, her face turning bright red. And then, feeling utterly helpless against Cole's boyish and childish imagination, she added, "But, we also had our ups and downs. It wasn't all peaches and cream and roses all the time."

Cole had to admit it to himself that she was right. There were plenty of times when they fought like cats and dogs. Afterwards, they wouldn't speak to each other for weeks, and this would drive Sal absolutely crazy because he loathed being caught between two feuding parties. If we could start over again, Cole thought, perhaps we would do things differently. Perhaps, we'd give love a chance to flourish.

"You know, I lost track of you right after high school. You went off to a college somewhere out west—what was the name of that college?"

"USC," Susan said, thinking that Cole knew perfectly well where she had gone to school. Didn't he send her dozens of letters, which she never answered? She was always too busy studying her political science and making new acquaintances and political connections.

"That's right, USC. I do remember, now that you mention it. You were sick of country living back then and wanted to get away from us farming types. Our lives were uneventful and too boring for you, as I recall."

"Not exactly," Susan said thinly. "I just wanted to see another part of the country, another part of the world, and to broaden my experiences and make new friends. You know how kids are at seventeen and eighteen years old. They think they know everything. I had to get away. Anyway, after graduating college with a degree in political science and foreign relations, I got a job as a writer with the *Los Angeles Times* covering politics in Southern California, and so I stayed." She paused. "But, I never forgot about you, Johnny. You have no idea how many times I had wanted to call you and drag you back to good old Tennessee, again, and back to this farm."

Cole smiled warmly and had no doubts that if anyone could have dragged him away from New York City and out of the clutches of the ambitious Gina Anderson and her father, the Honorable Senator James Anderson, it was Susan. He realized, perhaps too late, that his life would have been simpler and so much more satisfying here in Tennessee with Susan than in New York with Gina Anderson. Now, with a sense of melancholy, he asked Susan, "When did you return to country living?"

"It was shortly after mother passed away back in '77," Susan said sadly, her eyes tearing up. "You and Sal had already returned from Vietnam. In fact, it was several years later, after you had graduated from the University of Tennessee and had gone up to Boston to study law at Harvard. That's when I came home, while you were in Boston. Dad and Sal were taking mother's death pretty badly. I thought they needed me, so I just came home to be with them."

"You should have called me. Perhaps I could've been of some help. Why didn't you call? " Cole asked.

She sensed that he was angry and hurt. She scowled and dismissed Cole's objections with a casual wave of her hand. "Don't be angry with me, Johnny. I never told you because I didn't want anything to stand in the way of you and your career. And, I still believe even today that I made the right decision. It's plain to see that you've done quiet well for yourself in New York."

"I did all right, I suppose," said Cole wistfully. While all the time his heart was breaking and he was thinking about how he had wasted all those years living alone, living – if one could call it that - without Susan, without her lovely smile and delicate sense of humor. How much more exciting and enjoyable life might have been with her?

Then, Susan said something that shocked Cole. "Are you going to marry Gina Anderson?"

"Gina Anderson?" Cole exclaimed, his voice rising to a screech. "That brat? What ever gave you that idea?" He struggled to regain control of himself, and suddenly he felt awkward and embarrassed because he had never told Susan about Gina or that he and Gina were betrothed. "How did you know about me and Gina Anderson?"

"I read about it in the newspapers. In the society section."

"Oh! I see." Cole wanted to crawl away.

"Well?" Susan asked, though she thought she already knew the answer. "When will you and Gina tie the knot?"

"I don't know," said Cole, and he was shocked by the sound of his own words. "To tell you the truth, I'm not sure if we ever will 'tie the knot,' as you so eloquently expressed it. I just don't know."

It was dusk when Theresa, William, and Father McFarland marched onto the verandah with a pot of freshly-brewed hot coffee, a French apple pie, and a walnut cake. Theresa placed a silver serving tray of cups, saucers, and silverware on a small table. It was getting dark so William turned on the porch light, and then they sat there sipping coffee and eating pie and cake, while casually talking about politics and the economy till late in the evening. When they had finished, Father McFarland and Susan departed quietly and sadly. They were like two lost souls wandering off into the eternal darkness of an abyss, thought Cole.

While Theresa gathered the cups and saucers and stacked them neatly on the serving tray, William turned to his son and said, "Tell me something, Johnny, if you don't mind, what's the real reason you left New York City? It wasn't just to visit, was it? I remember reading something in the newspaper about the Tate/Bradshaw case. It said that you were the lead prosecutor for the state of New York. If that's true, what are you doing here?"

"William, what are you getting at?" Theresa asked. "Why don't you leave the boy alone?" She loathed it when William needled the boy for information. She had always thought that if their son wanted to tell them something—something that might have taken place at school or of a more private nature—he would. There was no need to pry or to force it out of him. He would tell them in his own good time.

"Do you remember when I told you about Black Hawk, Dad, and about how he had saved my life in South Vietnam?" Cole asked.

"Yes, of course, I do." His father was watching him carefully now and saw his profile outlined against the silvery light of the moon.

"Well, apparently, Black Hawk's in some kind of trouble back in South Dakota. He wrote a letter to Sal asking, pleading, for our help. Dad, I have to go to South Dakota with Sal and get to the bottom of this." He turned and looked at his father and his eyes scanned his face for a signal of his approbation. "You'd want me to do that, wouldn't you Dad?"

"Why, yes, of course, son, I would. It's like I've always told you. You have to do what you think is right," William said without hesitation. He looked at his son proudly.

Cole felt the clear meaning of his words. From as far back as he could remember, his father had taught him the difference between right and wrong. He knew his father would speak the truth, as he understood it. And it was this sense of right and wrong that now drove Cole to make the decision he did. He felt that responding to the plea in Black Hawk's letter was something he had to do.

Theresa had overheard the conversation between Johnny and his father and suddenly she sat back down again, her eyes teary.

As William attempted to explain to Theresa why her son had to leave again, Cole sat back in his chair and looked up at the millions of stars that were glittering light years away in the dark sky. Cole might have heard every word they were saying, had he not been lost in his thoughts, creating in the eye of his mind imaginary dots formed by the position of the stars in the sky. He connected the dots with an imaginary line and he wasn't exactly surprised what he saw in the stars. It was the image of Black Hawk—the Warrior—wearing an Indian headdress. His face had been painted red and he was dancing with other warriors, arching his back and raising his arms to the gods in the sky.

It could have been a rain dance, but Cole thought that it looked more like a war dance. Then, he saw Black Hawk charging through the jungles of Vietnam, and several paces behind him he saw Corporal Buccanon. They were shouting and screaming and firing their semi-automatic, M-16, rifles. Then, the terrifying sounds and images of war faded away and were replaced by the stars and the sound of an old warrior's voice—a voice he did not recognize— chanting, "The cradle rocks above an abyss . . . The cradle rocks above an abyss . . . The cradle rocks above an abyss. . . ." Cole instinctively placed his hands over his ears as if he could prevent the warrior's voice from reaching his soul.

"Darling! Darling! It's getting late. It's time we go upstairs to bed. I'll see you in the morning, darling. I'm so glad you've come home, even if it is only for a short visit." Theresa slowly climbed out of the rattan chair and kissed her son.

"Goodnight, Mother," said Cole tenderly, and then he added, "I love you."

"Goodnight, son," said William.

"Goodnight, Father," Cole replied.

Chapter 10 – Corporal Buccanon

Cole was alone on the porch. The night was extremely quiet and dark now, except for the sound of a door hinge squeaking somewhere deep inside the farmhouse. Theresa had opened and then closed the bathroom door, or was it a closet door? Cole recognized the soft, murmuring voices of his mother and father as they conversed contentedly with each other, reiterating pieces of conversation that they had overheard that night and thought was particularly interesting. They were complimenting one another on how well the evening had gone when Cole heard an owl hooting in the oak tree next to the barn. He looked up toward the sky as a chevron of geese flew overhead winging their way north. Then he heard the scurrying thump of a black and white rabbit as it streaked swiftly across the barnyard and disappeared safely into the fields, woods, and gullies beyond.

Cole actually jumped when the rabbit scurried across the yard. He followed it with his eyes as it ducked behind the corner of the stable; then he froze as a strange, ominous figure emerged from the shadows, from the darkness of the abyss. He stared at it for a long time and he recognized it as the shabby form of Corporal Salvatore Buccanon.

Now that he was spotted and recognized, Corporal Buccanon stepped out from the dark shadow of the barn and approached the farmhouse with T-bone, a viciously snarling-half-breed dog, at his side. Thin, wiry, and of medium height and stature, he stood facing the porch. His long arms were like rubber bands, almost out of proportion with the rest of his body. His dirty brown hair was parted in the middle and pulled tightly down over his ears and knotted at the back of his head in a ponytail. His eyes were dark, cold, and piercing, and were separated by a thin, but prominent, beaklike nose. His head and face, long from top to bottom, resembled a football. A scar stretched across his right cheek and was partly hidden by a filthy, unkempt beard. The figure of Jesus, crucified on the cross at Golgotha, was tattooed on his right arm, and a prostitute decorated his left arm. Beneath a black leather vest, a sleeveless black t-shirt covered a bony chest, bone-thin shoulders and a flat, emaciated-looking stomach. His hands, arms, face, and jeans and boots—also black—were splattered with caked dirt and blood. Overall, Corporal Buccanon looked sick and grotesque—as though he had just emerged from a bloody battle.

It seemed to Cole that Corporal Buccanon was an anachronism. Someone who was still living in the past, who was still living in the sixties, still living in South Vietnam. "Corporal Buccanon, reporting for duty, sir." Sal stepped forward and saluted Cole rather disrespectfully.

Cole said nothing and watched him curiously as every muscle in his body tightened.

"So you made it, Captain," said Corporal Buccanon, scowling, his black eyes piercing Cole's heart. "Susan said you had come back but I didn't believe her. Once a coward—"

"Well, it appears I've proved you wrong, again," Cole said quickly, stepping off the porch, and moving closer to Sal. They were now standing face to face and as Cole looked into his eyes, he saw fathoms of darkness, miles of eternal blackness, the culmination of years of envy, bitterness, hatred, and evil.

"Fifteen years is a long time, Captain. You look well. It seems that life's been good to you."

They studied each other with enmity, as if they were standing on opposite sides of an abyss and were about to engage in a struggle in which one was certain to fall to his death.

"I'm sure you'd like nothing better than to forget about this whole thing. I can see it in your face, Captain. It isn't something you might easily hide from a keen observer."

"Give it up," said Cole flatly.

"You'd like to go back to your comfortable, high-paying law practice up north and forget this, wouldn't you?"

"If you say so!"

"Forget about the one who carried you through the rice paddies and jungles of Vietnam."

"No, you're wrong. I haven't forgotten," said Cole, his face showing little emotion. But on the inside, Corporal Buccanon was doing one hell of a job tearing him apart.

"You haven't forgotten?" Corporal Buccanon said sarcastically, his voice suddenly rising while his face appeared devilishly convoluted. "I haven't forgotten either; no, not by a long shot. I've been living with the horror of Vietnam everyday of my life. It's like a recurring nightmare that returns to haunt me day and night. I don't sleep anymore—at least not like normal folks do. Sometimes, I can't even eat. It never ends. I might be a happy man again if I could only stop thinking about it. I expect that I'll carry it to my grave, Captain."

"Stop calling me Captain," said Cole. "I'm not your captain anymore."

"Listen, Captain, it's no secret how I feel about you. I have nothing to hide. You're not exactly the number one person in my book of favorite people. Before I had only hated you— now I despise you."

"Don't say that," said Cole softly, but as he looked at Corporal Buccanon's black eyes, he realized that there was no point in arguing with a madman. Once a crazy got hold of an idea in his head, regardless of whether the idea was sound or fallacious, the crazy would never let the idea go and could never be persuaded to think differently. Cole knew that Corporal Buccanon would rather take his irrational ideas and prejudices to the grave with him than to admit that he might be wrong. Cole sighed and shook his head.

"I hate you for what you did to us in Nam."

"Why don't you stop torturing yourself?" shouted Cole. But Corporal Buccanon would not stop. He had waited a long time to say this to Cole face to face, and he wasn't about to stop now. In fact, for a moment, Cole thought that the little bugger was enjoying it.

"You were unfit to command and you knew it. You never should have led us into that area without first checking back with our command post. But, you never bothered to check, did you?"

"And if I said I did would you believe me?" said Cole. For a moment they had become as one sharing pain and anguish. Now it became clear to Cole that Corporal Buccanon's whole purpose in life, since the end of the war, was to spread misery and pain, especially to those nearest to him. He thought about Henry, and Betty, and Susan, and how they must have suffered having to put up with Corporal Buccanon's outbursts and fits of rage. It had to be a living hell for them. And, now, Cole realized that he had become Corporal Buccanon's new target and that the corporal would keep popping away at him with his rife and his bullets of anger and hatred until he destroyed his target.

"You never called for support, did you? You never checked your map to find our precise location, did you? You didn't even know how to read the map—am I right?"

"Why do you want to keep torturing yourself over this? Can't you just drop it and forget about it?" Cole asked coldly.

"Like a fool, you lead us into an ambush, which nearly wiped out our whole damn platoon. Ten good marines died and five more were badly wounded that dreadful day. And, it's all because of you!"

Cole didn't want to hear anymore. He knew if he had been wearing a sidearm at that moment, he would have shot Corporal Buccanon right where he was standing just to silence him. After a few moments, which seemed like ages to Cole, Corporal Buccanon resumed his attack.

"You're lucky you're still alive. If it wasn't for Black Hawk, you'd have rotted away in the jungle long ago."

"We've been through all this once before, Corporal. When will you show mercy and stop? How many times are you going to relive this war and torture yourself? I won't relive it with you, again. I've told you that once before. As difficult as it might have been in Vietnam, I've learned to put it behind me, to move on with my life."

But Cole couldn't put it behind him. Now, he saw the platoon as if they were standing right in front of him, projected on a large black screen formed by the cosmic heavens and the universe.

Twenty-five young marines, cautiously walking along Route Nine in the jungles of Vietnam, and entering inadvertently an area that was heavily mined. It was late afternoon before they had realized they had made a mistake. It happened very quickly and without warning. The first explosion wiped out three American soldiers when the point man – Lance Corporal Taylor - stepped on a concealed mine. The force of the explosion had lifted his body ten feet into the air before he landed in the brush. Corporal Duncan and Gunnery Hamilton were killed with the shrapnel. Then Cole heard popping sounds like fire crackers on the Fourth of July coming from trees tops and from nearly every direction.

He saw his men fall, one by one. They were like the sitting ducks he used to shoot at with his pellet rifle when he was a boy attending the midway with his father and mother. Then, panic and pandemonium broke out among the young American soldiers. He saw them die, screaming, and writhing in pain as several more land mines exploded. Hypnotized by the stars and the black screen before him, Cole couldn't turn his head away. He couldn't close his eyes to what was unfolding before him. He checked their location on his map, and then yelled something to his radio operator. Private First Class Davis scrambled to get a message off to their command post for back up units and air support. But it was too late. Corporal Buccanon and Black Hawk had been pinned down some fifty feet away. Then a mortar round exploded close by and Cole realized that he had been hit, falling to the ground in a pool of blood. Flying shrapnel from the mortar riddled his body and rendered him practically helpless. His blood-soaked shirt and trousers clung to his body. Slowly, he lost consciousness.

When Black Hawk saw Cole drop to the ground, he responded like a marine. Leaping to his feet, he dashed forward under direct fire from the enemy and in total disregard for his own safety. Reaching Captain Cole, he shielded him with his body and dragged him into the brush, where he returned enemy fire. Despite the confusion surrounding him, Black Hawk was able to apply first aid and save Captain Cole's life.

As day turned into night, the forlorn and desperate marines began to withdraw, despite the Vietcong sharpshooters who had been perched in the trees above and leisurely picked them off, one by one, as if they were playing a game. For Cole, all the marine training Black Hawk had received in boot camp paid off, because it never occurred to Black Hawk that he ought to save his own skin and abandon Cole. Instead, he carried Cole on his back and when he couldn't carry him, he dragged him to a clearing in the forest—a makeshift, temporary landing site where several Hueys were waiting. Just as Black Hawk lifted Cole onto his shoulders and started to run the last ten feet to reach the landing zone, he felt a pain rip through his back and he knew instantly that he had taken a bullet. He managed to stumble a few more feet before dropping down and spilling Captain Cole in the tall grass.

As the marines at the Huey returned enemy fire, Corporal Buccanon scrambled to where Captain Cole and Corporal Black Hawk were lying. Straining every ounce of muscle that covered his bony arms, he quickly dragged one and then the other the rest of the way to the Hueys where the marines placed them on board with the rest of the wounded. Once they were safely in the air and away from the deadly canopy of the jungle, they were flown to a MASH unit.

Captain Cole and Corporal Black Hawk were eventually medevaced to a hospital in Yukosoka, Japan, where after several months they recovered from their wounds and where Captain Cole and Corporal Black Hawk became friends.

While on leave from the war, Corporal Buccanon had visited Black Hawk in the hospital on several occasions, but never once did he visit Captain Cole or even asked about his condition. As far as Corporal Buccanon was concerned, it was as though Captain Cole had died back in the jungle.

Now, as he stood under the canopy of glittering stars, reunited with his old friend after a separation of fifteen plus years, Cole felt the hatred between them. It had not subsided as he had hoped. If anything, the hatred had grown stronger over time. For Cole, Corporal Salvatore Buccanon brought back all the memories of the past—both the good and the bad.

"I'm doing this for Black Hawk," continued Corporal Buccanon. "What I have to do, I can do alone without you. I don't need the likes of you hanging around me to muck things up. In fact, I wouldn't have bothered you with this, if it were not for Black Hawk who had asked for you in his letter."

Corporal Buccanon reached into the inside pocket of his leather vest, produced a crumbled letter, the corners of which were fray, bent, and torn off, and handed it to Cole.

Cole looked at the letter warily and for a moment it seemed as if he was afraid; afraid to touch it; afraid of the power it had over him. Suddenly, he heard Randy Scott's voice echoing in his head: "What power does Black Hawk have on you Cole? It's more than a pledge or some cockamamie code of honor! What is it, Cole? What is it? I want to know! I want to know! Tell me! Tell me!" Perhaps, Randy was right. Cole felt there just might be some strange power, a power he couldn't understand yet, at play here, working him and Corporal Buccanon like pawns in a game of chess. He sat down on the top step of the porch and held the letter up to the solitary porch light. He read the letter silently.

"He doesn't say much, does he? Black Hawk was never one for long speeches and letters. He said he's living with his wife and young daughter and father in a small town just outside of Sioux Falls, South Dakota. He works for the Department of the Interior as a game warden, and he's been having some trouble with the locals. He said he needs our help; although, he never really explains what kind of help he needs," said Corporal Buccanon huskily. "But look at the last line of his letter—it's really a kicker, something about a cradle rocking above an abyss and common sense . . . or something. I don't get it. I think Black Hawk's been on the warpath too many times and it finally caught up with him."

But Cole recognized the words immediately, and he quietly repeated the line in its entirety, "The cradle rocks above an abyss and common sense tells us that our existence is but a brief crack of light between two eternities of darkness."

Corporal Buccanon's eyes widened and his jaw dropped onto his chest. With a dumbfounded expression on his face, he gazed at Cole.

"It's strange because I read that line in a book that was written by Vladimir Nabokov, titled *Speak Memory*, only two weeks ago, and ever since then my life's been turned upside down. And on top of it, out of the clear blue sky, I get a letter from you, and then a phone call, and now this," indicating the letter from Black Hawk. "You're right, Corporal, about the letter. He doesn't really say what kind of trouble he's having, only that he's having trouble, and that he needs our help." Cole thought it didn't make any difference what kind of trouble Black Hawk was having because he was a marine who had a problem and was calling for help. Cole knew that if Black Hawk hadn't responded like a trained marine Cole would have died somewhere in a jungle halfway around the world. He also knew that the code of honor that made marines brothers demanded that he do something, anything, to aid a fellow marine.

"When can you be ready?" Corporal Buccanon asked sharply.

"Tomorrow morning, after breakfast. I'll pick you up."

"In what? That!" said Corporal Buccanon, sneering and nodding his head in the direction of the BMW sitting in the driveway.

"Yes, why, what's wrong?" said Cole defensively.

"I won't be caught dead in a BMW, that's why, Harvard lawyer, Captain, sir. I'm taking my Harley."

"Oh, no! Don't tell me you're a HOG and still driving a Harley! Don't you think you're a little too old to be driving around the country on a Harley? Although, after seeing you in that 'get up,' I'm not the least bit surprised. It's a miracle, of course, you haven't killed yourself."

"Your bike's still in the barn, Captain Lawyer," Corporal Buccanon said thinly and without having to say another word, Cole knew that Corporal Buccanon had challenged him. He realized that if he intended to survive the next few days with the corporal, he would have to take risks and do things differently, just as he had done in South Vietnam and in the courts of New York City.

For the first time in fifteen years, he remembered he even had a Harley and wondered if he could even ride the old Softail again.

"Give me a day or two to get it into shape," Cole said, and suddenly he felt tired.

"Okay, Captain Lawyer, as you wish, you have a day, perhaps, two to get your Harley in shape. After that, I'm out of here, and you're on your own," said Corporal Buccanon snappishly. And then, without uttering another word, he and T-bone backed away and like phantoms were quickly dissolved by the darkness.

Chapter 11 - The Resurrection of the Harley

Early the next morning Cole heard an owl hooting in the orchard; then it fell silent as the sun peeked above the horizon and the sounds of day became more prominent. From his bed he heard the familiar noise of pots and pans clanking in the kitchen and water running in the sink. A moment later the heavy, solid footsteps of his father descended the stairs, the screen door on the back porch swung swiftly open and then closed with a loud thump. The hens bickered in the henhouse, and the rooster crowed and strutted proudly across the top of the roof. In the stable, the horses huffed and stamped their hooves, and from their pens the pigs and piglets squealed. It was morning and they wanted to be fed, and the cows wanted to be milked.

Then Cole heard the sound of a pickup truck pulling up to the back of the house and the husky, familiar voice of Jake Snow as he greeted Theresa at the threshold of the screened doorway. Theresa led Jake into the kitchen where breakfast was being served and where he would have an opportunity to meet with William and review the itinerary of chores that had to be completed that day. Cole knew the routine, having grown up on the farm under the watchful eye of his father.

The early sounds of morning were not the only things that had drifted up the steps and into the little room on the second floor. There was the sweet, eye-opening smell of bacon and eggs frying in the skillet, and piping-hot coffee brewing on the gas range.

Cole lingered in bed and thought about the events of last evening and how strange it was that some things never seem to change. For example, he recalled Father McFarland's propensity for political intrigue and gossip in the nation's capital. He'd been spouting the same rigmarole for years. Susan hadn't changed either. Cole thought that she was just as warm and sensitive a person now as when she had been an adolescent protecting stray kittens and dogs from the cruel and evil world. Although he had to admit that she was more than a little frayed and broken around the edges, she was for the most part intact.

Corporal Buccanon's late-night visit, on the other hand, scared the hell out of him and nearly convinced Cole that he should have listened to Gina Anderson and remained in New York City. Cole began to wonder if coming home again to Nashville was indeed a mistake and if going to South Dakota was an even bigger mistake. And what about Black Hawk? What was he up to? What did Black Hawk really want from his former marine buddies?

Cole reluctantly dragged his tired body out of bed. He took a long cold shower and dressed in working clothes his father had laid out for him the night before. Feeling almost human, and invigorated by the thought of seeing Susan again, he went downstairs to the kitchen where he joined his mother and father and Jake Snow for breakfast.

Jake Snow was short, handsome, and muscular. He was in his late fifties and was five or six years younger than Johnny's father. He reminded Cole of the television actor Rod Taylor, who had become famous and popular in the fifties playing a detective in Hong Kong.

When Cole entered the kitchen, Jake greeted the younger man as if he was the long lost prodigal son who had finally returned home. He shook his hand, slapped him on the back, and hugged him tightly while laughing merrily.

Theresa shouted, "Sit down, Jake! Sit down, Johnny, and eat your breakfast before it gets cold!" She poured a cup of hot coffee for her son and then looking up to examine his face, she said inquisitively, "Johnny, you look so tired. Didn't you sleep well last night? I wouldn't be surprised if you didn't get any sleep at all last night with all the talking I heard out there on the porch. Was that you?"

"Yes. I was talking with Salvatore Buccanon."

"He was here, last night?" she asked, surprised.

"Was T-bone with him?" asked William.

Cole nodded.

"Was he sober?" Jake asked.

"Sober enough to discuss our trip to South Dakota," said Cole softly, "In fact, I'll have to hurry." He shoveled two eggs into his mouth and gulped down a cup of hot coffee. "I have just one, maybe two days, to get my Softail in shape for the trip." He looked at his father and then at Jake. "Is it still in the barn?"

"Right where you left it, son," said William. He looked a little pale and under the weather from drinking and celebrating the night before. He felt as if someone was buried inside the center of his skull and was using a sledgehammer to break out. He held his head in the palms of his hands and cursed the wine and the incessant pounding that he thought would never stop.

"Yes, it's right where you left it, Johnny, but you'll have to dig it out because it's buried under a pile of junk," said Jake.

After breakfast Theresa started her chores while Jake, William, and Cole sauntered to the barn, a huge, red building constructed of wooden posts and beams and planks and boards of varying sizes. It had a silo for grain and feed storage.

William and Jake each took one of the huge wooden doors and swung them open widely, letting in columns of sunlight. The interior of the barn was dark and musty. To the left were a workbench and cabinets for storing tools, and to the right William and Jake had constructed additional storage bins containing all sorts of items such as furniture and cans of paint. In the middle of the barn were a John Deere tractor and seeder, and an International Harvester reaper.

Jake Snow climbed nimbly onto the John Deere tractor and started the engine. William jumped into his pickup truck and together they started out toward the cornfields in the west. Now, Cole was left alone. Carefully and slowly he searched the barn, finally arriving at the conclusion that his dad and Jake had made a mistake - the bike wasn't there. Then, he saw something in one of the dark corners of the barn. It was stowed away in a bin, covered by a canvas tarp under a load of wood, hay, and sticks of furniture. With his hands trembling, Cole anxiously cleared away the hay and the furniture that had been stacked on and around the mysterious object. Firmly gripping the moldy, dusty, rust-covered tarp in both hands, he pulled hard, sending it sprawling to the hay-covered plank flooring and unveiling a huge, dirty Harley-Davidson motorcycle—a 1960 Heritage Softail Classic with custom-designed flames and screaming eagles. The wheels were covered with spider webs. The seat was soiled and torn in several places, and the glass covering the odometer was broken. But to Cole the machine looked as if it had just been wheeled out of the showroom.

He was suddenly overwhelmed by a passion for the Harley. He wheeled it into the center of the barn so he could get a better look at the condition of the machine. A beam of sunlight fell upon it. He grabbed a rag from off the workbench and started rubbing and cleaning away the layers of grime and dust that had accumulated over the years. Slowly the Harley began to sparkle again. With a burst of spirited energy, he polished first the gas tank, then the fenders, the handlebars, and the triple-beam headlights.

When Cole was able to see his face reflected in the chrome of the V-twin engine and the long, elegant exhaust pipe, he smiled thoughtfully. Then he stitched closed the fissures in the seat and polished the leather saddlebags. Finally, he mounted the Harley, gripping its handlebars, and for the first time in years recaptured the feel of the Softail. For a moment, he was dreaming about the Softail and riding down to Memphis, where he had visited Graceland, the home of the king of rock and roll. Sometimes, he'd cruise to Chattanooga, and up to Lexington and Louisville, Kentucky, and back and forth between the farm and the University of Tennessee.

Cole was too absorbed in his thoughts about the Harley and the good old days on the road to hear the sound of Susan's Explorer as she and Salvatore Buccanon turned into the tree-lined driveway and parked alongside the barn.

When Susan peered into the barn, she saw Cole straddling the Softail and she thought he looked just like a schoolboy again—an overgrown schoolboy who had found a forgotten toy in the attic. She laughed and said, "You still have that old contraption?"

Cole looked up and saw Susan's bright eyes and cheery smile. He thought she looked quite beautiful in her blue jeans and her red and white checked shirt.

"I hope you're not thinking of driving that monster after all these years. Why, you'll kill yourself." Susan and Corporal Buccanon stepped into the shade of the barn to get a closer look at the Softail.

"Well? Are you gonna just sit there like a toad on a log in the swamp, or are you gonna see if you can start her?" Corporal Buccanon bellowed loudly. He grinned as his eyes ran over every inch of the Harley.

"Good morning, Susan," Cole said as he squinted his eyes and looked into the sunlight and at the two figures standing just inside the threshold of the barn, now partially cloaked in darkness. Suddenly Cole felt weird, as if he had been looking at two aberrations or ghosts hovering at an open door or tapping at a window. The next moment he felt a cold shiver run down his spine as he gazed downward and saw T-bone standing in Corporal Buccanon's shadow. The dog was snarling viciously, and Cole knew that he wouldn't have a pray of a chance if the dog should attack.

"We only have a day, Captain, so why don't you wheel that ancient Harley out here and into the sunlight so I can take a closer look at it?"

Corporal Buccanon stepped back out into the yard with Susan and T-bone, while Cole wheeled the Harley out of the darkness and into the sunlight. Suddenly, the Softail glittered and Corporal Buccanon was flabbergasted with its classic and elegant design and style.

"It's filthy, Johnny," said Susan, wrinkling her nose and frowning, "I'll help you clean it." As she turned in the direction of the house, she asked, "Is Theresa inside? I'll ask her for a pail of water and something to clean it up with."

"Don't bother," said Cole. I've already finished cleaning her up."

"You did?" She looked at Cole seriously and then again at the Harley. "Well, you could've fooled me. From the looks of her, I'd say you missed a few spots." She walked away, heading towards the farmhouse where Theresa was filling a bucket with water and soft detergent.

"Have you tried starting it?" Corporal Buccanon asked as he approached the Harley and gazed at the red-and-black screaming eagles.

A certified motorcycle mechanic and an aficionado of Harley-Davidson motorcycles, Corporal Buccanon appreciated what the Heritage Softail model had to offer. He admired its low seat height, its traditional fork, its skinny twenty-one-inch lanced wheel, and its deeply stepped two-place seat and sissy bar useful if the driver should pick up a rider along the way. The floorboards, the solid aluminum wheels, the wide handlebars, saddlebags, and staggered chrome exhaust pipes were from out of this world.

He turned to Cole. "The first thing we have to do is to put a little petrol into the gas tank and try to start it."

As Cole got the petrol and started to fill the tank, Corporal Buccanon went back to the Explorer to get his tools.

Susan and Theresa came out from the house carrying a pail of fresh water and a handful of rags and placed everything down next to the Harley. Theresa greeted Corporal Buccanon with a thin smile. "That thing hasn't been started for years," she said dryly. "Probably needs a new carburetor."

Once Cole had filled the teardrop with gas – just enough to turn over the engine - Corporal Buccanon straddled the Softail and concentrated on the Harley. He cranked it several times with his boot, but the engine wouldn't turn over. The Softail just sat there quietly, as if it were a tamed animal sleeping in the middle of the yard under the hot morning sun.

"Maybe the gasoline needs to work its way into the carburetor," said Susan thoughtfully.

"Yeah," Corporal Buccanon said sarcastically. He shook the Harley violently from side to side. After a few moments, he made a second attempt to start the Softail. Still nothing happened. Finally, Corporal Buccanon said, "It's probably the carburetor. I'll run over to Ned's with T-bone and pick up some parts."

Cole was glad Sal was running off to Ned's to pick up parts for the Softail because he wanted to be alone with Susan. He watched Susan pick up a swath of cloth, soak it in cleaning solution, and start scrubbing the leather saddlebags, and he was thinking that she was quite beautiful.

"This is beginning to feel like old times again, Johnny. I mean the three of us hanging out together, like we used to do in high school," Susan said dreamily, her face and eyes radiantly bright and glowing with life.

"Yes," said Cole thoughtfully, tenderly. "It does remind me of the good old days. I was always impressed by the way you hung in there with us. And, you know something, I was glad you were there being a part of it all. If you hadn't, it wouldn't have been the same. I thought I should tell you that, not that it makes any difference now." He reached for her hand and gently pulled her to her feet. "I was too young and too stupid to really understand what I was feeling at the time, let alone be able to express my feelings for you." Cole smiled and laughed. "I don't feel so very young right now—that's for sure. When I get up in the morning, this old body's full of aches and pains. I can tell you that. And, I'm actually going to ride this thing"—nodding toward the Harley—"across the country to South Dakota with that crazy brother of yours? I don't believe it. It's simply crazy."

"You'll take care of Sal for me won't you, Johnny?" Susan asked seriously. "Promise me. He's so unstable at times. When he's home on the farm, I don't worry so much, but when he goes out into town or travels alone, I'm afraid for him."

"Why should you be afraid?" asked Cole, deeply concerned. "I think he knows how to take care of himself. He made it through Nam."

"And that's why I'm afraid. Sure, he survived that terrible war, but there's not one day that passes when I don't fear for his life. I'm afraid he'll do something terrible and get himself into trouble," said Susan painfully. "I never know when he might snap. I'm warning you, Johnny. If you take Sal on this trip across the country to South Dakota, you're asking for trouble. Sooner or later, he's going to explode. If you provoke him even a little, he might turn into a raving savage, I'm afraid."

"Have you ever been hurt by him, Susan?" asked Cole.

"No. But I've seen him when he could be really dangerous. Do you remember Nathan Daniels, Jeffrey Miles, and Bobby Lake?"

"Yes, of course, they went to high school with us. They were into athletics. Played football and they were pretty good at it, too, winning city and state championship awards. Nathan was an all-

American quarterback. Jeffrey played the center position because he was built like a tank, and Bobby was a receiver. He was tall and fast," said Cole.

Susan smiled sadly. "They ran into Sal on his way home from South Vietnam. He was going to take a taxicab from the airport when he ran into them. He was still wearing his uniform. The boys were drunk but that's no excuse for what they did or what Sal did. Sal was hailing a cab when Nathan saw him and started an argument over the war. It was stupid, very stupid. Sal managed to keep his temper under control until Nathan spat at him—right smack in the middle of the face, and on the uniform, too.

"Well, if you know Sal, then you know he's not the kind of a man who would take that from anyone. He had served his country for four long years, and fought in a bloody war, and nearly got himself killed I don't know how many times. He was practically in tears when he lost control. I'm sure Daniels, Miles, and Lake didn't know what hit them. Sal took on all three at the same time, and when he had finished Nathan Daniels had a broken clavicle, Jeffrey Miles had several broken ribs, and Bobby Lake had several lacerations and a concussion, and lay unconscious in the gutter next to the taxicab. Sal was charged with disorderly conduct. The judge placed him on probation. Ah! Yeah! He received a real hero's welcome when he came home— one that he'll never forget."

Cole knew the story by heart. It was a story that was being lived all over America by veterans who had returned home from the war and had been abused by antiwar protectors. He often read about these stories in the newspapers, and they were the talk of Cambridge and Washington. There was no doubt in his mind that the war was unpopular, but he thought it was an outrage when soldiers returned to the states and were treated disrespectfully. Cole remembered how he felt when he first came home. He felt uneasy, as if he was an outsider, a stranger—an alien from another planet.

Although it took time to adjust to civilian life again, he often wondered what he would have done had he been confronted with characters like Daniels, Miles, and Lake.

"I can't promise you anything, Susan, but I'll try to do my best to keep him out of trouble," Cole said, reluctantly, but wanting to encourage her at the same time.

"You know, Farther McFarland was right when he said that Sal needed help. He's like a ticking time bomb that could explode any minute, any second. He can be ruthless when he wants to be, especially when things don't go his way. I often hear him at night screaming in his sleep. Sometimes, I can hear him calling out the name *Lai Choi*. Who is Lai Choi, Johnny? That's a woman's name isn't it?"

"Lai Choi," said Cole contemplatively, his mind racing back in time to the war years, trying to remember all the names and faces and villages he saw or visited. Then, after a long pause, he said, "I don't know. I never met a Lai Choi. She probably lived in one of the villages and came to camp looking for a handout. We saw it all the time in Nam," and then, he added, "Look. Let's take a break." He took the swath of cloth from her hand and threw it into the pail of water. "We've been working too hard. Let's take a walk." And, then he took her by the hand and led her past the henhouse, past the stables, and through an open field and meadow to a place in the woods where they could observe the cornfields and the Cumberland River.

They reposed under a tree and watched the Cumberland flowing gently and continuously past them. Cole studied the branches and twigs running along the surface of the river, and the sky overhead. It was clear and blue with only a wisp of clouds in the distance. He saw a dozen cows grazing in a field off to his left, and beyond them, in another field, he saw a half dozen horses grazing and prancing majestically. He saw the heat of late morning rising and shimmering from the good fertile earth. Then, he looked at Susan sitting beside him, and he thought that he was glad to be alive.

It was past high noon when they returned to the barn and found Corporal Buccanon working diligently on the Harley. "If I waited for you two love birds, we'd never get done," he snapped.

Parts from the Softail were strewn across the ground. Cole knew that while he and Susan were watching the river, Corporal Buccanon was busy changing spark plugs, the front and rear brake pads, the fuel-line, the carburetor, and the chain. I hope he's got the timing down right, thought Cole.

In the meantime, Theresa had brought out a serving platter that was stacked high with sandwiches and two tall pitchers—one of lemonade and the other of ice tea—and placed them on the table on the verandah. Then, William and Jake drove back in from the field and they were all standing around on the porch having luncheon.

Corporal Buccanon wiped the perspiration from his brow and grinning ate both a turkey and a ham sandwich. Theresa watched him with wide eyes as he drank down half a gallon of ice tea before returning to the machine.

It was late afternoon by the time Corporal Buccanon had completed his mechanical work on the Harley. Turning to Cole, he said, "We'll just need enough petrol in the tank to test it. Just in case we have to empty it again."

Theresa and Susan watched wearily as Cole filled the tank with gas and then mounted the Softail. Afraid that the Harley might explode in their faces, Corporal Buccanon, Theresa, and Susan instinctively stepped back a few paces, giving Cole plenty of room. Slowly, Cole gripped the handlebars, placed the gear in neutral, and positioned the boot of his right foot on the starter pedal. Then, rising to a standing position, he suddenly stepped down hard on the pedal with the entire weight of his body while simultaneously turning the right hand grip to feed and rev the engine with gas.

Nothing.

Cole tried a second time.

Still nothing.

On the third attempt, Theresa and Susan nearly jumped out of their skins as the engine roared to life, belching out smoke and fumes from its staggered exhaust pipes.

Corporal Buccanon shook his head and bellowed, "It sounds like a frog croaking, Captain. We'll have to fine tune it."

For the rest of the afternoon and into the early evening, Cole and Corporal Buccanon fine-tuned the V-Twin engine. When completed, the Harley sounded like a new bike, idling and shifting smoothly. Cole smiled to himself as he discovered he was pleasantly surprised at the thought of driving the Harley again.

Later that evening, after dinner and long after Susan and Corporal Buccanon and T-bone had departed, Cole was sitting on the verandah with his mother, and he sensed her fear. He knew that she was afraid she was going to lose her only son, again. Cole saw she had been crying.

She turned to her son and said, "Promise me you'll be careful, Johnny. Your father and I love you. If anything should ever happen to you . . ."

Cole embraced his mother, wrapping his strong arms around her frail shoulders, and said, "I know, Mother. I know. And, I love you and dad, too. But, please, please, don't be afraid. I'll be all right," and he almost believed it. Then more confidently, "Everything will be all right." He gently kissed her and they sat on the porch under the stars until late in the evening.

Part III—On The Road

Chapter 12 – Lord, I Was born a Rambling Man

At the break of dawn, long before anyone in the house had awakened, Cole packed his saddlebags with a few of his things and stealthily wheeled the Harley from the barn. He was careful not to disturb the hens scurrying across the yard or the rooster watching him warily from the peak of the roof. If you crow now, it will be the last crowing you do, thought Cole. After reaching the road, he looked back and saw the little farmhouse, dark and silent. In a few more minutes the sun would rise, and William would be the first to get up, to milk the cows and feed the horses and the pigs.

Cole pushed the Heritage Softail a mile or two to where Corporal Buccanon was waiting for him under a tree. The Road King was standing at the side of the road. Even in the twilight of dawn, Cole unconsciously contrasted the magnificence of the Road King to the shabbiness of Corporal Buccanon appearance.

No words passed between them. When Cole had reached the tree, Corporal Buccanon rose and gracefully slid into the seat of his Harley. He looked at Cole and frowned. Then they started their engines, donned their helmets and goggles, and in a flash they were gone, the sound of their Harleys rising and drifting softly in the early morning breeze.

At precisely that moment, Theresa rustled in her sleep. She had been dreaming of a young boy. He was five or six years old. She saw him running towards her in a field. Then, as he came close to her, he suddenly leaped into the air and threw his arms around her neck, and hugged and kissed her endlessly. For just an instant she thought she heard a sound, faint and far away. She couldn't make it out, so she thought it wasn't anything that could hurt her. No.

She turned uneasily in her bed. The sound was moving farther away now. When it was no more than a whisper in her ear, she drifted off to sleep again. Finally, it stopped. But by then she was dreaming again of the young boy, running in the field with his arms outstretched and reaching for her.

They were riding side by side—Captain Cole and Corporal Buccanon—as they made their way along Route 24, heading north through Tennessee and into Kentucky, past Paducah, and crossing over the Mississippi at Wickliffe, Kentucky, into Missouri. They proceeded along Route 55, breezing by Cape Girardeau and Jackson, following the winding Mississippi River north to St. Louis. Picking up highway 70, Cole and Buccanon continued biking along, passing through Columbia, and Marshall, stopping for the night at Independence, Missouri, just outside of Kansas City.

It was late when Cole and Corporal Buccanon turned their Harleys off the main road and found a quiet area to bed down for the night, near some trees in one of the fields. The large, red sun was already setting in the western sky.

Cole had collected some twigs and branches and started to build a small campfire when Corporal Buccanon pulled out his sleeping pack from the Harley and unraveled it over a grassy area under a tree. He heard a high pitched screeching sound as Corporal Buccanon started singing a song made famous by the Allman Brothers' Band, "Lord, I was born a ramblin' man, tryin' to make a livin' and doin' the best I can. And when it's comes to leavin', I hope you'll understand, that I was born a ramblin' man—"

"Will you shut up?" Cole spoke abruptly as he tried to light the campfire. "Look, we've been riding all day, and I'm tired. Would you just pipe down and stop that singing. It's driving me crazy."

"Listen, Captain, if my singing annoys you, you could bed down somewhere else. This is one hell of a big country out here, Captain, and there's plenty of space. It's not like New York City, where people live on top of one another like pack rats," Corporal Buccanon taunted.

The campfire was now burning and crackling. Red flames danced across their faces. "I'll stay right here," said Cole decisively, unrolling his sleeping bag. "You know, you might be a little more considerate."

Corporal Buccanon looked at Cole. "I don't think it's my singing that annoys you, Captain. I think it's me! I annoy you, don't I?" Corporal Buccanon took a step closer to Cole. "I remind you of something, right? It's as though I'm the ghost of Christmas Past, and it's your ugly past I remind you of." He stepped closer. "Everyone has done something in their past they'd like to forget. Right, Captain? I know because I've done plenty of things in my past, which I'd like to forget. And, you know what they are, don't you, Captain? In fact, I wouldn't be surprised if every time you saw my ugly face or heard my sour voice, you'd curse me and wish I'd fallen off the face of the earth or into an abyss. Is that right, Captain?" Corporal Buccanon took another step closer to Cole.

Cole began sweating and wondering if he'd be able to defend himself from this madman. No matter how puny and scrawny a madman might look when feeling calm and sunny, Cole knew that when agitated he could become fierce and strong. It's the adrenaline pumping through the body that could transform a weakling into a superman.

"Because whenever you see me," Corporal Buccanon continued, "you're confronted with something that frightens you. Isn't that right, Captain? Isn't it?" The blood had rushed to Corporal Buccanon's face, turning it bright red, and his voice rose swiftly to a high pitch.

Cole stood up and faced Corporal Buccanon squarely and firmly. "I'm like you, Corporal Buccanon, in that I have plenty of horror stories that I'd like to forget. But I'm unlike you, Corporal, in that I've come to terms with them. I've decided long ago not to look back, not to think about those dreadful days and nights in the jungle fighting the Vietnamese, destroying and burning villages, but to think only about the present and the future. It hasn't been easy, believe me. Once, I had even thought about attending a group therapy session that was offered by the VA, but when I heard that part of the therapy was to visit the Wall – the

Vietnam Veterans Memorial Wall - in Washington, DC, I canceled at the last minute."

"You coward."

"I've done nothing to be ashamed of Corporal, and I'll ask you just one more time not to refer to me in those terms again. Do you understand, Corporal?" Cole said crossly.

"And, I would appreciate it, Captain, if you would stop ordering me around. We're not in Vietnam any longer, and besides, the last time you gave me an order, I nearly got myself killed."

"Oh, shut up!" Cole shouted.

Suddenly, Corporal Buccanon lowered his head and tackled Cole, knocking him to the ground. "I should have knocked some sense into you a long time ago. Maybe more of our boys would still be alive today," Corporal Buccanon shouted wildly. His arms and legs flailed in all directions.

Cole defended himself as best he could, but when Corporal Buccanon unexpectedly leaped across the campfire and landed ponderously on his chest, his breath had escaped him. He gasped for air as they rolled and tumbled about wildly, locked together in a bear hug. Then, strangely as if someone had reached down and whispered something into their ears, they stopped struggling. Somehow, instinctively, they both sensed they were not alone in the field, that someone was watching them. Lying on their backs and looking upside down, feeling absolutely silly, Cole and Corporal Buccanon saw a young man in his early thirties sitting nearby under a tree.

He had been watching Cole and Corporal Buccanon as they fought in the grass. He smiled at them as a father would have smiled at his two sons wrestling at his feet on his living room floor in the comfort of his home on a Sunday afternoon. He was strikingly handsome with light blue eyes and long brown hair falling to his shoulders. His hands were folded in his lap on a neatly wrapped package that looked like a Christmas gift or a birthday present.

Cole and Corporal Buccanon quickly turned over onto their forearms. "Who the hell are you?" Corporal Buccanon asked gruffly.

"Where you did come from? And, how did you get here?" asked Cole, surprised by the sudden appearance of the young stranger.

He knew the man hadn't been sitting there a moment ago or they would have seen or heard him. No! It was as though the stranger had popped into existence from thin air. Cole had the idea that perhaps Corporal Buccanon had finally driven him over the edge and into the deep end of the pool resulting in a wild and crazy hallucination.

"I didn't even hear your approach," said Corporal Buccanon.

"What did you do, just pop in here like you're some kind of a ghost or a genie?" asked Cole. He thought about Major Anthony Nelson and how the genie in the bottle used to pop in and out of his life.

"You can get yourself into a hell of a jam, stranger, sneaking up on people like that at night, and in the middle of nowhere," Corporal Buccanon said. He stood up and faced the young man who was now leaning nonchalantly against the tree, smiling graciously.

Then the young stranger said something that shocked Cole. In fact, he would never have believed it had he not heard it with his own ears. In a calm voice, the stranger said, "The cradle rocks above an abyss, and common sense tells us that our existence is but a brief crack of light between two eternities of darkness. Do you believe this or do you believe in the eternal light from the Father, Captain Cole? Tell me. Don't be shy, Captain."

Cole stood up and shook the dust off his clothes. "I don't know what I believe right now, stranger." And, then he said, "Are you lost? Do you need directions? I have a map—"

"No," said the young man. "How can I make you understand that it's not me who is lost, but, you?"

"We're not lost," Corporal Buccanon said petulantly.

"I appreciate your kindness and hospitality, especially since you have offered it to a stranger." The young man nodded at Cole.

Cole noticed that a strange glow or light had mysteriously engulfed the young man as he spoke. "I've been searching for the two of you for a very long time, and now that I have found you, my prayers have finally been answered. Here you are," he said confidently, his eyes shining with a warm inner glow. "And, for the moment you're both safe."

"What do you mean 'for the moment you're both safe'?" asked Corporal Buccanon, his voice betraying his nervousness.

"Do I know you?" Cole asked, taking a few steps forward.

"Do not come any closer, please," beseeched the young man. "Yes, you know me, John, or I should say you know of me. And you, Salvatore, you know of me as well."

"You're mistaken, stranger, I've never seen you before in my life, and how the hell did you know my name?" Corporal Buccanon asked.

While Corporal Buccanon bantered with the stranger, Cole searched through the cobwebs of his mind to put a name and a place to the face of the stranger. What's his name? Where did we meet? Damn, where was it—Vietnam, Japan, California, Okinawa, perhaps in some geisha house in Tokyo? That's it. That must be it. I remember now. But he wasn't really certain.

"Oh, no, Brother, I'm not mistaken. I know you intimately, Salvatore. In fact, I had wept bitterly for you, not very long ago, when your father had no other choice but to shoot Roscoe when he had wandered out onto the road, alone, late one night, and was hit by a car driven by old lady Hanley. And, let us not forget your wife, Lai Choi, and your unborn son, whom you left in Vietnam. You could rest your weary mind about them, Corporal. They are at peace in the house of my Father and they are happy. So as you could see, I know everything there is to know about you, Corporal Buccanon. Everything; if you know what I mean."

"Who the hell are you?" Corporal Buccanon asked savagely. He was astonished and on the verge of tears, and in another moment he would have killed the stranger if Cole had not stepped in between them, seized Corporal Buccanon by the shoulders, and held him back with no little effort.

"And you, John. Why do you carry around inside of you all that guilt and shame? You've done nothing to warrant it. But what really surprises me, John, is how you've come to transfer your anger and hatred to the courtroom."

"I'm one of the best, most successful prosecutors in the State of New York. Why just last year alone, I had successfully prosecuted over thirty cases for the State—"

"I know . . . I know . . . spare me the details, John, I'm quite familiar with them," the young man politely interrupted Cole and waved his hand to silence him. "Nevertheless, John, the trial you are about to face is quite different, and in no way resembles anything you had ever experienced before—either in the classrooms at Harvard or in the marble hallways and courtrooms of New York City. Even your prestigious law school could never in a million years have prepared you for what you are about to face. Are you frightened, my son? Yes? No? Well, you should be. We shall see for ourselves all in good time, won't we?"

"What do you want?" asked Cole.

"I have a message and a gift for the both of you. First, my message is this: Do not fight amongst yourselves. Preserve your strength, my brothers, for the battle, the holocaust, the apocalypse is approaching and it will be upon you before you even realize it. If you endeavor to get through this trial, this battle, you will have to pray and demonstrate faith, my sons. Without prayer and faith, I'm afraid you'll be quite lost in the conflagration that will soon engulf you from the fiery furnace of hell. You'll have to control your fear, and press forward no matter what happens. Mark my words, and take my counsel—whatever you do, you must never look back or even think of turning back. Never! Do you understand?" He was adamant and Cole thought that he saw a worried look streak across his face.

"To help you through these trying times, I thought I might give you something—this gift," said the young man, softly. Then he gently tossed the neatly wrapped package to the ground and it came to rest at the feet of Cole and Corporal Buccanon. They bent their heads and stood looking down at it as if they were in prayer and posing for a picture. Their eyes fixed on the package that lay at their feet. "Use it wisely. And, remember, without prayer and faith, you are lost . . . lost forever."

When Cole and Corporal Buccanon looked up again, they weren't surprised to have found that the young man was gone. He had vanished from their sight and disappeared into the darkness of the night.

Chapter 13 - The Gift of the Revelation

"Hey, wait as minute! Come back! Come back!" Cole said, running to the spot beneath the tree where the young man had been a moment earlier.

"He's gone! Where the hell did he disappear to?" said Corporal Buccanon surprisingly, rubbing his eyes with the palms of his hands.

"I don't know, but we have to find him. Check the orchard and I'll check the cornfield."

Cole and Corporal Buccanon prowled around in the darkness, thoroughly searching the area for some time, and when they were satisfied that they couldn't find the young stranger anywhere, Cole called it quits.

He was exhausted and had been frightened by the sudden appearance of the stranger and what he had said. How could he have known the things he did? How could he have gotten that information? Collapsing before the campfire, Cole watched Corporal Buccanon as he picked up the neatly wrapped package and sat down to open it. He watched closely as Corporal Buccanon crossed his legs and held the package before him as if it was the Holy Grail. Then, cautiously, he unfastened the twine that crisscrossed the package. When this was accomplished, he carefully slid his fingers between the sleeves of the outer covering and the object and slowly removed the transparent tape and the plain brown paper that hid the gift.

Once he had removed the brown-paper wrapping, Corporal Buccanon viewed the object that he held in his hands studiously and suspiciously for a moment and then said, "It's the Good Book, Captain. And, there's a marker at Revelation Nine, The Fifth Trumpet."

Cole was certain he sensed fear in Corporal Buccanon's trembling voice.

"Do you think, he purposely marked this passage in the Book so we might read it?" Corporal Buccanon asked. "I don't like this, Captain."

"What are you afraid of, Corporal? It's only a book of words."

"I'm not afraid of anything, Captain—not this book, not the jungles in Southeast Asia, not the Vietcong," Corporal Buccanon said sternly.

"Well, I am afraid, Corporal. And, I'm not ashamed to admit it. Do you know what I'm deathly afraid of?"

"What?"

"I'm afraid I'm becoming more and more like the priest in Bergman's *Through a Glass Darkly*."

"Sure," said Corporal Buccanon sarcastically, and he thought, here we go again, the eminent Harvard lawyer and professor is ready to give his class another lecture. He remembered once taking a film appreciation course in high school, but all he could remember now was a few names and songs like Hitchcock, Fellini, and Bergman, and Marlene Dietrich singing "Falling in love again, what am I to do, didn't want to, can't help it."

"Do you remember the priest, and how he eventually lost his faith because of the silence of God in the world? It was so dreadfully obvious to me at the time. In fact, I became angry, appalled at the thought that after all is said and done, after living through all the tumultuous afflictions of this wearisome life, the only thing we might look forward to is a horrible death. And, afterwards nothing more than the silence, and the darkness, and the oblivion of an abyss for all eternity. That, Corporal, is what scares me."

Cole moved his blanket and sleeping bag closer to the campfire. It was dark now and the flames of the fire had turned their faces crimson and was reaching up and licking the sky. Cole thought he heard something, and then he thought it was only his imagination. When a black raven alighted on a branch in a tree in the orchard and stood watching them menacingly from its perch, he felt as if they were being watched by some unknown entity. It gave him the creeps.

When Corporal Buccanon saw the raven, he got up and threw several stones at the bird, but his shots all fell short or veered off to the left or to the right at the last moment. It was as if an invisible shield or some kind of force was protecting the raven. It cawed defiantly, and Cole thought that it sounded like laughter. Could it be laughing at us? He had the idea that if he had a gun, he would shoot the damn bird, the way Henry had shot Roscoe. But then again, he didn't think he would have been able to. He knew he could pull the trigger, but he felt that the bullets would be no more effective against the raven—this strange bird—than the stones Corporal Buccanon had pitched at it.

Corporal Buccanon gave up on the raven and returned to the campfire, feeling agitated and disgusted.

Cole continued. "Forget about that damn bird for now and listen to me. I'm talking about my childhood fears. I would rather face them, again, Corporal, than the abyss the strange young man was alluding to. Why, I'd embrace them eagerly and have a good laugh over them compared to what I've heard this evening and what I now fear. I could remember vividly my bedroom (wasn't I in the room only yesterday?) where I tossed and turned endlessly in my bed and where I saw shadows dancing on the walls. When I had gone to bed, I wouldn't usually fall asleep until the early hours of the morning. Sleep came to me grudgingly, and when it did, I'd usually have horrible dreams. It felt as if I was having an out-of-body experience. Often, I saw myself among a crowd of hysterical people running along a city street or running down a lonely, deserted dusty road in some lonely deserted town in the Midwest. I was petrified and afraid to look back over my shoulder because I knew that something huge, monstrous, and deadly was following us. Then I had the feeling that I was running in place and making no progress. My legs had become rubbery and heavy and almost impossible to lift. I was horrified at the thought that this unseen monster might crush me. Somehow I had gathered the courage to look over my shoulder so I might get a glimpse of the Godzilla or Rodan that was following us and destroying the city and killing everyone. But, all I saw through my weary, blood-shot eyes was the rubble of the buildings and the broken bones of frightened pedestrians and motorists that had been crushed beneath the foot of the Godzilla. Sometimes, I saw a city engulfed in flames that were being fanned by the wings of the Rodan. As I struggled to free my burdensome legs from the muck and mire that had been spewed over the street, I could hear the shrieking sound of the monster bellowing overhead. He was getting closer. And, then, suddenly, I stumbled and fell headfirst into the street where my face struck the tire of an automobile that had been parked at the side of the curb and was burning. Desperately, I tried to lift my face from out of the gutter, but I had discovered that I was frozen to the spot and could not move. All that I could do was lie there with my face against the wheel of the car and wait for the monster to crush me into the ground. I thought I was finished. I was going to be stomped and crushed into a fine, powdery dust by the ponderous foot of the monster or consumed in a fireball from hell near a burning car. And, then, thank heaven, miraculously, I would wake up, crying and sweating. When I looked around the room and particularly at the walls, I thanked God that the shadows were gone. But for how long? When would they return to haunt me?

"But it was still early morning and I knew that it was too early to get up and start my day, so I would lay back down to rest my eyes. And, I don't know why but I was always shocked when I would fall asleep again and found myself running in place. Running down the same street, looking over the same shoulder, looking for Godzilla and Rodan, and falling into the same curb, pinned against the same wheel, again and again and again." Cole paused momentarily to wipe the sweat that had gathered at his brow. His mouth felt dry and sticky.

Corporal Buccanon grunted and said, "Grow up, Captain. Everyone has crazy dreams when they're young. Most of us grow out of them."

Cole continued. "The horror and fear I felt as a child living with a recurring nightmare, Corporal, was nothing compared to what I feel this evening as a grown man after listening to that stranger. Did he think he was speaking for God? Was his the voice of God? I doubt it. Like Bergman's priest, I waited patiently for the voice of God, and I've heard nothing, nothing in return. I'm not ashamed to admit it that what I fear most of all is the silence, the loneliness, and the darkness and nothingness of the eternal abyss."

Then, suddenly, Cole raised his head to the heavens and said; "Oh, Lord and savior, if you exist somewhere out there in this universe or in our hearts, hear my supplications and save our wretched souls." When he was finished, he turned to Corporal Buccanon and said with an air of finality, "Read the passage."

Corporal Buccanon leaned forward turning the Book toward the campfire, so the light reflected and bounced off its glistening pages. With a husky voice, he read aloud from the first passage:

Then the fifth angel blew his trumpet, and I saw a star that had fallen from the sky to the earth. It was given the key for the passage to the abyss. It opened the passage to the abyss, and smoke came up and out of the passage like smoke from a huge furnace.

Cole and Corporal Buccanon looked at each other quizzically from across the campfire as they attempted in their own way and in their own mind to interpret the meaning of the words. From the orchard, the raven watched them. It sat motionless and Cole sensed that it was still there in the dark, though he could no longer see it. After several minutes, the trancelike atmosphere dissipated like a misty fog and Cole and Corporal Buccanon slid into their sleeping bags and blankets and retired for the night.

Chapter 14 - The Funeral Procession

Early the next morning, Corporal Buccanon quietly made breakfast and stowed the Good Book in the saddlebag on his Harley, while Cole searched the orchard one last time for the stranger and the raven whom they had met the night before. The sun was just peeking over the horizon, casting a bright hue of color—reddish blue—on the stalks of corn and the cherry trees by the time Cole returned from the orchard.

Corporal Buccanon watched as Cole hungrily ate his breakfast. He thought that the last time Cole ate breakfast so fast was in Vietnam and that was because the Vietcong were on their tail so they had to move quickly. And, there was one thing more, he had almost forgotten: they were afraid—afraid of being caught by the VC with their pants down.

When he had finished his breakfast, Cole packed up his gear and prepared for the road. After everything had been stowed away and the saddlebags had been buckled shut, he and Corporal Buccanon climbed onto their Harleys and started their engines. Cole pulled the map from his breast pocket and studied it for a few moments. Satisfied, he stuffed it back in his pocket and drove north along Route 29, passing Kansas City, Missouri, and then snaked up the Missouri River. Toward midmorning, Corporal Buccanon pulled alongside Cole and pointed to his gas tank. Shortly afterwards, Cole stopped at a service station for gasoline in the town of St. Joseph's.

It was around high noon when Cole and Corporal Buccanon had crossed the Missouri River and entered Nebraska, the Corn

Husker State. Here, they had deliberately opened the throttle on their turbo engines and raced recklessly and feverishly down the long and narrow highway. Driving at horrendously neck-breaking speeds and averaging one hundred miles per hour, they sped across undulating prairies and fields of corn, wheat, rye, barley, and alfalfa.

Then Corporal Buccanon shot past Cole, leaving him in a cloud of dust to inhale and choke on toxic exhaust fumes. He laughed wildly, savagely at the thought of beating Cole. Corporal Buccanon was well aware that since the war and the ambush at Nam, Cole had become more than just a friend whom he had gone with to high school. In fact, he was more than a war buddy, and his captain. He had become his nemesis and enemy. Somehow in his mixed-up mind, he thought Cole was no different than the Vietcong he had killed in Vietnam. And, like the Vietcong, Cole had to be stopped. He had to pay for his mistakes—deadly mistakes that had resulted in the deaths of young marines.

There, Captain! How do you like it when someone shakes and rattles your cage? If I could shake you up and rattle your cage so you might fall off your Trojan horse, I would have a great laugh at your expense and it would make my years of suffering all the more palatable, even worthwhile. Yes, indeed.

A moment later, Corporal Buccanon heard the sound of thunder in his ears and before he could snap out of his reverie and make the necessary adjustments, Cole had regained the lead, pushing his Softail hard and fast along the highway.

"You son of a bitch," thought Corporal Buccanon, and then he leaned forward and downward onto his Road King, his chest pressed up against the gas tank. Reducing wind resistance, he slowly and methodically closed the gap between himself and Cole.

When Cole managed to look over his shoulder, he saw Corporal Buccanon coming up fast and closing in on him. Every time he looked, he perceived that the distance separating them was getting smaller: ten feet . . .five feet . . .two feet. Now they were riding neck to neck, like two racehorses coming down the home stretch in the Kentucky Derby. Cole knew that Corporal Buccanon was a worthy competitor and his raw talent and skill as a cyclist should never be underestimated. He also knew that Corporal Buccanon would pursue the race relentlessly and recklessly. He was a fool who would drive his Road King to the limit, even if it meant killing himself or Cole in the process.

They were racing just south of the town of Tekaman when Cole and Corporal Buccanon looked up and saw a line of cars crawling before them and coming up fast. At the head of the line was a horse-drawn black hearse with narrow pillars and glass on all four sides. Two black horses with plumes of black feathers crowning their heads pulled the hearse at a slow pace. The driver was wearing a black top hat and a long black coat. Behind the hearse and moving just as slowly along the highway were five vintage cars from the fifties, sixties, and seventies. Each had been decorated lavishly and gaudily with highly polished chrome and accessories.

Cole wasn't certain if the procession was a wedding or a funeral. He approached the last car in the line - a 1955 DeSoto Fireflite - and reduced his speed so he might lag behind the procession. After awhile, he moved to the left and sped up so he might ride alongside the DeSoto, a long car with tapering tail fins, two-tone exterior finish, and bench seats. As he pulled up the car, he looked through the window and was shocked when he recognized the driver. It was Bellows Hanley, an old codger, and sitting next to him was his wife, Carmela. He remembered it was Carmela Hanley who had been driving the car that had hit Roscoe and which caused Henry to shoot the dog while his son looked on. He remembered that Bellows was having a heart attack at the time and she was taking him to the hospital driving fast and recklessly. They had been neighbors for some fifty years after Bellows bought the Coopers' house on Chestnut Road.

After passing the DeSoto, Cole pulled alongside a white 1955 Ford Thunderbird, a two-seater sporty convertible. Apprehensively, he looked at the driver of the Thunderbird. He was a heavy, stocky gentleman. Cole didn't recognize him at first because he was wearing a bright red fedora and had an expensive Havana cigar clenched between his teeth. Sitting next to him was a sexy woman with long brown hair and a voluptuous bosom. She was tightly wrapped in a fancy dress and would have spilled out of it if she hadn't been leaning against the man in the front seat. She reminded Cole of Rita Hayworth and Eva Gardner, but she was more primitive, yet at the same time sophisticated. She had a bottle of Smirnoff in her right hand, and the next moment, Cole saw her pour the contents of the bottle into Mr. DeForest's rapacious mouth. Suddenly, the gentleman turned to Cole and smiled broadly, with a grin that stretched from ear to ear.

Oh! God, thought Cole, I must be hallucinating—that's Mr. DeForest, my high-school English teacher. Why was he wearing a red fedora and smoking a Havana cigar? And why was that woman pouring vodka into his mouth? Cole had an idea that Mr. DeForest was only a phantom of his imagination, and he could prove it. He remembered Mr. DeForest was a heavy drinker and had died from cirrhosis of the liver. Cole was at Harvard at the time of his death and found out several days later when his mother had sent him a copy of the local newspaper and he read about him in the obituary column.

Cole frowned and pulled up to the next car in line. It was a blue 1970 Dodge Dart Swinger, a two-door hardtop. At the wheel he saw a woman who reminded him of one of his aunts—Aunt Lucille. She was an elderly, frail woman. She was wearing glasses, a flowery cotton blouse, and a silk scarf around her neck. Cole couldn't remember when he had last seen her. He was a young boy then, and she used to take him to places like Virginia Beach, Ocean City, and Wildwood in New Jersey. He recalled the time when she was sick, dying, for more than a year and had eventually succumbed to emphysema and blood cancer. He was at her bedside in the hospital when she passed away, spitting up her insides. He gritted his teeth as he passed the Dart Swinger, and the wind stung his face as it wiped away a tear from his eye.

Cole next came to a green 1960 Cadillac convertible with a chrome grill, a sleek body, and tail fins. It was rocking from side to side. Inside Cole recognized four of his classmates from high school: Bobby Canary (he was given the sobriquet The Grand Canary), Benjamin Saltzman, and Danny and Donald Wu. From the looks of it, Cole thought, they were having one hell of a time, enjoying the ride, telling stories, and getting drunk on beer. Then Donald flipped an empty beer bottle out the side window of the car and it struck Cole's Softail causing him to swerve to the side of the road and nearly crash. The bottle shattered into a million pieces, but no one seemed to have noticed. Cole had to remind himself that this wasn't really happening. It was all just a figment of his imagination.

Driving ahead of the green Cadillac was a two-tone 1957 Plymouth Fury hardtop coupe. Cole pulled up alongside and looked in. He wasn't at all surprised when he saw Jake Snow driving the car, and sitting in the backseat were Cole's mother and father. William was drinking wine and Theresa was crying and dabbing a corner of her eye with a white handkerchief she held awkwardly in her trembling hand.

Wearily, Cole pressed forward and when he reached the black hearse, he realized that the procession wasn't a wedding procession but a funeral. He was afraid to look. He knew there had to be a coffin riding in the back of the hearse. But the question that haunted him was whose coffin was it? Turning his head into the wind that had suddenly kicked up from the northwest, Cole peered through a diaphanous curtain hanging like a drape over the side of the hearse. He wasn't surprised when he saw the black coffin. It was closed and nailed shut. Nevertheless, Cole perceived – as though he could see right through wood and fabric—an outline of a man lying within the coffin. He shivered because he recognized the man. It was his own image he saw lying there. Cole turned away and looked at the driver of the hearse. The man had a long, leathery face. He was partly bald, and his black hair formed a horseshoe around the back of his head. Cole had noticed his hair was long and fell to the collar of his black overcoat. His eyes were set close together like snake eyes. They were flaming red and black, and truculent. Sitting atop and cocked to one side of his head was a tall black hat. It was dirty and ragged and the rim appeared as if it had been chewed. He was grinning ominously, and Cole felt a dark foreboding when he saw his gaping maw and his sharp wolfish teeth. Cole realized that this was no ordinary person; he was possessed by something evil, something indefinable, and something dark and bottomless as an abyss.

Suddenly, Cole heard the sound of a horn blasting furiously, and when he looked up again, he saw the intimidating grill of an approaching eighteen-wheel tractor-trailer. Gritting his teeth and gripping the handlebars until his knuckles turned white, he turned the Softail to the left just in time to avoid a head-on collision. He steered the Softail into a field of corn and pressed his legs against the bike to prevent himself from falling off. Then he applied his brakes gradually until the Softail came to a stop.

Buccanon, on the other hand, skidded off the road and penetrated deeper into the cornfield where he was thrown from the Road King.

The driver of the black hearse leading a procession of vintage cars slowly and ceremoniously down the highway was undisturbed by the near collision of the tractor-trailer and the two Harleys. In fact, he never looked back maintaining a speed of ten miles an hour.

Pivoting his Softail, Cole drove deeper into the cornfield in search of Corporal Buccanon. He didn't have to go very far. Corporal Buccanon was just thirty feet away lying face down under a stalk of corn. His Road King was lying on its side. Groping for his canteen of water, Cole ran to Corporal Buccanon and surveyed the damage.

"Buccanon! Buccanon! Is anything broken? How do you feel?" Cole asked, gently turning him over as if he were a broken porcelain doll.

"I'm all right, I'm all right," Corporal Buccanon said languidly, his face turning blue from a lack of oxygen. "I just had the wind knocked out of me—that's all." He took several deep breaths. "I'd like to catch up with the driver of that tractor-trailer. He nearly killed us!"

"Well, Corporal, we were riding on the wrong side of the road— or don't you remember?" said Cole sharply. "But more importantly, did you get a look at anyone inside the cars or at the black hearse as you had passed them on the road?"

"What? No, I was too busy driving. I didn't see a thing," said Corporal Buccanon briskly, and then he looked away nervously.

Cole thought he was lying. He looked at Corporal Buccanon's face and his bloodshot eyes, and saw something there that he hadn't seen in many years—not since South Vietnam. He saw fear in the face and eyes of Corporal Buccanon and it made him sick and weary. Firmly gripping Corporal Buccanon under the arm, Cole slowly pulled him to his feet, and said, "I know you saw something."

"I didn't see anything, I tell you!" shouted Corporal Buccanon irritably, and then after a moment, after thinking about it, he said softly, "I didn't see anything." He turned to his Road King and grunted awkwardly as he set it upright and wheeled it back to the road. The tractor-trailer and the funeral procession were long gone. The road was now empty, quiet, except for the sound of a flock of geese flying north. Cole looked up and saw a chevron formation. Corporal Buccanon was trembling. He knew what he saw, but he would rather swallow nails than admit it to Cole, who would think he was going out of his mind. "Oh, Lord, what did that young man in Independence, Missouri, say? Did he say something about an abyss? Was it something about smoke and fire? Why can't I remember?"

Chapter 15 – Moose Mulligan and the HOGS

A minute later, Cole came trudging up from the field of corn with his Softail and joined Corporal Buccanon at the side of the road. Then, he sighed wearily and said, "I suppose you'd like to know what I saw back there."

"Not particularly," Corporal Buccanon said, roughly. His face was pale and he tried desperately to suppress the tremors shaking his body. He was scared but he didn't want to admit it to Cole. He didn't want to know what the hell Cole had seen back there, because something deep in the pit of his gut was telling him the thing tormenting them was evil. It wasn't anything that anyone might outrun on the open road or on a racetrack. And it wasn't anything like Cole's silly recurring nightmare of Godzilla and Rodan, where you're comforted by the realization that it is merely a dream that will shortly come to an end. In the deep recesses of your mind, you feel as if you're still in control and could easily wake up from such a nightmare by merely concentrating or thinking about it long enough. He sighed wearily.

"You wouldn't believe it, but I thought I saw someone who looked just like my Aunt Lucille," said Cole in a low trembling voice. "Do you remember my Uncle Chic from my mother's side of the family? Everyone called him Chic Brown. Well, he was married to my Aunt Lucille. She was driving the Swinger. She died years ago in the hospital, and I was there at the end." After a pause, he said, "I also saw Benny Saltzman! And Bobby Canary!

And Danny and Donald Wu! Do you remember them? They were classmates of ours—back in high school."

Corporal Buccanon said nothing. He suddenly felt sick and had the urge to vomit. He stood there leaning against his bike and watched Cole suspiciously. He thought Cole was going mad; they were both going mad.

Cole wiped the sweat from his brow and shook his head miserably and wearily. "And that's not all. I saw Mr. DeForest, our English teacher, and Mr. and Mrs. Hanley. And do you want to know who I saw riding in the Plymouth Fury, directly behind the black hearse? It was Jake Snow. He was driving my mother and father. They were sitting in the backseat. My mother had a worried look on her face and she was crying."

"You're imagining things. You've been in the sun too long. Your brain must've fried like an egg in your helmet. You couldn't possibly have seen all that," Corporal Buccanon grumbled nervously. He didn't like it when Cole talked like this. It was strange talk. He had always thought Cole was a rational person— as rational as they come—and was someone he could count on for having two feet on the ground. This kind of talk was giving him the creeps, making him nervous, making him break out in a cold sweat.

"Listen to me! For a moment, just listen to me!" shouted Cole. "I thought I saw a coffin lying in the back of the hearse. And somehow I was able to see inside the coffin where I saw something that scared the hell out of me. I recognized the person lying in the coffin. I was that person!"

"Come on! You were hallucinating! " Corporal Buccanon said.

"No, listen to me! I saw myself or it was something that looked like me. I saw it as clear as I see my hand before my eyes. It had turned its head just as I drove up alongside the hearse and I saw my own image staring back at me. Oh, God, it was ugly and horrible. It was dead, and yet it looked as if it was still alive. Oh, God!"

Corporal Buccanon mounted the Road King. He said, unsympathetically, "I told you you're imagining things. You must've hit you head back there when you came off the road. When we get to Tekaman, we better stop and have a doctor take a look at you."

"Listen to me. Just before the tractor-trailer drove us off the road, I got a glimpse of the driver of the black hearse. He was partly bald and he was wearing a black overcoat and a top hat. His skin was translucent, and I could see every bone in his body. He had big red, bloodshot eyes, and big flaring nostrils. And his teeth were well...they didn't look like human teeth at all, but more like fangs. When he turned and looked in my direction, I felt as if all hell was watching me. He grinned and I heard him say, 'you're next.' It was as though he was talking directly to me. His thin lips didn't move, but I heard his voice in my head just the same. Did you see him? Tell me, you saw him, Corporal Buccanon. He was the devil! I'm almost sure of it," Cole said, desperately. "I know you saw him."

"No!" said Corporal Buccanon coldly. "I didn't see anything. Now, climb on your bike and let's get the hell out of here. I'm sick of this place. It gives me the creeps." He opened the throttle, and stepped on the starter. Nothing happened. He made several attempts to start the Harley but it wouldn't turn over. It just sat there. After the third or fourth attempt, Corporal Buccanon jumped off the Harley and savagely kicked it three or four times before it toppled over and crashed to the ground. A string of profanity spouted from his mouth.

While Corporal Buccanon nearly trashed his bike in a burst of rage, Cole leaned back against his Softail and watched, his face frozen into a mask of cold stone. Through tinted shades that hid his hard eyes, he observed Corporal Buccanon reach into his saddlebag and pull out a tool kit. Cole was amazed how quickly he had figured out that the fuel line had been severed in the accident.

"Damn," shouted Corporal Buccanon loudly. "I found the trouble. It's the fuel line—it's been severed—I'll have to replace it with a new part. Damn! Damn! Damn! You'll have to ride ahead into Tekaman and get me a new one." He tried to read Cole's face, but it was useless. With those damn aviator sunglasses sitting across his face and covering his eyes, he couldn't tell what kind of mood Cole was in.

Imperceptibly at first, Cole felt a tiny vibration. He sensed it more than felt it. Then, he felt the gravel trembling under his feet. He got up, walked out to the middle of the road, and saw the asphalt was trembling there as well. He looked up and down the road in both directions and saw nothing. Nevertheless, he knew instinctively that something was coming—something was coming towards them. Then, he thought *Something Wicked This Way Comes*, the title of a book written by Ray Bradbury. Yes. It was a story about two boys—William Halloway and Jim Nightshade—who lived in Green Town and went to the Cooger and Dark's Pandemonium Shadow Show where strange things happened on a carousel. Wasn't that what he had just witnessed with the funeral procession—a kind of rolling carnival on wheels? A shadow show? He thought he heard the sound of the calliope, but he wasn't sure. He knew the idea went further back than 1962. In fact, it went back to 1605-1606, when Shakespeare wrote Macbeth, in which the second witch said, "By the pricking of my thumbs, something wicked this way comes."

He could hear it in the distance now—a low, rumbling sound. Then he saw a speck, like a dot on the horizon above the asphalt road, shimmering in the heat. And as the speck grew larger in size, the constant rumbling of the engines became a cacophony of shattering thunder.

Cole and Corporal Buccanon stepped back off the road as the Capital Harley-Davidson Owner's Group (H.O.G.s) from Washington, DC, came cruising along the highway. There had to be more than a hundred riders—men and women, husbands and wives, friends and lovers, young and old, the wealthy and the not so wealthy—driving steadily in pairs one behind the other. Everyone drove a Harley, and there were Harleys of every size, model, and color—red and black Sportsters, yellow Panheads, white Softails, metallic gray Road Kings, silvery Low and Wide Riders, metallic blue Fat Boys, soft blue Ultra Classic Electra Glides, and black and gold V Rods.

Moose Mulligan, a large, bearded man wearing thick glasses and a tightly fitting black leather jacket and cap, was riding a black and red 1995 Ultra Classic Electra Glide, and his wife, Barbara, a round and bulky woman, was riding alongside of him snuggled up in a sidecar. She had a leather cap covering her white curly locks, a pair of goggles protecting her soft hazel eyes, and a red and black scarf around her neck that flapped in the wind.

Moose Mulligan was a veteran of World War II, a commander who fought courageously in Europe and was awarded a Purple Heart. When Mulligan saw Cole and Corporal Buccanon standing wearily on the side of the road, he knew he couldn't simply drive by without first offering a helping hand. So he pulled over, breaking away from the line of Harleys, and came to a stop directly behind Cole and Corporal Buccanon. He recognized Corporal Buccanon's field jacket and suspected that they were soldiers and had fought in Vietnam.

"Good morning," Mulligan said enthusiastically. His eyes sparkling brightly in the morning sun. "If I didn't know better, I'd say it looks as if you boys have some kind of a problem here. What can I can do to help you boys get back on the road?"

"I suppose, you don't happen to have an extra fuel line with you?" Corporal Buccanon asked, gruffly.

"Good Lord, no," Moose Mulligan said, laughing.

"Good morning," Cole said cordially. "My name's John Cole and this is Corporal Salvatore Buccanon. The corporal here had a slight accident with the Road King earlier this morning and he damaged the fuel line."

"That's unfortunate. I'd ask if either of you were hurt but I can see for myself that you're both fine," Moose Mulligan said heartily. He then looked across at Cole and Corporal Buccanon with a curious eye. "I'm Moose Mulligan, and this is my wife, Barbara."

"It's a pleasure," said Cole cordially, shaking hands with each in turn.

"Likewise," said Corporal Buccanon.

"You're lucky neither of you was hurt in that accident. You know out here, in the middle of nowhere, it could take some time before an ambulance would arrive. And, unfortunately, even a short delay could be fatal. Gentlemen, I'm a doctor at Georgetown Medical Center, in Washington, DC. I've seen many roadside accidents in my time and I believe that responding quickly is critical if a seriously injured party is to have any chance of survival. In Washington, as in all large urban cities, one of the greatest obstacles we have to overcome is the traffic. Could you imagine what it's like idling in traffic with a seriously injured person in the back of your ambulance and all you can do is sit there and look at your partner? Out here, in the Midwest, the greatest obstacle to overcome is the distance between towns—these great open spaces. Oh, they're beautiful, all right. But, they're also a killer."

"And that's not all that can kill you out here," interjected Barbara seriously. "Ravens! Perhaps, you've seen them. Sometimes they fly together and other times you might see them alone. I don't know where they come from, but they're out here, nevertheless, and they could be mighty vicious. I've heard stories from people who've camped out in these parts and said that the ravens are wild and could kill a person if they had a mind to. If you see one, I'd stay clear of it if I were you."

Listening to Barbara mouthing off about ravens, Cole remembered the raven he and Corporal Buccanon saw back in Independence, Missouri. It was the night they had met the stranger sitting under a tree in an orchard. Cole remembered how Corporal Buccanon threw several stones at the raven to scare it off, but nothing he had done seemed to faze it. In fact, it appeared as if the raven wasn't afraid of anything. In his mind's eyes, Cole could still see it just sitting there, defiantly, on a branch in the tree and watching them all night with its red and black eyes.

"A person could easily bleed to death out here and no one would ever be the wiser—at least not for some time," said Moose Mulligan and then he shrugged.

"I get your point," said Cole, and then he nodded toward the group of riders cruising joyfully along the road. "I've never seen so many HOGs in one place before. What's the occasion?"

"We're on our way to Sturgis, South Dakota, boys," Barbara Mulligan enthused, looking at Cole and Corporal Buccanon and smiling broadly.

"For the annual meeting of the Harley-Davidson Owners' Groups at Sturgis. At this very minute, there are thousands of Harley owners from all over the country converging on the sleepy little town of Sturgis, South Dakota," said Commander Moose Mulligan, grinning in a friendly manner.

"It's not going to be sleepy much longer, sugar," interjected Barbara. "Sturgis is putting on a big party and for the next two weeks, the little town will be inundated with all types of people—most of them HOGs. And, I know what you're thinking. You're thinking that these fellows are over-the-hill sleazeballs. Well, you're wrong. You'd be surprised to learn that many of them are management types—CEOs, lawyers, accountants, and presidents of corporations and companies. Don't let corporate America fool you. They know how to party," Barbara said playfully. She turned to her husband and asked, "Isn't that right, Moose?"

"That's right, darling," he replied cheerfully. Then, as if he suddenly remembered why he had stopped in the first place, he said, "Oh, there's a parts dealership about ten miles up the road in the town of Tekaman. They should have whatever it is you're looking for."

"Thanks," said Cole, as he watched the last of the HOGs cruise by.

"Well," said Moose Mulligan, cheerfully. "If there's nothing more we can do for you boys, we'll be on our way. Hope to see you in Sturgis."

"See you in Sturgis, boys," Barbara Mulligan said and she waved good-bye as Moose released the brake and accelerated steadily, guiding the Harley and the sidecar back onto the road and into the line of Harleys and HOGs.

Chapter 16 - The Harley-Davidson Dealership

Corporal Buccanon adamantly refused to leave his Road King in the cornfield unattended, so he solicited Cole to proceed alone to the Harley-Davidson dealership in Tekaman to get the necessary part for his motorcycle.

"All right," said Cole grudgingly. "I'll go. But, you owe me one." He climbed onto his Softail and, sweltering under the hot sun, drove to Tekaman alone.

It was midafternoon by the time Cole reached Tekaman. He drove down the main street and found the dealership at the end of town. What caught his eye was the Harleys parked in front of and alongside the building. He saw a sign hanging above the entrance. Printed in bold letters was the name of the shop: Lucifer Johnson's Harley-Davidson Dealership—Where We Sell More than Just Motorcycles. HD is our lifeblood! Cole climbed off his Softail and walked along the front of the red brick building. He peered through the large glass picture window and saw a showroom jam-packed with Harleys, customers, and several salesclerks.

Cole stepped inside where it was cool and refreshing. The air conditioner was working on overtime, thought Cole. He shivered as he surveyed the dealership, admiring the Harleys. He ran his fingers gently along the smooth, highly polished surface of the gas tanks and fenders and chrome exhausts, admiring their custom designs. He touched the screaming eagles and flames, and suddenly withdrew his hand with a jerk as if he had been shocked with a current of electricity. He stared at the screaming eagles and flames, and for a moment, he thought of the stranger, and the red-eyed raven in the orchard, and the funeral procession. He pushed the images out of his mind and turned his attention back to the magnificent machines on display. Examining the sensuous lines and curves of the Softails, his heart began to race. Then, he sensed more than felt the heaviness and strength of the Electra Glides, and the dominance and overbearing power of the Road Kings. The Low Rider was easy, the FXSTB Fat Boy was haughty, and the popular Sportster was speed.

Beyond and to the right of the Softails, Cole saw a young man struggling to squeeze into a fine black leather jacket that had been hanging from one of the racks of clothing. Several feet to his right, a tall, lean blond was checking out the tee shirts. And further to his right, an elderly couple was looking at decorative whiskey glasses, pen and pencil sets, and paperweights for the desk, pet collars, and mugs. Next to the elderly couple, a man with a white beard and wire-rim eyeglasses stood with his fiancée browsing through copies of *The American Iron Magazine's Hot XL, Rodder's Digest, America's Motorcycle,* and Harley-Davidson's *Enthusiast.*

Cole eventually found the parts counter in the back of the dealership. It was partly hidden behind several racks of leather jackets and display cases of sundry items. As he approached, Cole saw a man of medium height with broad shoulders leaning ponderously against the counter. He was wearing a white shirt that had tassels dangling ornamentally from his sleeves. It reminded Cole of the western style shirts worn by cowboy rodeo stars in carnivals and sideshows. He was talking to Johnson, the owner of the dealership, and he was writing down his address on an order form. He said huskily, "Have the manufacturer send the merchandise directly to my address in Baton Rouge, Louisiana."

"Yes, sir," Johnson replied pleasantly. He was a mammoth of a man, easily weighing over three hundred pounds. His barrel chest was covered with a dirty tee shirt and a leather vest. A gray-black beard clung to his huge, craggy face like icicles. He had a crooked nose that looked as if he had been in one too many barroom brawls. His neck was thick and bulky and reminded Cole of a Japanese sumo wrestler. His teeth were jagged and stained from drinking too much coffee. And his head was covered with a skullcap and goggles. "Give it a week or two," Johnson told the man. He then completed writing the order and courteously thanked the customer.

As Cole stepped up to the counter, Johnson greeted him in a friendly manner as he would any customer. Apparently he's enjoying the increase in business the rally in Sturgis is bringing his way, thought Cole.

"Good afternoon, partner," the mammoth said. "My name's Lucifer Johnson, and I'm the angel of light from above that fell from the skies and heaven. I'd like to welcome you to Tekaman, partner. I suppose you're heading to Sturgis like everyone else. Well, now, how might I help you?" He looked across the counter at Cole curiously, his dark blue eyes shinning brightly in what appeared to be a solitary bolt of afternoon sunlight that had mysteriously penetrated the skylight in the showroom and landed squarely on Lucifer Johnson's face. It was as if a powerful searchlight or a beacon from a lighthouse along the rocky coastline had suddenly been switched on to guide wayward ships to a safe harbor during a dangerous storm.

Cole was mesmerized by the phenomenon: the glow around his head looked distinctly like a halo. Then, as if divined by Providence, a cloud passed in front of the sun and the last ray of sunlight faded away. At that moment, everything went dark, except for two red-burning eyes, now staring intently at Cole.

Cole shifted his weight uneasily from one foot to the other as the darkness suddenly surrounded him. He sensed more than felt the loss of the sunlight and throughout his body his nerves started to tingle. For a moment, he was reminded of ominous caves and subterranean labyrinthine caverns, whose winding and narrowing tunnels and precarious rock and crystal formations are deadly. He had once taken Gina to the Crystal Caverns in Pennsylvania, and after he had descended into the depths of the earth, he imagined he was a groundhog or a mole. Now he had a preternatural premonition, a feeling that he had fallen into an abyss and might be lost forever in the bowels of the earth, beneath layers and layers of earth and rock. Then, he snapped out of his trance and he looked curiously at Lucifer Johnson.

"Good afternoon," Cole said, his voice shaking a little. "I'm looking for a fuel line for a 1996 Road King. Would you have something like that in stock?"

"Let me see . . . a 1996 Road King." Johnson entered the information into his computer and stared at the screen.

Cole noticed Johnson's eyes. They reminded him of the undertaker who had been driving the hearse.

"Hummm . . . Here it is! The part number is 335670. I'm sure we have it in stock. Excuse me for a moment while I check in the back." Lucifer Johnson disappeared behind a row of metal shelves.

From the corner of his eye, Cole saw Johnson darting back and forth in an awkward and confused manner. Cole waited anxiously, and when he thought that Johnson had been gone long enough, he glanced at his wristwatch. He got a sick feeling in the gut of his stomach when he noticed that the second hand had stopped moving. It might be just the battery, he thought. Nothing to worry about. But that didn't settle his nerves at all. He tapped the face of his wristwatch and concluded the battery was dead. He drummed the countertop nervously with his fingertips as he saw several customers leaving the shop. He had noticed that the two salesclerks who were busy helping customers had suddenly disappeared.

Perspiration was now beginning to run in rivulets down the side of Cole's face and soak his shirt collar. Taking a handkerchief from his back pocket, he wiped the sweat from his brow, and then, for the first time, he heard the sound of heavy, irregular breathing coming from somewhere behind the metal shelves. He couldn't see that far back into the darkness, but he could certainly hear Johnson's voice speaking from within. It was a strange, deep, and ugly voice. Cole thought he heard Johnson muttering something obscene and incoherent. Was the woolly mammoth losing his mind? Cole heard something violent: a crash. It sounded as if Johnson was throwing parts down onto the floor and smashing them into little pieces.

Then, from inside the abyss, the woolly mammoth turned toward Cole, his prey, and stepped out of the darkness. He moved swiftly and powerfully and reminded Cole of a malignant, savage creature—a Beast. Cole nearly screamed and fainted when he saw

Lucifer Johnson standing before him. He wasn't the same bike-loving HOG who had stepped behind the metal shelves two minutes ago. He had changed into something horrible, something dangerous—something discernibly evil.

Cole glanced down at Johnson's hands and what he saw frightened him. They had become talons with sharp, razorlike nails. And on his head two pointed nubs resembling baby teeth had emerged. Protruding from his mouth were two jagged fangs that dripped foam and salvia. His nose had metamorphosed into a pointed beak and his head hung forward like the head of a vulture. Cole noticed immediately that the smiling, friendly face of the woolly mammoth had transformed itself into a grotesquely evil mask. A streak of silver gray ran through the creature's wild hair. It was as if God had sent a bolt of lighting down from heaven to kill the creature before it had a chance to devour and destroy the world—His creation.

The mammoth extended his claw and laid it on the counter. His fingers wrapped tightly and firmly around the fuel line that Cole so desperately needed. Cole saw the fuel line and bravely reached across the counter to grip it with his right hand. At that moment, he felt a bolt of electricity pass through the fuel line and into his hand and up his arm. He realized instantly that the mammoth—the Beast standing before him—was possessed with an evil spirit, the same evil spirit that had possessed the driver of the black hearse.

Cole's body began to shudder and twitch convulsively, helpless beneath the towering evil force. He tried to pull his hand away, but it was useless. His body felt paralyzed, every nerve ending frying and sizzling like bacon in a hot skillet. As he looked into the murky red eyes—the fuming, flaming portals of the abyss—he wanted to scream. Never before had he felt as shamelessly frightened and horrified as he did now.

Johnson really didn't know what was happening to him. One minute he was searching for a motor part, and the next minute he felt that an evil force had invaded his body. He felt his strength increase tenfold and his nostrils dilate, his eyes grow large and red. He didn't recognize his own voice when he admonished Cole. "Turn back! Leave the land of the Sioux! If you listen to your friends and false prophets, you will be annihilated, cast into an abyss, into Gehenna, where there is nothing but fire and brimstone!"

Cole tried to pull away from the Beast but his arms and legs were paralyzed. Then, the creature roared, "The young man you met in Independence is powerless against me. Ha . . . ha . . . ha." He laughed wildly. Then, he thrust his head back and bellowed loudly, "You fool!" He glared at Cole menacingly. "You think you can help Black Hawk or the old chief? Ha . . . ha . . . ha . . . ha!"

"What are you talking about?"

"The door to the abyss was left open, and now I have my freedom. I am finally free! Free! After a thousand years of confinement, no one will ever lock me up again. Do you understand me? Not even after a thousand times a thousand years. Never! Never! Never!"

The woolly mammoth suddenly leaped over the counter to seize his prey, and Cole instinctively retreated wildly to the showroom, where he fell into a line of Harleys, toppling them to the floor. He didn't bother to look back to see if the Beast was following him or if anyone else was in the shop. He flew frantically from the cavern of horrors.

The Beast laughed triumphantly from the doorway of the Harley-Davidson dealership as Cole leaped onto his Softail and fumbled with the starter. Leaning forward, Cole opened the throttle and drove recklessly down Main Street, Tekaman. As he sped away, he could hear the creature bellowing, "You're powerless! Powerless! Powerless against me! Captain Cole!"

He was several miles out of town before he realized what it was that he was holding so tightly in his clenched hand. It was the fuel line. He had had it all the time—amid all that frantic commotion. He looked at it wearily now and silently thanked God that he had got away from the Beast and out of Tekaman alive.

Chapter 17 - The Raven

Thirty minutes after Cole left the campsite and drove his Softail to Tekaman to visit Lucifer Johnson's Harley-Davidson dealership and purchase a fuel line for Corporal Buccanon's Road King, the raven had returned. Corporal Buccanon was quite alone now, preparing his lunch over an open campfire. He had opened a can of beans and franks and was heating the provender in a skillet. The campfire crackled softly as he stirred everything together with a wooden ladle. Now that Cole was gone, he sang his song loudly, "Lord I was born a ramblin' man. Tryin' to make a livin' and doin' the best I can. And when it comes to leavin' I hope you'll understand that I was born a ramblin' man. Lord, I was born a ramblin' man...Lord I was born—"

Just then the raven alighted on the handlebars of the Road King and Corporal Buccanon saw him. He stopped singing abruptly as he stared at the creature. He sensed instinctively that this was the same raven he and Cole had seen back in Independence. Oh, yes. It was the same raven, all right. Corporal Buccanon recognized the penetrating red and black eyes of the bird. And just as in Independence, it wasn't afraid of anything, least of all mankind.

"Well, I'll be damned! It's the raven," Corporal Buccanon said in a friendly manner, and got up slowly. No fast movements, now. Everything has to be done nice and slow, he thought. Inside, he sensed danger and felt his body grow tense. An alarm went off in his head telling his muscles and nerve endings to wake up. Then, he remembered the words of Barbara Mulligan, "Ravens! Perhaps, you've seen them. Sometimes they fly together and other times you might see them alone. I don't know where they come from, but they're out here, nevertheless, and they could be mighty vicious. I've heard stories from people who've camped out in these parts and said that the ravens are wild and could kill a person if they had a mind to. If you see one, I'd stay clear of it—if I were you." He heard her voice clearly, as if she were standing next to him and whispering her admonishment in his ear.

He said to the bird nervously, "You're a long way from Independence, raven." Despite his friendly manner, Corporal Buccanon was aware that the raven was looking at him menacingly. He smiled, then laughed, thinking it would be better to hide his fear from the bird. If he showed the raven he was afraid, it could take that as a sign of weakness and attack. Don't show it you're afraid, dummy.

But, he sensed the raven could see right through him and look deep into his very soul and mind. Corporal Buccanon saw a picture of himself bleeding to death in the cornfield miles from nowhere, while Captain Cole was out somewhere joy riding. He cursed Cole and then clenched his fists.

He could smell the franks and beans burning in the skillet and he slowly moved away from the campfire. He thought that perhaps he'd offer some of the franks and beans to the raven as a peace offering, when it leaped forward, flapped its wings, and flew in a beeline towards Corporal Buccanon's head. Within seconds, the raven had closed on its prey and would have plucked out the corporal's left eye had he not ducked and lowered his head. Nevertheless, the raven struck him on his forehead, creating a gouge two inches above his eye. A cataract of red blood cascaded down his face and for a moment he was blinded by the blood. He reached for his handkerchief and wiped the blood from his eyes. He pivoted and followed the bird as it flew away and then he saw it turn and circle around. It's coming back, he thought. The damn bird is coming back to finish the job. He held his handkerchief over the wound and applied direct pressure to stem the flow of blood and to promote clotting. Wasn't that what they had taught him when he was at high school attending health and gym classes and in Vietnam?

Now Corporal Buccanon was angry, and he wanted to kill the raven. He felt his heart pounding in his chest, blood racing through the arteries in his neck. The bird had circled around and was now coming in for another attack. "You mother—" Corporal Buccanon said angrily, never taking his eye off the raven as it swooped down in a kamikaze dive and struck him squarely in the face, throwing him backwards and into the campfire. The skillet of franks and beans spilled over into the dirt next to the fire, which was now smoldering under Corporal Buccanon. Gripping the raven with both hands so as to prevent its talons from digging into his neck, he tossed the bird roughly away from his body.

A moment later, the raven was circling overhead again. As Corporal Buccanon watched the bird, he realized that without a weapon or a gun, he was no match for this devilish creature . . . this fiercely plundering bird . . . this monster . . . this deadly Beast. He glanced around and saw the cornfield, and he thought the corn stalks might afford him safety. As the raven started back, making a beeline for Corporal Buccanon, he ran as fast as his tired legs could carry him to the cornfield. He crouched under the stalks of corn and cupped his hand to protect his eyes. The bird was still coming, driving forward fearlessly, like a locomotive or a skier heading downhill. He soon discovered that this raven was no ordinary bird, but sought its prey relentlessly. A moment later, the crazy bird had crashed into the cornfield, flapping its wings, and was getting closer. As he ran, he felt the bird on his back, digging its sharp talons into the soft skin of his neck while pecking at his head.

He raised his arms over his head so he might grip the bird and tear it from the back of his neck, but the bird was too strong and he couldn't get enough leverage. Then Corporal Buccanon came into a clearing, and he flung his body onto the ground hoping that he would crush the bird. He found some relief after the raven released its grip and flew away, alighting on a signpost at the opposite end of the barnyard in which Corporal Buccanon now found himself.

His mind tried to interpret what he was seeing. He shuddered at the idea that he was at the mercy of some preternatural force. He thought that part of it had to do with the raven. He looked at the raven perched on the signpost, and its red and black eyes stared back at him coldly. To the right of the signpost was a wooden fence that led to the barn. It was a typical western barn—beam and post construction—with a hayloft and silo. Its red paint was worn and faded in several places. Some of the boards were missing. Corporal Buccanon saw huge double doors hanging on rusty hinges, left open and revealing a gaping black maw. Twenty-five feet to the right of the barn was a wagon containing bales of hay and a pitchfork. Another twenty-five feet to the right, he saw a farmhouse—dilapidated and in ruins. Its windows and screens were broken and torn, reminding him of a haunted house.

He was now feeling weak from the shock of the attack, the fierce relentlessness of the raven, and the loss of blood. He collapsed in the middle of the barnyard, and he thought if the damn raven were to attack him again he would probably die in this blasted barnyard, surrounded by a blasted cornfield, and no one would be the wiser. He told himself he would give anything to see Captain Cole's face when he returned from Tekaman and found his body in this godforsaken place. He laughed, and then he looked at the raven perched on the signpost, and this time he looked at it with new respect and fear. It has proved to be a worthy adversary, he thought.

After several minutes had passed and the raven did not attack, Corporal Buccanon thought that the worse was over. The bird was obviously bored and, perhaps, it would soon leave so that he might be able to return to his campsite, where he'd find Captain Cole pacing back and forth, worried sick. He was starting to feel better when he heard the snarling sound of a dog, coming from the barn. He squinted, his eyes barely seeing the shadows and silhouettes of two dogs standing side by side. The tremors in his arms and legs had returned, and his head was beaded with droplets of sweat and blood. He could taste the salt and blood in his mouth. His stomach seemed to flip as the snarling sound grew louder. He looked at the gaping maw of the barn and suddenly he saw the two dogs. He didn't recognize them at first, but then after a moment, it struck him like a bolt of lightning from the sky.

"Roscoe! T-bone!" Corporal Buccanon said, and then he realized he was hallucinating. He also imagined that the raven was somehow responsible for this and was the source of his pain and suffering. This couldn't be real, he thought. Roscoe is dead. Dad had shot him years ago on the road when he was broadsided by Mrs. Hanley's car. I saw him pull the trigger, and Roscoe died in my arms. He's dead! And T-bone! I left him back in Tennessee with Susan. When he thought of Susan, he heard the rusty hinges of the screen door screeching.

Someone had opened the door, and that someone might help him. He turned and saw three figures stepping out onto the rickety porch. He thought he had lost his mind when he saw his mother and father and sister standing there. His father was cradling a Winchester rifle in the fold of his arm and Corporal Buccanon knew that it was the same rifle that he had used to kill Roscoe.

Then, the raven flapped its wings and cawed loudly and horribly, and T-bone stepped forward as if on cue. Corporal Buccanon knew he didn't have a lot of time to sit and think about what he should do. If he wanted to survive, he had to do something and do it right away. T-bone must have read Corporal Buccanon's mind because the next second, the dog leaped across the barnyard and charged. Corporal Buccanon scrambled to his feet and raced toward the farmhouse. He had reached the wagon containing the bales of hay when he felt a pain shoot up his leg and into his head. He looked down and saw T-bone holding on, teeth firmly imbedded in his flesh.

Corporal Buccanon lurched forward, and his hand fell upon the shaft of the pitchfork. The pain was so great that he couldn't think of anything else to do but to raise the pitchfork and bring it down forcefully into the shoulders of the dog. T-bone howled in pain, and then fell where he stood. His mouth finally releasing Corporal Buccanon's profusely bleeding leg.

Corporal Buccanon knew the raven had more tricks. Without hesitating he ran to the porch where his mother and father and sister were waiting and watching the horrible scene before them. He didn't have to look back to know that Roscoe was already charging across the barnyard, his mouth wide open and his fangs glistening in the sunlight and dripping with foam and saliva. He knew the raven was watching. He knew that in a few seconds he might be dead. He clambered up the porch and just as Roscoe jumped, Corporal Buccanon seized the Winchester from his father's arms, pivoted, and squeezed the trigger. Three shots were fired and Roscoe fell like a sack of potatoes hitting the floor. He then looked at his father, who was standing with his head hung low and nearly touching his chest, and he thought, this was your job not mine.

He then turned to the raven perched on the signpost, raised the Winchester, took aim, and clicked off three more shots. Corporal Buccanon was an expert marksman, who had developed his skills in the forests and meadows of Tennessee, while hunting with his father, and on the battlefield of Vietnam. He knew he had the raven dead center in his sights, and it should have been killed if not wounded. Yet the raven cawed loudly, flapped its wings, and escaped. Corporal Buccanon saw it flying away and disappearing over the cornfield.

Up to that moment, it had never occurred to Corporal Buccanon that his mother and father and sister had been watching him and, moreover, hadn't said a word. He turned to them now and looked at them suspiciously.

Henry was the first to speak. "Son, you can't kill—"

"Something that's already dead," interjected Betty.

Then, Susan said rather calmly and stoically, "Turn back, before it's too late."

Corporal Buccanon turned away. They're not real, he thought. They're only figments of my imagination, spectral ghosts, shadows, and preternatural phantoms. Then, he looked back and wasn't surprised to discover that his mother and father and sister had disappeared. And so had the dogs—Roscoe and T-bone. The raven took them, he thought. That was the only sane explanation.

He hobbled to where the raven had been perched and looked at the signpost. He didn't know what to expect, except that there might be another message scribbled across the face of the sign. He saw the words printed with black paint in bold, block letters: No Trespassing! Proceed at your own risk!

Corporal Buccanon snickered, and then he hobbled as best he could through the cornfield and back to his campsite, where he laid down on his bedroll, pulled out a bottle of whisky, and drank until he passed out.

Chapter 18 — Turning back

The red, hot sun was low in the sky casting long, great shadows by the time Cole made it back to camp. As Cole rode up and pulled the Softail to the side of the road, he saw Corporal Buccanon sleeping in his bedroll, an empty whisky bottle and the Good Book lying next to him. He was snoring loudly, fitfully, and Cole thought it sounded quite irregular. He approached Corporal Buccanon and looked at him closely, and he was shocked when he saw the bloodstains on his face, neck, and legs.

"What the hell happened to you?" asked Cole as he reached for his canteen. He dampened his handkerchief and wiped off the blood from Corporal Buccanon's face and neck. "Corporal Buccanon! Corporal Buccanon! Pshaw! You're drunk!"

"I'm not drunk, Captain, and if I were so what," Corporal Buccanon said harshly. His voice sounded as if he had a pound of gravel stuck in his throat.

"I suppose the raven returned and drank that bottle of whisky," Cole said angrily. He remembered the conversation he had with Father McFarland and his mother around the dinner table back in Tennessee. He recalled how they had accused Corporal Buccanon of being a drunkard. His mother said that he was despicable and filthy, that he was a bully and a womanizer who liked to brawl in public. Cole supposed that it was only a matter of time before Corporal Buccanon would turn to the bottle. Well, now he had, and Cole wasn't sure what he should do about it. They could hardly drop in on the next AA meeting. No, Cole knew that he would have to be firm with Corporal Buccanon before he went on a deadly binge.

"It did," Corporal Buccanon said seriously. He wasn't laughing or smiling now. Cole saw it in his face and stony eyes that he was dead serious. "The bloody raven returned while you were away."

"And, it attacked you, right?" said Cole and he wasn't sure if he should believe him.

"No. I did this to myself!" Corporal Buccanon shouted sarcastically, indicating his bloody face and the wounds on his neck and legs. "That little bastard nearly killed me. Drove me into the cornfield and clear to the other end, where I stumbled on a barnyard and farmhouse."

"A farmhouse?" Cole asked. He still wasn't sure whether Corporal Buccanon was telling the truth. But the least he could do was to listen to his yarn, and then he would decide for himself.

"Yes, a farmhouse and a barn. But that wasn't all I found. I saw two dogs that looked remarkably like Roscoe and T-bone. You think I'm going crazy, right? But, I have the proof that they were there. Just look at these wounds."

Cole looked again, examining the gash in Corporal Buccanon's forehead, the puncture marks on the back of his neck, and the teeth marks on the back of his leg, and he confirmed at least in his own mind that they were real.

"Where's the raven now?" Cole asked.

"It flew away after I tried to pop it with a Winchester!"

A Winchester?"

"Yes."

"Where did you get a Winchester?" Cole inquired.

"From my father. He was standing on the porch of the farmhouse with my mother and sister. They were all there. First I had been attacked by the raven and then by T-bone. I killed T-bone with a pitchfork. Finally, there was Roscoe. He came after me and I ran to the farmhouse. Dad had the Winchester, so I grabbed it and shot Roscoe, and then I tried to shoot the damn bird, but it flew away. Thank God! Thank God, it flew away!"

"Just like it did in Independence," said Cole with a sigh of resignation and worry.

"Yes, just like it did in Independence. I had the bird in my sights when I clicked off three rounds, and I knew I had hit it.

But, it didn't die. The bloody creature simply flew away as if nothing could touch it, as if it was impervious to bullets."

"I see," Cole said. "Was there anything else you saw or heard?"

"Yes. Mom and Dad said that there are some things in this world that you just can't kill - something that's already dead, for instance. And Susan said that we should turn back, before it's too late."

Cole said, "We have to get the hell out of here, and right away. Oh, yeah, here's the damn fuel line you needed. You can't imagine what I had to go through to get it." He frowned and tossed the fuel line to Corporal Buccanon.

Then, Corporal Buccanon tossed the empty whisky bottle into the cornfield, looked at the fuel line, and turned to Cole. "What do you mean?"

Wearily, Cole collapsed before the campfire. "I mean, when I was at the dealership in Tekaman this afternoon, the strangest thing happened. Something had taken over the body of Lucifer Johnson, the owner of the dealership. He was possessed. Do you hear me? Possessed!" Cole laughed nervously. "I must be losing my mind—one minute he was fine and the next minute, he was acting like . . . like a—"

"A Beast?" asked Corporal Buccanon seriously.

"Yes, that's right—a Beast. But how did you know?"

"It's all here, in this book." Corporal Buccanon held up the opened book. "It's written down here in Revelations. In fact, the young man from Independence had placed a marker in the book for us to make sure we would read it. It says the Beast lived in an abyss, and after a thousand years the door was opened and the Beast got out and now roams freely."

Cole turned pale and weak. He thought he was slowly going crazy and hallucinating. This couldn't be happening. This is madness. "We have to turn back," he said desperately. "We have to turn back tonight! Right now! Fix your damn Harley and let's get the hell out of here."

Corporal Buccanon reached into his pocket and pulled out a smoke. He lit it and sat back watching Cole very carefully. "We can't leave now, Captain. It's too late. In another fifteen minutes, there'll be no more sunlight, and how am I to change the fuel line in the dark?" Corporal Buccanon said impatiently. "It'll have to wait till the morning. And there's another thing, I'm not turning back." He said this firmly, stubbornly, and Cole had a picture in his mind of a dusty old prospector leading a stubborn mule across the desert in Arizona. He saw them descending the red cliffs and narrow paths of the Grand Canyon, and the prospector was furious with the mule when it stopped and he couldn't get it to move from its spot on the edge of a precipice. He tugged and pulled on the reins, but the mule, like Corporal Buccanon, would not budge.

"You haven't seen this Beast, Corporal, up close like I have. You don't know what he's like, what this evil, sinister force can do to you."

"Oh...I think I do."

"It's like nothing you've ever seen before," Cole said tremulously. He wished he were back in Tennessee with Susan or back in New York with Samantha, Leo, and Joe—anywhere but here.

"I don't care. I'm not leaving, Captain. In the morning, I'm going on to South Dakota to meet Black Hawk as we had planned. He needs us, Captain, or have you forgotten?" Corporal Buccanon spoke defiantly.

"No. I haven't forgotten. But that Beast said there's nothing we can do for Black Hawk, or for the old chief. Of course, I don't know what he meant by that, but whatever it means, I'm sure it's not very good for any of us."

"The young man from Independence said we have to have faith, Captain. And, we have to pray," Corporal Buccanon said, solemnly. He took another drag on his smoke and began to feel good again.

"What does he know? I tell you, I saw this thing . . . this Beast . . . and there's no way that we're going to beat it. He said the door to the abyss was opened and we'll never be able to close the door again . . . not for a thousand years . . . not for a thousand times a thousand years."

"I'm not turning back," said Corporal Buccanon, angrily. He picked up the fuel line and walked over to his Harley. "But, of course, Captain, if you want to leave, you can do so. I won't stop you. And, it won't change my opinion of you."

Cole knew deep inside of him that he couldn't go back, that he was trapped on a highway to hell and that he couldn't abandon Corporal Buccanon or Black Hawk. He felt pessimistically that somehow someone had set him on this path—perhaps God—and that wherever the path would lead him, he would have to go— even if it meant walking into the valley of death. He knew how Corporal Buccanon felt about him, and he didn't care. Cole felt that everything he had done, every decision he had made on the battlefield was the right decision and was made for the benefit of his men. No one could tell him differently. Although he had some regrets, he had decided long ago not to second-guess his decisions lest it would drive him mad. So, Cole cried silently, carrying his decisions and his regrets with him, carrying them inside of him day and night like a burden on his shoulders. Then, one day he buried the war and his feelings, and for a long time he never spoke of them—until he received the letter from Corporal Buccanon. And then, everything—the memories, the feelings, the fear—came back.

After satisfying his hunger with coffee and stew that Corporal Buccanon had cooked for dinner, Cole wearily unraveled his sleeping bag and prepared for sleep. Lying on his back, looking up at the stars, he said to Corporal Buccanon, with a sign of resignation in his voice, "Corporal, I think you ought to re-evaluate your plans and consider giving up this lost cause. I don't think you fully understand what you're dealing with here."

Corporal Buccanon sat up and looked at Cole contemptuously. "First of all, Captain, we're doing this for Black Hawk, and I don't consider doing anything for Black Hawk a lost cause. And, secondly," his face turned pale and stony, "I think I know what we're dealing with here." He took another long drag on his smoke and scowled.

Chapter 19 - Lai Choi

"Remember this afternoon, when we were almost killed by the tractor-trailer while trying to pass that damn hearse that was crawling along the road like a snail, you asked me if I saw something?"

"Yes. I remember," said Cole as he lay studying the stars and the planets and thinking how extraordinarily peaceful and beautiful they looked in the dark sky. He was also thinking about the raven that had nearly killed Corporal Buccanon and the Beast that had possessed the driver of the hearse and Lucifer Johnson. And what about Mr. DeForest, his English teacher from high school, and his Aunt Lucille, and his classmates Bobby Canary, Benny Saltzman, and Danny and Donald Wu? He had also seen Jake Snow, and his mother and father. His mind was spinning like a carousel, and all he really wanted to do was to get some sleep and then in the morning to skedaddle before first light.

"Well, I did see something," Corporal Buccanon said seriously. "I—I—I saw something that scared me half to death. Would you like to know what I saw?" Corporal Buccanon said.

"If you'd like to tell me," said Cole. He sat up and looked at Corporal Buccanon across the campfire, which was crackling softly and burning brightly. He found himself thinking back to a time when he and Corporal Buccanon were Boy Scouts again, roasting marshmallows over a campfire. Those were the happy days, he thought, when they were young and fresh, spending their long days hiking through the woods, fishing for trout in clear, cold streams, singing, and telling stories around the campfire. But, that was long before Nam, where he had discovered just how much he feared the woods and the dark and the stories of the lost and fallen.

"It was Lai Choi, my wife, and our unborn child, my son."

"Your what?" Cole said and stared at Corporal Buccanon intently. He had known Corporal Buccanon almost all his life and he thought he knew him well. But this! Cole was discovering that he really didn't know this drug-smoking-pot head. He never imagined that Corporal Buccanon had a wife, that he had married a Vietnamese woman and had a child. He realized that there was always going to be a few knuckleheads in the field who would try to get it on with the women hanging around camp or in the village. And, he had always frowned upon it.

"I never told you about Lai Choi, Captain, did I? Well, right after you and Black Hawk were wounded in the ambush on Route Nine, the platoon, that is—what was left of it—was ordered to Da Nang. We held up there and waited for replacements. Every night women from the surrounding villages would come to Da Nang looking for handouts. Well, one evening while on guard duty, I ran into Lai Choi. You should have seen her, Captain. She was beautiful. She had long, black hair, skin smooth as silk, and a lovely smile. I'll never forget her smile. I gave her some c-rations, and that was my big mistake, Captain, because she returned the next evening and every evening after that. I couldn't get rid of her. But to tell you the truth, I didn't want to." He paused and looked up at Cole. 'I loved her. I knew what the regulations said about fraternizing with the women, but I loved her. And she got pregnant, Captain. Pregnant! Do you have any idea what that meant for her and our baby and how I had compromised them among their own people?"

Cole quietly listened as Corporal Buccanon continued. "If her people had found out about her pregnancy, she would have been ostracized, shunned, despised, and thrown out of the village, which, as you know, is like a death sentence. You might as well take a gun and blow your brains out, or hang yourself from a tree. I almost wished I had known about the pregnancy—then perhaps I would have done something to get her out of the country. But, I didn't know and I didn't get her out.

"Several months passed and we were ordered back into the area to help with the relocation. Our objective was to relocate the village, her village, and to blow up any tunnels we found there. We had entered the village in the late afternoon. The engineers were right behind us, blowing up tunnels and bomb shelters—one after another. The village was in total chaos and pandemonium. I was instructed to clear out the civilians. Many of them were stubborn and wouldn't move. Just as we'd get them together and start herding them out, they would stop and run back to their hooch or house. I remember hearing Sergeant Conners shouting, 'Get the lead out.' He wanted me to hurry up. So he kept yelling at me, 'Get the lead out . . . move them out . . . move them out! The women were screaming and the babies were crying. Some women were on their knees praying to Buddha. I was going mad— I couldn't concentrate. I was losing it, Captain. I was in a real quandary. The engineers were on my tail and wanted to blow the next tunnel. I was standing in front of this tunnel and I could hear women and children in there. Of course, the VC was in there as well, holding them hostage. I didn't know for sure. I had looked into the tunnel, but I didn't see anyone or anything in there. It was pitch black. I imagined that they were trying to be quiet but I could hear them moving around. I asked them to come up. I got down on my hands and knees and begged them to come out. I even spoke to them in Vietnamese—a few words I had picked up hanging around the village, but they were frightened. I was frightened too. I was getting a very bad feeling about this. And then the engineers came, and I turned to Sergeant Conners and pleaded for more time; I begged for more time. I know I could've got them out if he had only given me a little more time. But it was chaos and everyone was screaming and shouting. And then I heard one of the engineers yelling, "Fire in the Hole!" and the next thing I knew the tunnel blew up, and everything in it, and there was a fire, with tremendous flames bursting forth out of the small opening in the ground. I just turned and walked away, but I was sick. I was really sick of this. Later, I learned from one of the villagers that Lai Choi—and our unborn son—had been hiding in that tunnel."

"I'm sorry,' said Cole. "I never knew—"

"How could you have known? Well, this afternoon, for the first time in twenty years, except in my dreams and nightmares, I saw Lai Choi, or a very good likeness of her. I saw her in the black hearse, lying in the coffin with our unborn son sleeping on her breast." He looked up at Cole and added, "I didn't say anything this afternoon, because I thought I was going out of my mind—I was frightened."

"It's strange how we both saw something different when we looked into the hearse," said Cole.

"Yes, it is strange. But, I told you all this, Captain, not because I wanted to frighten you, but because I wanted you to know that I understand what's happening here, and even though I'm afraid I'm not going to turn back and abandon Black Hawk."

"I didn't think you would," Cole said. "Good night, Corporal. Get some rest. We're going to need it."

Chapter 20 – Corporal buccanon's Dream

Despite Cole's suggestion that they ought to get a good night's rest, Corporal Buccanon slept restlessly, tossing and turning in his sleeping bag all night long. His restlessness stemmed from several dreams—actually four successive dreams—that tormented his mind.

In his first dream, he saw Cole creeping stealthily from one foxhole to another, checking on the condition of his men along a perimeter that had been established just south of Con Thien. He was telling his men to stay put and to keep alert. "This is only a respite. They'll be back and the next time they'll return in greater force and probably hit us with everything they have. Alternate the watch every two hours. Got it? Okay!"

Then, he saw Cole jump into the foxhole and look at Black Hawk. "Stay alert! Don't let them catch you off guard. Black Hawk, wake up! You look like you're a hundred miles away. What's wrong with you?"

Black Hawk's muscles had tightened as he looked at Captain Cole. "Nothing, Captain. I was just thinking about my people back home. I was wondering what they might be doing right about now. If I close my eyes, I could actually see parents as if they were standing around in the kitchen, cooking a turkey or a ham. God, I wish I was home in the Sacred Black Hills of South Dakota again."

"Don't think about it," Corporal Buccanon told him. "You'll only drive yourself crazy. When I first got here, I used to think about home all the time and ask myself all kinds of silly questions. It would drive me mad. Do yourself a favor and just forget about home."

Corporal Buccanon twitched in his sleep and moaned something indistinctly. Then, he found himself in a fishing boat— a twenty-five foot cabin cruiser—with five other fishermen. He saw Captain Cole standing at the helm on the upper deck and struggling with the wheel, turning it first one way and then the other. In the stern of the boat was Black Hawk. He was dressed in his native attire and his face was painted red and black. Standing alongside Black Hawk was another Native American whom Corporal Buccanon didn't recognize. He was an old man, short and fragile. From his attire and headdress, Corporal Buccanon guessed he might have been a chief of some tribe. Then the cabin door swung open and the undertaker from the funeral procession, wearing his black top hat and overcoat, emerged from the cabin below, followed by Lucifer Johnson who was wearing his skullcap and goggles. It wasn't long before a gust of wind swept the black top hat from the undertaker's head and carried it out to sea where it was swallowed up by the ocean and the darkness. The undertaker uttered a curse and Johnson told him to shut up. Then a black-footed albatross or gooney alighted on the railing next to Corporal Buccanon. Despite the pitching of the boat, the gooney clung to the railing with its webbed feet. It cawed wildly and then the bird metamorphosed into a raven. Its screams could be heard over the sound of the waves mercilessly pounding the vessel, until it finally broke up into a million pieces.

Corporal Buccanon found himself in the water. He swam to a section of the starboard that was floating nearby and pulled himself onto it. It was frightfully small, no larger than six by four feet, but it was large enough to carry him to safety. All night long, he held on desperately to that little board.

By morning, he discovered that the ocean current had guided his raft toward a small island. It was a beautiful island with sandy beaches and palm trees. He paddled as best he could under the circumstances, and when he got close enough he swam to shore, where he collapsed on the beach. It was not until Lai Choi appeared and gave him food and fresh water that he fully recovered his senses.

Lai Choi was young and incredibly beautiful. She had long, shiny, dark hair that fell seductively over her bare shoulders, and her eyes were a dazzling bluish-green. Her sparkling white teeth glistened in contrast to the tawny complexion of her lovely, smooth skin. She was beautiful, and when he first laid eyes on her he fell in love instantly.

The first week on the island, Corporal Buccanon set to work building her a tree house at the edge of the jungle. They labored together like newlyweds, cutting bamboo, collecting leaves and twigs, making twine, stripping bark from trees, and mixing clay and mud. When it was finished, the tree house looked appalling, but it was their home, and it was safe and warm.

In the mornings, he would wake her with a gentle kiss. Then, he'd race along the coastline of the island, chasing after her like a seagull flying wildly. When exhausted, they'd collapse into reassuring arms and sit on the beachhead to watch the sea as the waves lapped gracefully on the shore and caressed their sand-covered toes.

Corporal Buccanon imagined he was Robinson Crusoe and she was his Friday. He asked her, "Do you know what I wish for more than anything in the world?"

She smiled into his beaming face and shrugged her shoulders.

"I wish I could remain here with you forever. Just the two of us on this lovely island." Then, he leaned forward, lowered his head and kissed Lai Choi passionately.

Suddenly, the sound of an explosion nearly ripped his ear off, and Corporal Buccanon found himself in the war again. A barrage of mortar shells was falling from the ominous sky, pounding their position. Desperately holding onto their helmets with trembling hands, Corporals Buccanon and Black Hawk pressed their bodies closer together and deeper into the fox hole.

"This is it!" shouted Cole and then he was gone, running back along the perimeter. "Get ready, stay alert. This is it."

Corporal Buccanon saw the village and the burning tunnel. He heard the marine engineer shouting, "Fire in the hole," again, and the sound of women and children crying and screaming. He saw the tongues of flames burning fiercely in the dark, consuming everything and illuminating the dark, Vietnamese sky. And, he was crying in his sleep.

In the morning Cole and Corporal Buccanon began the last leg of their journey, crossing over the winding Missouri River and entering South Dakota, where they stopped at what they thought would be their final destination—the small town of Wolf Creek, just outside of Sioux Falls.

Part N—Wolf Creek, South Dakota

Chapter 21 – Chief Long Wolf

The sun was low in the sky that afternoon when Cole and Corporal Buccanon approached a run-down ranch house sitting on 160 acres in a deserted, wooded area of Wolf Creek, South Dakota. As the Softail and Road King came to a stop before the ranch house, an old man—an octogenarian—appeared in the doorway. Cole watched him as he emerged gingerly from the house and stood on the front porch, his hand firmly gripping a rifle. Cole recognized it immediately. It was a Winchester, and the old man had cocked the trigger and held the rifle lengthwise across his chest. Perhaps he was expecting trouble, thought Cole.

The old man was a Native American and he was thin and short, standing perhaps five-foot, two-inches tall. He had a golden, reddish-brown complexion that resembled the red rocks of canyon walls. His face was leathery and wrinkled, baked from the burning sun. His long, grayish-white hair was pushed straight back and tied in a ponytail. His high cheekbones were like granite rocks set against thin lips, a furrowed brow, dark piercing eyes and a pronounced hawk nose. He seemed to swim in his faded blue jeans, his loose-fitting white shirt, and his boot moccasins. A colorful bandanna was wrapped around his head to absorb the beads of sweat that were forming there under the hot sun.

"What do you want here?" Chief Long Wolf asked as he looked at Cole and Corporal Buccanon suspiciously.

"We're looking for a friend. His name is Black Hawk. I believe he lives somewhere around here," said Cole, pleasantly, as he removed his helmet and goggles. "If you know of him, perhaps, you could give us directions; we would appreciate it, friend."

"I am Long Wolf, chief of the Sioux Nation. Welcome!" said the old man, lowering his rifle and holding it down at his side. "Black Hawk was my son, and this is the home of Black Hawk."

"I am John Cole, and this is—"

"Corporal Buccanon, at your service, Chief."

Chief Long Wolf motioned to Cole and Corporal Buccanon. "Come inside out of the sun so we might talk in peace."

They dismounted from their Harleys and followed Chief Long Wolf into the ranch house. He led them into the kitchen, which was sparsely decorated. In one corner there was an old stove and in another a Philco refrigerator. Cabinets ran across the length of one wall, and like everything else in the house, they were old and cheap looking. The varnish was worn out in spots and the wood had splintered at the edges. On the opposite wall facing the cabinets, there was a small window that looked out toward the front of the house. Through it, Cole could see the long driveway and the Harleys parked out front. The window was decorated with water-stained curtains and below the window there was a rusty sink. From where he was standing in the kitchen, Cole was able to look through an archway and see the combination dining and living room.

His heart sank when he looked into the dining room and saw the condition of the wooden table and chairs. The table wobbled and shook terribly whenever anyone leaned against it and the chairs—there was something about the wooden chairs. Two of the four wooden chairs had split apart and had been repaired with Elmer's Glue. He sighed when he glanced into the living room and saw the sofa and walls. The sofa was shabby and threadbare and the paint on the walls had faded to a dull color of straw yellow.

One thing, however, immediately caught Cole's eye. It was the Sioux ceremonial buffalo skull hanging above the sofa. He whistled and studied its features for a few moments, examining the black, hollow depressions that had once been its eye sockets and the white feathers with their black crowns and edges hanging limply from opposite cheekbones. At one end of the sofa there was a recliner upholstered in brown vinyl that had cracked and was held together by layers of strips of black adhesive tape. At the other end of the sofa, there was a small table with a reading lamp.

There were three small bedrooms in the house and they were in the same dreary condition as the living room, being sparsely decorated with old furniture, Hopi Kachina dolls, a wooden Ojibwa male effigy doll, several Indian peace pipes that the old chief had carved himself, and a coup stick. The playful warriors of the Plains Indians used a coup stick to show how brave they were in battle. Instead of killing their opponents, they would touch them with the coup stick.

Chief Long Wolf invited Cole and Corporal Buccanon into the dining room where they sat around the table and watched the chief as he prepared refreshments for his guests. He was a proud old man and served them coffee and corn bread. Then, sitting down opposite Cole, he said gravely, sincerely, "Captain Cole, Corporal Buccanon, I would like to thank you for answering my letter." He paused to observe and to study their reactions. Unceremoniously, he added, "Don't be so surprised, Captain. I wrote the letter! I wrote the letter and I prayed to Wakan Tanka, the Great Spirit, that you would come. And my prayers have been answered because you are here. Wakan Tanka did not fail me."

"Where's Black Hawk?" Cole asked curtly. He didn't like the idea that the old chief had hoodwinked him. If the old chief and not Black Hawk was the author of the letter Corporal Buccanon had received several weeks ago, then he had been deceived, lured here under false pretenses. Cole could hardly control his anger as he looked at the old man, the so-called chief of the Sioux Nation. He had several questions he needed answered: where's Black Hawk? And, why—why did the chief deceive us? Why did he lure us here with a fake letter? A letter he had written himself and then signed it with his son's name: Black Hawk?

"I live here alone with my granddaughter, Captain. My wife, Running Deer, died shortly after Black Hawk and White Cloud had been murdered. That's right, Captain Cole, my son and his wife are dead," said Chief Long Wolf mournfully.

"What?" Cole was utterly shocked by the news.

"They were killed by poachers. Poachers and hatred."

"Those bastards," gasped Corporal Buccanon loudly, and then he pounded the table with his fist, until the cups and saucers tipped over spilling their contents onto the table and floor. Cole saw Corporal Buccanon make the sign of the cross and lower his head into his arms. He groaned, and Cole thought that he was crying.

"Good God!" exclaimed Cole, mournfully. The corners of his mouth turned down as he gritted his teeth. Although he had not seen Black Hawk for more than fifteen years, he was deeply hurt by the loss of his friend. He knew if it had not been for Black Hawk, he would not be alive today, and this weighed heavily upon his mind. Now, if Cole had wanted to help his friend, he would have to resort to what he knew best: the law. He looked at Chief Long Wolf and said, icily, "Have the miscreants been caught and brought to trial? Has justice been served?"

"No, Captain Cole," Chief Long Wolf said sadly, his eyes welling up with tears. He then reached into his pocket for his handkerchief and wiped his face.

"I'm sorry, Chief." Cole knew from experience that time was of the essence and that with every passing day, the unsolved case would become more difficult to solve. If the case hadn't been cracked by now, he surmised, there was a good chance that it would never be solved. A terrifying sense of hopelessness and despair overwhelmed Cole at this moment. Even with modern technology, solving a cold case without any substantial clues to go on was like looking for a needle in a haystack. He didn't know what else he could say to the chief to adequately express his commiseration.

"It is unfortunate, Captain, that even now, long after the white man had tamed the west and conquered my people, there still exists an implacable hatred toward the Native Americans. I would ask you, what didn't your kind do to destroy our culture and way of life? You killed our buffalo, scoffed at our religion, desecrated our burial grounds and holy sites, and silenced our songs and dances that portrayed life and death, as we knew it to be. And, to add insult to injury, you've made us dependent on your government for rations and subsistence." The old chief fell silent, so he might contemplate and give his hot blood a chance to cool off. After a few moments, he continued. "But we are friends—you and I—we are like brothers—you knew Black Hawk and he spoke well of you. We shall smoke the peace pipe, together."

Sliding out of his chair, Chief Long Wolf tottered into his bedroom, and shortly afterwards, returned with a long-stemmed, hand-carved wooden pipe and a pouch of cherry tobacco. In the threadbare surroundings of the ranch house, with an air and demeanor of ceremony and regalia, Chief Long Wolf carefully filled his pipe with tobacco before lighting it with a match and taking several long puffs. Then he gave the pipe to Cole, who looked at it apprehensively.

"Go on!" Corporal Buccanon said impatiently, as Cole fiddled with it indecisively. "Go on and smoke it! It's not what you think, Captain Lawyer, it's only tobacco."

Hesitantly, Cole lifted the pipe to his lips and inhaled slowly. Satisfied that the tobacco wasn't spiked with a narcotic like opium or marijuana, he became more relaxed, though he quickly passed the pipe to Corporal Buccanon who immediately inhaled several long drafts of smoke and then heaved a sigh of relief. Corporal Buccanon continued to smoke the peace pipe, while Chief Long Wolf and Cole resumed their powwow.

"After Black Hawk returned from Vietnam, he spoke very highly of you, Captain Cole, and you, Corporal Buccanon. He told us everything there is to know about how bravely and courageously you had fought in the war."

Corporal Buccanon choked and coughed suddenly. "He did?" Cole shot him a glance and Corporal Buccanon frowned and held his tongue.

"I feel as though I've known you all my life," Chief Long Wolf said persuasively, his eyes now dark and piercing. He was like a sorcerer with a great natural power who could look into your eyes and see deeply into your soul to discover what you are thinking and what you are made of. He did so now, as he looked deeply into the gleaming eyes and souls of Cole and Corporal Buccanon. And what he saw pleased him. He sensed the qualities and traits of character that only men and women display after having lived through difficult straits together. Those were the qualities of honor and loyalty. "It was your destiny, Captain, that you should meet with me here today so we might travel the same dusty path together, to the same dusty, dark abyss."

Cole looked at him wearily.

"You see, Captain, we are like a pack of hyenas or wolves living on the Great Plains. To survive, they must band and hunt together. They have to depend on one another or else they would starve to death. We must do the same thing. We must depend on one another. When we band together, Captain—you, Corporal Buccanon, and I—we shall become as one, don't you think?"

Cole said nothing, listening to Chief Long Wolf with a heavy heart.

"Black Hawk told us about South Vietnam, the Rockpile, Ka Sahne, Route Nine, the patrols, the search and destroy missions, napalm, the Hueys, the flying gunships, relocating villages, and the deadly ambushes. When he was wounded, I prayed to the Great Spirit—Wakan Tanka—and asked him to use his power to heal Black Hawk so that he might survive. His mother, Running Deer, was a Christian, so, of course, she prayed to the Christian God—to Jesus and his Almighty Father—for her son's recovery.

"It was at this time that I had visited Starfire, the medicine man, the shaman of the Oglala tribe, and asked for his counsel. He told me to go to the Sacred Black Hills, to build my tepee on a plateau, and to meditate and pray to Wakan Tanka. He said I should go alone, and fast, and wait for a sign from the spirit world. When I told Running Deer what I was planning to do, she argued and begged me to stay home. But, I would not bend like a reed in the wind this time. During the night, I went off to the Sacred Black Hill, and when she discovered I was gone, she became angry and sick because she thought I would do something stupid or that something terrible would happen to me. Day after day, she waited patiently, praying to her Christian God for Black Hawk and now for me. For days, she sat solemnly on the back porch watching the sun sink behind the trees and hills and beneath the horizon. She went to church every morning and evening to pray and to light candles for us.

"Finally after three days of fasting, I received a vision from the spirit world. It was a vision of the rising sun and a wolf and a hawk racing across the Great Plains, playing together in the valleys and red canyons of the desert, climbing atop the mesas, and leaping across flowing riverbeds, streams and gullies. Yes! They were chasing one another, as they danced and sang their songs of life and death and it was all quite natural. After the vision, I made peace with the world, accepting whatever fate the spirits had decided. So, I struck camp, carefully packed my tepee, and returned home, where Running Deer was waiting for me. She was as angry as a wounded buffalo, but being a good Christian who wanted to please her God, she forgave me and cooked my favorite meal.

"And then we waited for him and when we received no word of his coming home, we began to panic, because we thought that Black Hawk had died in the hospital from his wounds and he would never return to us. One evening while I was working in the garden, I was watching Running Deer through the kitchen window. She was standing at the sink rinsing the dishes. Then, I saw her as she raised her head and looked through the window. I realized she was staring at someone—a lonely figure walking, or rather limping, along the road. He had a cane and he was moving slowly, uneasily toward the house. Suddenly, I heard a shriek and the sound of a plate crashing against the floor, and I thought immediately that something had happened to Running Deer. Before I could run into the house, she had already descended the steps of the front porch and was now running down the road toward the lonely figure she had recognized. When she came face to face with him, she stopped abruptly, burst into tears, and collapsed into his arms. Even with a cane, he had the strength of a bear. He wrapped his massive arms around her and kissed her tenderly. In the meantime, I waited patiently on the porch for Running Deer and Black Hawk to return to the house and stand before me. I stared back at them with a face like a rock, because I would not dare to show the joy in my heart for fear Wakan Tanka, the Great Spirit, would grow angry.

"I was proud of Black Hawk, Captain. He served his country bravely and he often reminded me of Lieutenant Jack C. Montgomery, an Oklahoma Cherokee, and Lieutenant Ernest Childers of the Oklahoma Creeks, both Native Americans who were awarded Congressional Medal of Honors for their heroism in World War II."

"Yes," said Cole, solemnly, thoughtfully. "I was also very proud of Black Hawk."

Chief Long Wolf fumbled with his wallet before laying a wallet-sized photograph of Black Hawk on the table in front of Cole. It was faded and torn at the edges. Black Hawk was wearing his military dress uniform, and he was smiling handsomely. Cole and Corporal Buccanon examined the picture closely, and then gave it back to the chief, who carefully placed it in his wallet again.

"Within six months after returning to South Dakota, Black Hawk had enrolled in college, gotten a part-time job with the Department of the Interior, and started dating White Cloud, a beautiful, long-hair Brule Sioux whom he met in one of his classes. After graduating from college, Black Hawk and White Cloud got married and he started working full-time as a game warden and ranger.

"He loved his job, Captain. It was the type of job that allowed him to work outdoors. He was passionate, almost obsessed with the idea of protecting the wolves and other endangered species from poachers who often hunted in our woods. He told me once that his job made him feel as if he was restoring and preserving what little was left of our natural resources and game, especially after the white man had taken so much from the land. He was a good son, and I loved him.

"One night he was strolling the fields with White Cloud when they came upon a hunting party that had already killed two wolves and were about to kill the cubs. Without warning, they opened fire on Black Hawk and White Cloud and shot them dead—point blank. What distressed me more than anything else, Captain, was the fact that they knew my son and his wife— everyone around here knew them. They knew he was a game warden, and they knew they would be arrested and sent to prison for killing the wolves. Yet, they did it anyway. They killed the wolves, and then, Black Hawk and White Cloud. And, indirectly, they had killed Running Deer. She died shortly afterwards from a broken heart. And, in the meantime, the poachers got away.

"It's the Battle of Wounded Knee all over again, Captain," Chief Long Wolf said, sadly. "I am eight-five years old. I am tired and weak. And, there is very little time left for me in this life. I am waiting for my death song and it will come to me in a vision. Perhaps, I shall receive it tonight. If I do, I shall sing it for you, Captain. Then, I shall be ready for the funeral pyre. I tell you I am in the cradle of life rocking fiercely above an abyss. And should I tumble out of the cradle, I shall fall headlong into eternal darkness."

Chief Long Wolf wiped away a tear from the corner of his eye. He glanced at the coffee cups on the table, saw that they were empty, and he thought that he was a poor host. He rose from the table, wobbled to the stove, and returned with a pot of hot coffee and a bottle of whiskey. He filled the cups almost to their rims with coffee, leaving just enough room for a shot or two of whiskey.

When Corporal Buccanon saw the whisky bottle his eyes lit up and his mouth began to water. Suddenly, he felt mighty thirsty. Cole refused the whisky, but Corporal Buccanon made up for it, allowing the old chief to pour a double shot into his coffee cup. Then, Chief Long Wolf turned to Cole again.

"I know, Captain Cole, that you are a big lawman in the east. I have read many stories about you in the newspapers and I have seen you on the evening news. You must realize by now it was your destiny that brought you to the land of the Sioux. The Great Spirit, Wakan Tanka, had ordained it before you were even born. He has done this because he knows that there is something you can do for his people, my people—the Sioux, the Oglala, the Brule, the Hunkpapa, the Miniconjou, the San Arc, the Two Kettle, the Blackfoot, the Cheyenne, and the Arapaho—here in South Dakota.

"Black Hawk has a daughter. Her name is Little Flower. She is seven years old. I am too old to care for her. She needs you, Captain Cole, and you, Corporal Buccanon. I have no one else I could turn to for help. If she remains in Wolf Creek, she will get caught up in the ongoing battle of Wounded Knee. But, with your help, perhaps, there is a chance that Little Flower might live her life in peace and in honor. Is she not, after all, the granddaughter of the chief of the Sioux Nation?"

Chapter 22 — Little Flower and the Naming of black Hawk

Sometime later, Cole heard the sound of an approaching vehicle. Looking out from the kitchen window and standing where Running Dear had been standing when she first saw Black Hawk as he was limping home from the war, he saw a yellow school bus turning into the driveway and coming to a stop in front of the ranch house. A moment later, the yellow doors swung open and a schoolgirl approximately seven or eight years old jumped off the bus—a book bag dangling from one hand—and ran like the wind along the dirt path, up the rickety steps, and into the house. Cole turned and faced the door as the young girl burst into the kitchen like a whirlwind. She stopped abruptly when she saw Cole and Corporal Buccanon—strangers—sitting with her grandfather. She ran to her grandfather, kissed him on the cheek, and clung to his side, entwining her frail arms with his.

"This is Little Flower, my granddaughter and the daughter of Black Hawk and White Cloud," said Chief Long Wolf.

In the chief's eyes, Cole saw a mixture of emotions—pride, love, and sorrow. Cole thought that the girl was tall for her age and quite beautiful. She had long, black hair—silklike—which she got from her mother, no doubt—falling back away from her fair face and revealing her light, green eyes that stood in stark contrast to her soft, tawny complexion. Her brow curved ever so slightly above a small nose, and her teeth glittered brightly when she smiled. At first, she seemed naturally shy and suspicious of Cole and Corporal Buccanon. For a long time, she sat very quietly at the table when doing her homework, but as the evening wore on, she became more friendly and started conversing more freely and gaily with them about her school, and her grandfather, and other things.

From her conversation, it became clear to Cole that Little Flower was extraordinarily intelligent. Her mind was quick, pragmatic, and logical. With a little schooling, he thought, she could become a fine lawyer when she grew up. He stared at her for a long time, studying her lovely features as she completed her math homework with Corporal Buccanon looking over her shoulder and checking her work. Cole wanted to laugh aloud because Corporal Buccanon was never any good at mathematics when he was in high school. Even with extra tutoring from Cole and Susan, he had barely passed his math courses.

As Cole looked at Little Flower, he could clearly see her resemblance to Black Hawk. He realized Little Flower was all that there was left of Black Hawk and White Cloud, and for that matter, Running Deer and Chief Long Wolf. She represented the end of a long ancestral line, and this idea made Cole feel melancholy. He realized that all of their hopes, dreams, and desires for the future were wrapped up in this frail, young child. He grew angry as he thought of the injustice and unfairness of Black Hawk's untimely death. But when was death ever fair, and when was it ever timely? Black Hawk had been sent to Nam as a young recruit, where he fought in some of the bloodiest and deadliest skirmishes and battles in the history of the marines, only to be shot and murdered back at home by some dimwit miscreant.

Cole understood the inevitable question had to be asked: What would become of Little Flower? And, he believed that there was no one except, perhaps, the old chief who was prepared to give an answer. With no little effort, Cole tried to dismiss the question from his mind, thinking that she was someone else's problem. A relative or a friend of the family should take her in and see to her education and welfare, he thought. He finally told himself that she would be fine. He really didn't want to think of anything else.

When he looked across the table at Chief Long Wolf, he felt stupid and humiliated because he had been sent on a wild goose chase by an old man who *said* he was the chief of the Sioux

Nation. Yeah! Right! And, I'm the Great Spirit, Wakan Tanka! But now he knew the truth, and so he soothed his raw and jittery nerves by persuading himself that this great misadventure would soon come to an end. Tomorrow he would pack his things in the Softail and return home. He would return to his law practice in New York City and to Gina Anderson. That is, of course, if she would take him back. He thought she would, but like all things concerning women, he wasn't exactly sure. Then he thought about Susan and what it would be like if he were to settle down in Tennessee and resume his life with her. Life might be much simpler and easier, he thought, and that could be a good thing, too.

While Cole was lost in thought, musing about the future, Chief Long Wolf tottered to the kitchen where he busied himself making dinner for Little Flower and his honored guests. When Cole saw the so-called chief of the Sioux Nation preparing dinner for him, he became uncomfortable. This is crazy, he thought. Instead of the chief making dinner for us, we should be making dinner for him and his granddaughter. But, when Corporal Buccanon tapped Cole on the shoulder and told him that he should be grateful for the chief's invitation and that if he complained, he would only make the chief angry, Cole accepted the chief's hospitality.

After dinner, Chief Long Wolf, Little Flower, Cole, and Corporal Buccanon squared everything away in the kitchen, washing and drying the dishes and returning everything to its proper place in the dilapidated cabinets. Later, they went out back and sat in rocking chairs on the rickety old porch where they breathed in the fresh air and drank hot coffee. For a long time, Chief Long Wolf stared contemplatively at the vast, dark sky, observing the stars overhead, glittering and pulsating in the great expanse.

"Look! A shooting star, grandfather! A shooting star!" shouted Little Flower, excitedly. She was sitting next to her grandfather, looking up into the sky and then into his big dark eyes. "Grandfather, why are there so many stars in the sky?"

Chief Long Wolf embraced Little Flower and smiled warmly. "When I was a young warrior, your great grandfather, Chief Standing Bear—a great and wise leader of the Sioux Nation—once pointed to the stars pulsating in the heavens and said they were the souls of our ancestors. He said that they were living in harmony and peace with the earth and with the Great Spirit. And, from their mountain perch, our ancestors could observe all things here on earth."

Then, Little Flower said eagerly, "Grandfather, would you tell me again how father got his name?"

"Child, I've told you that story a hundred times. You know perfectly well how your father came by his name."

"Tell me again, grandfather. Please! I'm sure Captain Cole and Corporal Buccanon would like to hear it," Little Flower pleaded.

Corporal Buccanon was puffing away at the peace pipe and every so often a cloud of smoke would drift up into the air and float on a gentle breeze. The porch soon had the distinct smell of sweet cherry tobacco and French Vanilla coffee. Cole was leaning back in his rocker, staring into the darkness that surrounded them like a blanket and thinking about his journey home, when he heard Little Flower's request. He always thought Native American Indians had strange names, and he often wondered how they came by them.

"Yes," said Cole. "I'd like to hear how Black Hawk got his name. Why don't you tell us, Chief?"

Chief Long Wolf smiled and then told his story. "All right. I shall tell you the story again. I remember it as if it was only yesterday when the tall, skinny boy—your father—came running into my room screaming. He said he had a nightmare and he wanted me to interpret his dream. Running Deer picked him up and sat him on our bed, and he recited his dream song for us. It went like this: He saw a young boy wandering in the prairie—crossing the Great Plains—when suddenly a dark and ominous gathering of clouds covered the earth. He looked up at the angry sky and trembled, and when he looked down again at the earth he saw hundreds, thousands, hundreds of thousands of men plundering and desecrating his homeland. They were white men. He saw his people dying from the disease and hatred they carried in their bodies, hearts, and minds. Oh! It was awful! He saw them murdering his brothers, killing the wildlife—the sacred buffalo—their source of food and life, the very lifeblood of the Sioux Nation. He saw them laying iron tracks in the desert for the arrival of an iron horse that would bring more white men. And everything he saw had frightened him. He said the young boy then prayed to the Great Spirit, Wakan Tanka, for help. And suddenly, a great sacred black hawk appeared in the sky and drove back the intruders. It drove them eastward, back into the waters of the great ocean. Your father woke up screaming and crying, and after he had told us his story, Running Deer cried loudly, blissfully, 'Black Hawk! Black Hawk! That is what we shall call you! Yes! Black Hawk!' And from that moment onward, we called him by this name: Black Hawk."

Chapter 23 - The Ambush on Route Nine

Cole sat quietly in his rocking chair, ruminating and enjoying his strange surroundings, his new friends, and the stillness of the night. Again, he thought sadly and mournfully about Black Hawk and how he had been killed senselessly and tragically here at home in South Dakota, after having survived all those months in the war in South Vietnam. He heard an owl hoot in the night, and saw a gray rabbit scurrying swiftly across the backyard and into the woods. The air was cool and refreshing as it blew gently across his face. Although he couldn't see them, he heard the leaves of the birches, cottonwoods, oaks, and dogwoods swaying languidly, almost imperceptibly, in the gentle breeze.

South Dakota was lovely, and suddenly he felt tired and angry, especially when he thought about the poachers and Black Hawk's unsolved murder. If only he had been notified immediately of Black Hawk's murder, he would have hired the best detectives and bounty hunters money could buy to track down the miscreants and bring them to justice. But, now, it was too late, he thought. And, if it's too late to help Black Hawk, then what the hell was he doing here?

Chief Long Wolf turned to Cole, saw the worried look on his face and said, "You are very quiet, Captain Cole. I never imagined that a famous lawyer such as yourself could be so shy and quiet."

"Shy?" said Corporal Buccanon boisterously. He was surprised by the chief's assessment of Cole. "Captain Cole, shy? I don't think so, Chief."

"Oh, shut up, Corporal Buccanon! What would you know about it?" said Cole sharply, and then he leaned back in his rocker and gazed into the faces of Chief Long Wolf and Little Flower. "I'm sorry, Chief, I was just thinking—"

"I've read about you in the papers, Captain. You're a fine lawyer up in New York City," said Chief Long Wolf, interrupting him.

"I've done all right, I suppose," said Cole.

"Don't be so modest, Captain," grunted Corporal Buccanon from behind a cloud of smoke. "Believe me, Chief, whatever shyness Captain Cole might have had when he was a young boy, especially when he was trying to date my sister, Susan, he lost it the minute he stepped off the bus at Parris Island, South Carolina. It was brutally stripped away. You see, boot camp was a culture shock for him, Chief—a real culture shock."

"Do you have to bring that up again?" Cole looked at Corporal Buccanon coldly, knowing very well that once the corporal got on his soapbox it was virtually impossible to shut him up. Anything less than pugilism would be futile.

"I'll never forget the look on the captain's face—it was June, middle of the morning, about ten o'clock, when Captain Cole and I first stumbled into boot camp. After a grueling ride on a delightfully, filthy little school bus from the airfield, we were ordered to stand at attention by one of the ugliest and meanest looking drill sergeants I ever saw in the United States Marine Corps. A phantom from my worst childhood dreams couldn't scare me more than he did." Corporal Buccanon laughed loudly, slapping the side of his leg with his hand. Then he looked at Chief Long Wolf and Little Flower with his dark, piercing eyes, a wide grin across his face. He took another drag on his smoke.

"We stood at attention for two hours baking under the hot South Carolina sun until we were finished on both sides. Our ugly, dust-covered faces were drenched with beads of sweat that fell in a cascade like the cataract of Niagara Falls. And, God forbid if the drill sergeant saw you wiping the sweat from your brow," said Corporal Buccanon angrily. "That son of a—"

"That's enough, Corporal!" Cole said sharply.

For a moment, Corporal Buccanon had lost track of time and place. He thought he was back in Tennessee sitting around

General Lee's Bar and Grill with a few of his rowdy friends from town. Then he saw the faces of Chief Long Wolf and Little Flower staring at him strangely. "I'm sorry, Little Flower," he said apologetically. "For a minute, I thought I was back home again sitting around a bar and talking to a few friends about the lovely time I had in boot camp." He laughed sickly and wretchedly. "Whenever I think of Matthews—he was our drill instructor—and how he used to yell with that southern drawl of his—very condescendingly—as if we were some hicks off a farm—"

"We were just that," interjected Cole. Then he turned his face back toward the darkness, his mind and senses mesmerized and hypnotized by its vastness and nothingness.

"I just wanted to throttle his big, fat neck." Corporal Buccanon paused to wipe the sweat from his brow with his handkerchief. Then he added, "I can still hear him shouting, 'Wipe that smile off your face, recruit,' and he'd be standing right in your face like a bull dog. 'When I speak to you, I want your complete and undivided attention, children. Is that understood? Because what you could learn here today might save your life someday. I don't want to hear any whining or crying. And when I ask you a question, you're to answer me like a man, like a marine! I want you to raise your voice and speak loudly and clearly, so I can hear you. Is that understood?'

"Nevertheless, I have to give them credit. The US Marine Corps knows how to develop the killer instincts in their recruits. They go about it quite deliberately and cleverly. First, they brutally harass you, physically and mentally. They tear you down until you actually think you're lower than dirt, and then they begin the resurrection, building up your confidence and strength. And when it's all over, you actually think you're immortal. Within the short time of six weeks, we were all miraculously transformed from shy country bumpkins into aggressive instruments of death," said Corporal Buccanon, feeling pride and shame simultaneously.

"Of course, we were in a hell of a mess in Vietnam, and the North Vietnamese Army made it perfectly clear to us on our first day in country that we weren't immortal. And, with officers like Captain Cole—Ha!" Corporal Buccanon said this disparagingly and mockingly with a sense of irony and sarcasm in his voice.

Then he looked at Cole with scorn and hatred. "It's a miracle anyone made it out of there alive."

Cole's blood began to rise feverishly, despite his lethargic appearance. He was sitting quietly next to Chief Long Wolf and Little Flower and except for the gentle and slow rocking of his chair, one might have thought he was asleep. Yet, he was awake and alert, leaning his head back against the headrest of the rocking chair and watching the stars pulsating in the eternal darkness of the heavenly abyss. He desperately tried to block out the sound of Corporal Buccanon's irritating and gruff voice, as he portrayed the traducer.

"I used to be like Captain Cole," Corporal Buccanon said contemptuously. "I used to accept whatever anyone said at face value, as if it was the truth. Often, I'd ask myself, why would anyone lie? What benefit would anyone possibly derive from lying to me? So I accepted naively whatever they said and whatever they offered as the truth.

"I remember vividly one evening at dinner, I asked my father, an avid reader of politics and the war, what he thought about our American boys being sent into Southeast Asia and into an escalating conflict. He paused to light his pipe and then he said, 'Well, son, as I see it, we have a vested interest in that part of the world. It wouldn't be right if we were to just sit back and allow the communists to walk right in and take it over. No. No. That wouldn't sit well with our vested interest.' A vested interest, indeed! In that part of the world!" Corporal Buccanon repeated emphatically.

"Father McFarland, a priest from St. Patrick's parish, had dropped in for dinner that evening and he said, 'Containment! Containment! I believe we have to contain the communists or else they'll spread over the entire earth like a plague of locusts.' My sister, Susan, a real liberal and anti-war protester, questioned Father McFarland about the accuracy and veracity of his statement. She said, 'Surely, Father, you're exaggerating. Is it really that bad?' To which he replied, 'Yes, child. It's that bad. If the communists were to succeed, or if we were fail to stop them where they live, then someday we'll be fighting them in our own backyards, in the middle of Main Street, in our gyms and schools, in libraries and pharmacies, in homes and apartments all across America. Even on the front lawn of the White House.'

"And then Father said authoritatively, 'I'm sure, Susan, President Johnson, and President Kennedy before him, thought long and hard on the subject, and consulted with expert advisors in Washington and in Congress, and I should think that they have the interest of the American people foremost in their minds.'

"And just as Father said, 'We should be proud to have the opportunity to go overseas and give those poor lads some good old American advise and ingenuity,' Mother came into the doorway with a tray of saucers and cups and a pot of hot coffee. She was frowning because she had overheard our conversation, and she was irrefutably against the war. She said, 'I wish you wouldn't talk about it so nonchalantly, dear, like everything was all right. The only thing that I ever hear about nowadays is that frightfully wicked action in South Vietnam. Why, it's escalating into a honest-to-goodness war, and I don't think those fools in Washington know what the hell they're talking about or doing by sending our young boys into harm's way. Excuse my language, Father McFarland, but whenever I read the newspapers and see all this evil business on television, it infuriates me to think we have intelligent, grown men in Washington, supposedly representing our interests, and all they do is make incredibly absurd and stupid decisions. Our boys are dying over there! Why don't they settle this conflict diplomatically and peacefully?'

"Father McFarland leaned forward, stroking his chin meditatively and said quite conscientiously, 'I suppose they would if they could. But, yes . . . yes . . . your point is well made. I understand completely and I agree. It's a pity, a real pity. Nevertheless, Betty, I believe we shall prevail. It is God's will. Have faith in the Almighty Father. In the end, everything will be all right. Yes . . . yes . . . everything will be all right. You will see . . . you will see.'

"I was only eighteen years old when I joined the US Marine Corps. They didn't waste any time shipping me overseas to Southeast Asia. And, I have to admit that I was still naive, thinking that everything was going to be all right. Well, as soon as I got to South Vietnam, I discovered something quite differently. I was aboard a C-130, Hercules, military cargo plane, which was transporting grunts and medical supplies to an airstrip in Chu Lai, when I started getting a very bad feeling about this, you see. I was so nervous that I couldn't stop my legs from shaking. As the plane approached the airstrip, one of the landing gears collapsed and the plane crashed, sliding along the runway for several thousand feet before it came to a stop at the edge of the jungle. Another hundred feet and we would've hit the trees. Luckily, everyone got out safely. But it was a horrifying experience, nevertheless. I realized then and there that everything was not going to be all right, that some things were inevitably doomed and marked for disaster. I thought about my father and Father McFarland then and how they had lied to me. Of course, I didn't think they purposely lied to me; I believe they had only wanted to protect me from the cruel world and the reality and horrors of war. After the crash landing, however, I was confused and I kept asking myself, 'Can I survive this? Will I survive this, dear God? And what the hell am I doing here?'"

As Corporal Buccanon commented about his induction into military life and the discovery of truths and lies that could only be discerned on the battlefield, Chief Long Wolf sat quietly, thinking about the young soldiers and his son, Black Hawk. But now, he had to speak up and hear it from the captain himself. "I'm sure, Corporal, it was difficult and everyone tried to do the very best they could under very bad circumstances." He turned to Cole and said, "Captain, did your men act bravely under fire? Did they act like brave Indian warriors? Black Hawk told me the story many times, but now, I would like to hear it from you."

Cole didn't answer right away as the heavenly abyss captivated his attention. Then, he turned to the chief. "Yes, Chief, they acted like brave Indian warriors, each one of them," said Cole sadly. "And, I shall never forget how bravely my warriors had died in an ambush along Route Nine, a major east-west highway—"

"It was more like a little dirt road," snapped Corporal Buccanon. Then he turned and looked off into the darkness again, smoking his pipe.

Cole took up the narrative. "Route Nine runs the entire width of Vietnam just south of the DMZ, a demilitarized zone. Our major bases - Gio Linh, Cam Lo, Alpha Three, Con Thien, the Rockpile and Khe Sanh - were located along this route.

"We were patrolling the Rockpile, a notoriously dangerous hill, when Private Davis, my radio operator, received a call from our command post, informing us that M Company had been hit pretty badly, and we were to go out and find the survivors and bring them back.

"The platoon was proceeding quickly, at a running pace, along Route Nine. Lance Corporal Taylor was at the point, and Corporal Duncan and Gunnery Hamilton were following right behind him. Then, Lance Corporal Taylor stepped on a concealed mine and that was when he was blown to pieces by the explosion. His body had disintegrated and what was left of it landed in the brush. Corporal Duncan and Gunnery Hamilton died shortly afterwards from shrapnel wounds. Right after that, I heard what I thought was the sound of firecrackers exploding on the Fourth of July. The popping sound was coming from nearly every direction. And, then I saw the men begin to fall, one by one.

"Everyone scrambled for cover, jumping into the ditches alongside the road, and then I turned to Private Davis and told him to contact the command post and to tell them that we needed a medevac and artillery support.

"Corporal Buccanon and Corporal Black Hawk were pinned down some fifty feet away. And then I heard another explosion on my left—a mortar round—and it sounded loud and close. Afterwards, all I could remember was the pain and how it took possession of my body. For a moment, in my delirium, I thought I was back on the farm. Yeah, a young boy, running eagerly toward a woman who was standing before a farmhouse and waiting for me with open arms. I could remember how lovely she looked. She was beautiful. Her face and her smile were inviting, warm and tender. When I reached her, I fell into her arms, and that's when I blacked out. I can't remember anything else happening after that—nothing more than blackness and silence, like the blasted abyss I've been dreaming about and can't get out of my head for the past few weeks.

"Later, while I was recuperating in a hospital in Yokosuka, Japan, I learned from Sergeant Connors what had happened next." Now, Cole turned and looked at Little Flower, who had been listening pensively alongside her grandfather. Gazing into her big, luminous eyes, which were sparkling like the stars, and which reminded Cole of the Vietnamese August moon, he continued in a low, steady voice.

"I had been hit by a mortar round and was bleeding pretty badly from shrapnel wounds. While under intense fire from the enemy and with a total disregard for his own personal safety, Black Hawk jumped up and ran fifty feet along Route Nine to come to my aid. I was falling in and out of consciousness and bleeding profusely. Somehow, your father prevented me from going into shock and dying. I remember waking up and he was talking to me calmly and reassuringly in a low, whispering voice. His was the last voice I heard before blacking out.

"Under the cover of night, we began to withdraw from our position, but only at great sacrifice and expense of human life. Many of our boys fell to sniper fire."

Corporal Buccanon leaned his back wearily against the post of the porch and closed his eyes as Cole continued.

"The fortunate ones had crawled to safety, while the less fortunate—the wounded, the dying and the dead—had to be carried or dragged out by fellow marines. Black Hawk carried me and when he could no longer carry me, he dragged me along the ground like a sack of potatoes, refusing to leave me to the enemy." Cole slowly ran his hand over his face and eyes.

"A few of the marines had actually made it back to a landing zone, about three clicks or kilometers to our south, where several Hueys, helicopters had set down in an open field that was approximately 300 to 400 square feet. It took hours—practically all night—to travel three clicks. When the marines finally emerged from the jungle, they were confronted with an obstacle – an open field. They needed to cross an open field to get to the helicopters. Crouching low and shielding their eyes and ears from the dust and the roar of the rotating helicopter blades directly above them, they made their way to the Hueys, but not before many of them had been picked off by sniper fire which was pretty intense at the time.

"The helicopter pilots were getting nervous and shouting, 'Let's go! Let's move it! We can't stay here very long!'

"Several soldiers jumped out of the helicopter and started firing into the jungle. Three marines fell in the open field—Langley, Ortiz, and Curtis. Black Hawk had prayed to his Great

Spirit, and despite the fear that must've gripped him, somehow he flung me over his shoulder and ran as fast as his sturdy legs could carry us toward the waiting helicopters in the field, which were about to take off. Just before Black Hawk reached the Huey, he stumbled and fell.

"Then, Corporal Buccanon leaped forward and dragged me and Corporal Black Hawk the rest of the way to safety. A few moments later, three Hueys rose quickly into the dark sky and disappeared behind the treetops. We were safe . . . we were safe . . . we were safe for now. Later, on board the helicopter, we found out that Black Hawk had taken several rounds in the back."

As Cole concluded his story, he looked up at Chief Long Wolf and felt melancholy when he saw him sitting there proudly and honorably. Then, the chief noticed that Little Flower was crying silently. He embraced her and made a vow to himself that he would watch over her. Just let the Beast try to stop him!

"Yes, Chief, I was very proud of my men. They were good marines—good and brave Indian warriors—the very best the Marine Corps had to offer and sacrifice."

Later that evening, Cole and Corporal Buccanon were shown to a room where they stayed the night.

Chapter 24 - It's Over—black Hawk's Dead

The next morning, Cole woke up slowly, as a ray of sunlight streaked through a hole in the patched window shade and fell gently onto his squinting eyelids. For a moment he thought he was at home again, back in his room in Nashville, that his dad had started the chores and his mother was in the kitchen fixing breakfast. He thought he heard the back screen door banging against the house.

Then he was startled by the sound of a drum—just outside his window—and the chanting and raving of an old warrior chief. He opened his eyes and listened attentively for a few minutes. What was the chief doing out there so early in the morning? Praying to his Great Spirit?

Cole heard Corporal Buccanon, breathing rhythmically. Turning his head to the side, he saw the silhouette of Corporal Buccanon's tall, angular, body under a heap of covers. He lay sprawled out awkwardly on an old army cot that was made of canvas and wood. It had short stubby legs and reminded Cole of the type of cots that had been issued to soldiers during World War II.

Cole sat up in bed, yawned, passed his hands over his face, then shook his head like a mangy dog or a wolf in the wild. Though his body and mind still yearned for another hour of sleep, he got up, took a few steps, and stumbled, inadvertently, in the dark bumping into the cot where Corporal Buccanon was sleeping.

An angry, raspy voice rang out from beneath the covers, "Good God, man, watch where you're going!" Then Corporal Buccanon grunted, turned himself over, and fell back to sleep.

Pulling the shade away from the window, Cole peered outside and saw a copse of trees, and behind the trees, a big, red sun rising slowly above the horizon in the east. It's going to be another scorcher, he thought.

He saw Little Flower, in the backyard, looking up at a green great horned owl that had made a nest in a cottonwood tree. She was cradling a drum against her side and pounding it with a drumstick. But when that failed to scare away the owl and any evil spirits that it might have brought with it to the tree and to their house, she started motioning and flailing her arms in the air. Little Flower believed in the legends and myths of her ancestors that had been passed down from one generation to the next, and she imagined that the appearance of the green great horned owl always preceded the arrival of evil spirits. Though she understood that her notion about the owl was simply based on superstition, she had decided she wouldn't take any chances. She was going to get rid of the owl to save her grandfather.

Cole was amazed when he thought about the Native American Indians and how their lives were still wrapped up in superstition and myth.

"Shoo! Shoo!" Little Flower said anxiously, waving her arms wildly. Sensing that there was no immediate danger, the green great horned owl closed its large, round eyes and drifted off to sleep. The night air—cool and refreshing—was already surrendering to the heat of day.

When the beating of the drum had ceased, Cole turned to Corporal Buccanon and kicked the cot. "Get up. It's about time we get the hell out of here."

Corporal Buccanon groaned and then a stream of profanity flowed freely from his mouth. Sitting up, he rubbed the sleep from his bloodshot eyes. With loathing he looked at Cole. He said, "What's the idea of getting up so early, Captain? Can't you let a guy get some sleep? We're not exactly on patrol, you know."

Cole slipped on his trousers and shirt, and said calmly, "Black Hawk's dead, there's nothing more we can do here. We came all this way for nothing. It's time we head back to Nashville."

"And what about the girl? What about Little Flower? Are you taking her back to Nashville with you?" Corporal Buccanon said thickly, as he searched the small room for his trousers.

"No!" said Cole emphatically, and then he added condescendingly, "Don't be stupid. She belongs here with her grandfather and with her people."

"But the chief said he was going to die soon," Corporal Buccanon said sadly, "What will happen to Little Flower then?"

"Look! Chief Long Wolf is old, but he'll outlive both you and me together," Cole said definitively, as if to say he had heard enough from Corporal Buccanon and didn't want to hear another word on the subject. In fact, he had lain wide-awake most of the night, tossing and turning in bed and thinking about Little Flower. What's to be done with her? He was almost angry with Chief Long Wolf for making such an asinine proposition. As if he could just adopt Little Flower and take her back to Tennessee with him. As if there weren't any Native American families that would have been honored to adopt the granddaughter of the self-proclaimed chief of the Sioux Nation. He thought it was crazy and madness that he should be given this honor instead of any one of the more worthy families of the tribe. Yet, he wondered.

Now Corporal Buccanon began pacing up and down in the small room. Finally, he faced Cole and said furiously, "And what about the young man in Independence, Missouri? What are we to think about him? What about the funeral procession we saw on the road just outside of Omaha? How do you explain that? And, what are you going to do about the Beast in Tekaman?"

"Me?" Cole said angrily.

"Just turn your back and run away! Run back home to New York City and bury your head in the sand like an ostrich and pretend that it never happened?"

"Yes," said Cole firmly, coldly. "It's inexplicable. I can't explain the weird hallucinations we've been having ever since we left Tennessee. Nevertheless, I won't be dragged into this, either by you or Chief Long Wolf."

Upon hearing the clamorous voices of Corporal Buccanon and Cole, rising in pitch and volume, Little Flower ran quickly to the house to join her grandfather. He had sauntered quietly into the kitchen during the raucous and started a meager breakfast of eggs and biscuits for Little Flower and his guests.

The showdown between Corporal Buccanon and Cole continued unabated for some time. Corporal Buccanon said, vehemently, "I had supposed you would think that—that we were just hallucinating or losing our minds or something. And that the things we saw on the road didn't really happen." He was pacing again, back and forth, like a caged animal, ready to spring at his prey.

"It doesn't make any difference, now, Corporal. It's over!" said Cole harshly. "Black Hawk's dead! And, I'm truly sorry. But we were brought here under false pretenses by a little old man, an old man who thinks he's the chief of the Sioux Nation, who had decided to write a letter to his son's old army buddies and tell them that he was in trouble and to come quickly. Why? What was it all for? Only to have us travel all this distance and end up here in this godforsaken wilderness, just so he could say that he had a few visitors stop by and not feel so terribly alone. Or what's worse? That he tried to foist his own granddaughter onto us, as if she were some kind of Hopi Kachina doll that one might sell or give away?"

Cole started for the bedroom door, and then suddenly stopped with his hand resting on the doorknob. Without looking back, he added in a low, whispering voice, "I'm sorry, Corporal. It's over. There's nothing more we can do here. It's over." He quietly opened the door and walked out, leaving Corporal Buccanon in a state of abjection, sitting on his cot with his elbows on his knees and his head cradled in his hands.

Chief Long Wolf and Little Flower waited patiently for Cole and Corporal Buccanon to appear for breakfast, and being proud and gracious, they pretended as if they hadn't heard a word of their argument. To Cole, however, it was quite painfully obvious that everyone within a quarter mile of the ranch house had to have heard the shameful dispute between himself and Corporal Buccanon. He thought he would have to brace himself against their stolid and sad countenances sitting across from him at the breakfast table, but instead Chief Long Wolf and Little Flower had only smiled politely. For a while, Little Flower attempted vainly to engage Cole and Corporal Buccanon in conversation with one another, but the feuding parties only grunted and snarled at each other from across the table.

Then, Chief Long Wolf turned to Cole and Corporal Buccanon and said, "Before you leave, Captain Cole, and you, Corporal Buccanon, you might do me the honor of accompanying me to the Wolf Creek Cemetery. There you will be able to see for yourself where we have put him. He lies next to White Cloud and he is only a short distance from Running Deer. I know he would have wanted you to see his Mountain of Everlasting Happiness where he will dwell for eternity. Consider it a request from an old Indian chief who doesn't have long to live."

"It's the least we can do, Captain, " said Corporal Buccanon, pleadingly.

"Yes, of course," said Cole resignedly, yet he was thinking that if he and Corporal Buccanon were to leave immediately after breakfast, as he had hoped to do, they might avoid any further entanglements with Chief Long Wolf and Little Flower. Perhaps, they might avoid the breaking of promises and hearts, which only leads to bitterness. Yes, it seemed to Cole that he had no choice but to get the hell out of South Dakota—as soon as possible.

While Chief Long Wolf and Little Flower washed and dried the breakfast dishes, and carefully stacked them in one of the kitchen cabinets, Cole began to understand a few things that at first appeared to be unrelated incidences, but which he now saw as pieces of the same puzzle. He realized that the young man from Independence, Missouri, the funeral procession on the road, his encounter with the Beast at Tekaman, and Nabokov's haunting words, "The cradle rocks above an abyss. . . ." were somehow interconnected and related to Chief Long Wolf and Little Flower. He didn't relish the idea, but found it intimidating and scary. And, if it were true, he rationalized with his lawyer's mind, then what about Vietnam? What about Black Hawk's detail to his platoon, the fatal and fateful ambush that took so many young lives—brave marines and Indian warriors—and let us not forget Lai Choi, Roscoe, Father McFarland, Susan, his own mother and father, Henry and Betty, Golgotha, and Black Hawk's death? Were they not also connected to Chief Long Wolf and Little Flower and to his own destiny? What evil purpose was behind all this?

Cole asked himself these questions and despite all his years of experience and training in logic and clear thinking, he could not arrive at an answer that would satisfy his curiosity.

Chapter 25 - Wolf Creek Cemetery

After breakfast, the same little yellow school bus that had dropped Little Flower off the day before had returned. It waited out front as the little princess scrambled for her books, kissed her grandfather on the cheek, made Cole and Corporal Buccanon promise not to leave before she had a chance to say goodbye, and then ran out the front door, down the steps and into the bus.

The driver, a short and stocky San-Arc Sioux maiden named Roxy, smiled and waved at Chief Long Wolf, as she turned a handle that automatically closed the door of the school bus. Suddenly overwhelmed with a feeling of melancholy, Cole and Corporal Buccanon watched the little school bus pull away. They saw Little Flower leaning out the side window and waving vigorously. She shouted, "I love you, grandfather. I love, you!"

It had been decided earlier that Cole would drive the chief's red pickup truck and Corporal Buccanon would follow in the Road King. After twenty minutes of steady driving across flat, barren land, Cole finally saw a tall, white, steeple in the distance. Chief Long Wolf nodded sadly toward the steeple and said, "That's it. That's Holy Rosary."

Holy Rosary Church and the Indian cemetery that stood next to it were located in a desolate area outside of town. As Cole pulled up in front of the church and came to a stop, he realized just how closely its design resembled the architecture of churches in New England with their customary white steeples, white picket fences, and cemeteries.

Chief Long Wolf clambered out of the truck and led Cole and Corporal Buccanon through a gate and along a stone path that brought them to the last row in the cemetery where three tombstones were nestled close to the fence.

It was a solemn and melancholy occasion. Corporal Buccanon respectfully made the sign of the cross, knelt before the stones, and began to pray. Chief Long Wolf went from one grave to another, standing several minutes before each one, meditating and chanting. Cole watched the old chief with a sense of commiseration, knowing very well that there was nothing he could do to erase from their memories the pain and anguish associated with losing a loved one. He felt as if Providence had cheated him of the opportunity to repay Black Hawk for saving his life.

After wiping the tears and sweat from his face and brow with a small handkerchief, the chief turned to Cole. "Running Deer always wanted a Christian burial. She made me promise her that if she or Black Hawk were to die first, I was to arrange such a burial. She was an adamant woman when it came to her religion, Captain. She would never listen to anyone except the pastor of her church and scripture—the word of God. She was a devoted disciple." Then, he nodded toward Corporal Buccanon, who was still kneeling and praying at Black Hawk's grave. "And, very religious like Corporal Buccanon."

Cole realized the old chief was right; he could testify to the fact that Corporal Buccanon was a devout Christian and practiced his faith religiously whenever possible, despite his seeming apostasy. His drinking, cursing, brawling, and womanizing came much later, he remembered, after he had been inducted into the US Marine Corps and was sent off to fight in the jungles of South Vietnam.

An image came to Cole's mind of a young boy wearing a long robe with arm-length sleeves billowing and fluttering behind him. He was walking down the center aisle of a church and the hem of his robe swept the marble floor. Corporal Buccanon was an altar boy at Saint Patrick's Church and Father McFarland was a young priest just out of the seminary. Cole remembered how Corporal Buccanon would wake up at five o'clock in the morning, so he could serve at the seven o'clock mass with Father McFarland.

Henry would drive him to town before he started his chores around the farm. Cole recalled that for a while, Corporal Buccanon had seriously considered the idea of entering the seminary and taking the vows of priesthood.

At the time, Cole was a young man and couldn't even imagine living such a life—a life bound by restrictions and rules—where turning the other cheek was lauded. Then, shortly after joining the US Marine Corps, Cole saw Corporal Buccanon's astonishing metamorphosis.

His change was gradual and innocuous at first, but Cole, nevertheless, recognized it for what it truly represented—the beginning of the fall of the angel Buccanon. First, he took up smoking cigarettes, and then he switched to marijuana. Next, he started drinking on the base with the other soldiers and carousing with women. His language became rude and petulant. It wasn't long before he starting disregarding his personal hygiene, bathing and washing clothes only once a week. He literally stank. His hair and beard were dirty and filthy, though at first, he tried to maintain them. Then, he got the notion to cover his arms and shoulders with tattoos. He thought it was a cool way to make a statement. Cole found himself disgusted with Corporal Buccanon because he had sought the unconventional and had let himself become more like a ragged renegade than a marine.

Yet, despite all the changes that had occurred in Corporal Buccanon's life—transforming him from a shy teenager and high school graduate from Nashville, Tennessee, who had the world literally lying at his feet, to a wild, brawling marine—he never lost his faith. At least that's what Cole thought as he looked at Corporal Buccanon, kneeling and praying, at the foot of Black Hawk's tombstone.

"Where is your faith, Captain?" Chief Long Wolf asked, rather surprised by Cole's blatant display of irreverence and apostasy.

"My faith?" Cole sneered. "Corporal Buccanon has faith, and yet the minute he steps outside the house of God he's back to swearing, lying, and cheating. If he's what you consider to be a great example of Christian faith and reverence, Chief, then I'm the Archbishop of Canterbury!"

Corporal Buccanon ignored Cole and continued his praying at the foot of the tombstone. But Cole was determined to speak the truth, and to let Chief Long Wolf know exactly what kind of Christian Corporal Buccanon really was.

"Corporal Buccanon doesn't understand the meaning of the words *forgiveness* or *Christian charity*, Chief. That man will never forgive. Do you know he blames me for the ambush in Vietnam, and to this very day he holds me personally responsible for the deaths of over twenty good marines? He'll never forget and he'll never forgive." Cole frowned, shook his head, and walked back to the pickup truck, leaving Chief Long Wolf and Corporal Buccanon in the cemetery.

Chapter 26 - Starfire—Oglala Shaman

When Chief Long Wolf was finally ready to leave the cemetery, he took Cole aside and said quietly with a sense of urgency in his voice, "I must visit Starfire!"

"What?" Cole asked curiously. "Starfire? Who is he?"

"Starfire is an Oglala medicine man—a shaman! I must see him now! Immediately! Today, Captain! Do you understand?" Then, without waiting for an answer from Cole, Chief Long Wolf tottered to the red pickup truck and climbed into the cab where he meditated and waited patiently for Cole and Corporal Buccanon.

Chief Long Wolf gave Cole the directions to Salem, a small town northwest of Wolf Creek, where they were to meet with Starfire, the medicine man or shaman of the Oglala Sioux tribe.

Starfire lived with his wife, Morningstar, in an old trailer park that contained approximately a hundred decaying trailers. Starfire's trailer was located along the northwest edge of the perimeter, bordering a natural wild preserve—the same preserve that Black Hawk had patrolled and where he was murdered by poachers. In the field directly behind his trailer, Starfire built several tepees, which he used to attract tourists during the spring and summer months. He would often attract the same visitors year after year. Most of them were heading either to Sturgis, the Badlands National Park, or Mount Rushmore. A shrewd businessman, Starfire would charge a fee for a tour of his tepees, which were made of buffalo and deerskins stretched and fastened to poles with cords made from the hide of animals and the bark of trees. During a typical tour, Starfire would stress the authenticity of the tepees and explain how they had been preserved and passed down to him from his ancestors. He would also sing and dance for them, often beating his drum, shaking his rattle, and chanting long dirges.

Even before the pickup truck and the Road King had come to a stop before Starfire's dilapidated trailer, Cole saw an elderly man emerging from one of the tepees waving a rifle in one hand and a Colt .45 in the other. He looked more like a wild man who had escaped from someone's nightmare than a medicine man. He was approximately sixty years of age, of medium height and built. His rough, angular face of dark-red leathery complexion looked exactly like a mask that had been frozen in time. He had a sharp, hawklike nose, and his long, black hair looked disheveled. His mouth turned down naturally at the corners, and his eyes looked sullen, and deceitful like those of a fox. He hardly ever smiled but when he did, one would be inclined to shudder and cringe. This morning he was wearing a bandanna, a white shirt with quail feathers, leggings and moccasins. Around his neck was a string of beautiful beads and shells.

Starfire's knowledge of herbs and homemade remedies was vast, and as a result he was a very popular person among the Sioux Nations. It was not uncommon for Teton Sioux to travel hundreds of miles over rugged terrain and through burning deserts to visit the famous shaman. They would come from as far east as the Missouri River, as far north as Canada, as far west as California, and as far south as Arizona. Visits with the medicine man were usually brief. What the visitors wanted mostly was to purchase a small bottle of Starfire's lifesaving, pain-reducing potion—a potion which he made from the herbs he found in the forests and woodlands. Some of the visitors would sit before his tepee and listen to the sound of his melodious voice, the graceful rhythm of his rattle, and monotonous beat of his drum.

Apostates decried loudly against his antics, claiming that the shaman's power was nothing more than hocus pocus and superstitious pagan rites. However, after being coaxed to spend an evening with the shaman under the stars and within his honored tepee, where they would witness his supernatural and phenomenal healing power, they would emerge in the morning with wide eyes and with a new sense of understanding. Indubitably, the apostates were charmed by the power of the shaman.

When Starfire saw Chief Long Wolf and Cole climb out of the truck and Corporal Buccanon dismount from his Road King, he lowered his rifle and Colt .45 and grinned widely. He placed his arms around Chief Long Wolf and hugged him affectionately like a mother bear would have hugged her cub. Then, he greeted Cole warmly and looked at Corporal Buccanon suspiciously. It seemed to Cole that they had caught Starfire at a bad time. The old medicine man seemed disoriented and alarmed by their presence and unexpected arrival. Standing before his tepee, he was constantly looking over his shoulder and down the road as if he were expecting someone else to show up.

Starfire turned to Chief Long Wolf and said, "It's a good thing you came when you did, Chief Long Wolf, because I am getting ready to leave. I am packing up and heading to the Badlands for the Sun Dance celebration. I have to get an early start this year. I'm sorry I do not have the time to explain everything to you now. I cannot wait much longer." And, as he said this, he took another look over his shoulder anxiously. "Come, come, let us step inside, into the tepee." He hurried them inside.

Inside the tepee, Cole found the air to be extremely warm and humid. Beads of sweat formed immediately upon his face. Corporal Buccanon looked around curiously.

"I suppose, I could spare a minute or two for you, Chief. Please, sit down." Starfire motioned to the rug that was spread out in the middle of the tepee. Then, Starfire lit a peace pipe and invited everyone to smoke. As the pipe made its way around the circle, Starfire appeared to grow calm and less irritable as if he had been tranquilized by a sedative. He looked at Chief Long Wolf and said hauntingly, half-laughingly, "When I first heard the motorcycle approaching the camp, I thought you were the avenging spirit of death, Chief, coming to take poor old Starfire to the underworld."

"Ha . . . ha . . . ha," Chief Long Wolf laughed warmly, merrily, as he passed the pipe to Corporal Buccanon, who took it eagerly. "Why are you so suspicious of everyone, Starfire? What have you done? I have no need for you if you've been drinking again. I need pure medicine—medicine that has not been polluted by alcohol or drugs. I need your medicine."

Starfire leaned toward Chief Long Wolf and whispered, confidentially, "Lame Horse's mother passed away yesterday." He got up quickly, stepped to the opening of the tepee and looked outside. Seeing no one there but his wife carefully packing the car with camping gear and deer and buffalo skins, he returned to his guests.

"Lame Horse's mother had bronchitis, and after a week she developed pneumonia and died. Lame Horse came to me and I told him that she was old and there was nothing I could do for her. He would not listen to me. The fool is so damned superstitious. He begged me to go and see her in the hospital, to use the old medicine and perform magic. At first, I refused, but later I went to satisfy the old lady. She believed in me, and she thought that I could save her," Starfire said solemnly. "For seven days, I prayed for her, and when she died, Lame Horse took it very badly." He scowled and looked at his old chief. "And now, he wants to kill me."

"I will speak to Lame Horse, and perhaps we can settle this without bloodshed," Chief Long Wolf said uneasily, knowing very well that Lame Horse may already be plotting and scheming a death trap for the old medicine man.

"I cannot wait for that. I am leaving after dark for the Badlands, where I shall camp out in the hills with Morningstar and wait for the beginning of the Sun Dance ceremony," said Starfire.

Cole saw the fear in his face, a fear he recognized all too well from his own experiences dealing with desperate and frightened men in times of war. Now, it seemed Starfire was fighting a war of his own.

"Listen to me, old friend. Before you leave, I need your advice," Chief Long Wolf said with an air of finality. "I have prayed to Wakan Tanka, and I have decided to step down as Chief of the Sioux Nation."

When Chief Long Wolf declared his intentions, Starfire's eyes widened and his jaw dropped. He looked at the chief, incredulously.

Cole frowned and looked at Corporal Buccanon, who was sitting there in a state of total bewilderment. Cole didn't know what this meant exactly, but he was certain it would entangle him even further into the lives of Chief Long Wolf, Little Flower, and now possibly Starfire.

Starfire got up, stepped over to the drum, and started beating it fiercely, wildly. He sang a strange chant, in the old language of Algonquin. The chant lasted several minutes, and when he had finished, Starfire turned to Chief Long Wolf and said in a low, dreadful voice, "The cradle rocks above an abyss, and common sense tells us that life is but a brief moment of light between two eternities of darkness."

Cole was flabbergasted by the phrase—the same phrase from Nabokov that had been tormenting his mind for the last few weeks. And now, Starfire, a wild shaman, recites the phrase. This has to be more than coincidence. Suddenly, there was silence, and a moment later, Starfire began chanting again, but this time his chanting was accompanied by the sound of the rattlers. Taking one in each hand, he shook them fiercely and rhythmically.

While Starfire danced around the tepee, Cole leaned toward Chief Long Wolf and asked nervously, "Chief, what the hell are you talking about? What do you mean you're stepping down as chief of the Sioux Nation? You mean to say that you really are the chief of the Sioux Nations?"

"Yes," said Chief Long Wolf softly.

"Then, if you are what you say you are, you can't do that!" said Cole.

"Give me one good reason why you should step down as chief of the Sioux Nation," Corporal Buccanon said harshly, roughly.

"Listen to me, Captain Cole, Corporal Buccanon! I have thought about this for a very long time, and I have come to the decision that I must step down. I am an old man. I will die shortly and Little Flower will be left alone. If I live to see another harvest, I would consider myself lucky. I do not fear for myself, Captain, but for Little Flower. In the meantime, I have a responsibility that I must perform. I have to select a chief, a worthy warrior, who will replace me when I am gone. I shall make my announcement at the Sun Dance ceremony."

"The Sun Dance ceremony! What the hell is that?" asked Corporal Buccanon.

Suddenly, Starfire had stopped dancing around the tepee, turned to Cole and Corporal Buccanon and said solemnly, "For the Sioux Nation, this is very serious business. For the Sioux, selecting a new chief is like electing a president—like electing the President of the United States."

"The Sun Dance ceremony is a beautiful dance, Corporal," Chief Long Wolf said proudly. "For the warriors and braves who participate in the dance, it is a source of power and vision, and to our numerous tribes, it brings good fortune. Once each year, warriors and braves from the Sioux, the Apache, the Comanche, the Pawnee, the Kiowa, the Crow, the Navaho, and many others from all over North America, which make up the Sioux Nation, will come together to celebrate and participate in the Sun Dance. You have to see it for yourselves, gentlemen, to fully appreciate the magic, wonder, and splendor of the Sun Dance."

"You have to live it like a warrior, like a Sioux in days long past," Starfire said proudly. "Once you have seen it, you'll never forget it."

"Sounds interesting, Chief," Corporal Buccanon said thoughtfully. "I used to get a lot of powerful visions, too, when I was in Vietnam. I remember the time when—"

"Shut up, Corporal," said Cole angrily.

"Long ago, it was the custom of our tribe—especially our warriors and braves—to perform a dance before a sacred tree. For eight days and nights, they would dance while holding a cord that connected them to a sacred tree both physically and spiritually. They would dance until they collapsed at the foot of the tree, usually in a trance or a coma. While in this state, they would have a vision and communicate with the Great Spirit, Wakan Tanka," said Starfire.

"In recent times, however," Chief Long Wolf continued, "the Sioux had turned the Sun Dance into a ritual of self-torture. First, they would pierce the skin of their chest with a small stick or a small piece of wood, the ends of which had been whittled to sharp points. Next, they would attach one end of a long cord or a long piece of twine to the stick and the other end to the sacred tree. When this had been accomplished, they were then ready to begin the Sun Dance. They would dance around the sacred tree and tug or pull against the cord until it was ripped from their chest. It usually ended in a bloody mess.

"In 1910, the US Bureau of Indian Affairs had the dance forbidden. But now, we are allowed to dance again. In their wisdom, they have come to believe that self-torture was no longer practiced openly by our people. It is true that the signs of self-torture are no longer visible to the naked eye, but that doesn't necessarily mean it is no longer practiced. If you look close enough, Captain, you might see the scars."

"Where do you perform this Sun Dance ceremony, Chief?" Cole asked.

"In the Badlands, Captain, in the Badlands of South Dakota." Chief Long Wolf paused, took another puff on the peace pipe, and then added, 'The Badlands National Park. Many people will come to watch our Sun Dance. They come by motorcar, motorcycle, recreational vehicle, pickup truck, bus, train, and some even walk. And where do they come from? They come from Sturgis, and from as far away as California, New York, Canada, and Texas. They come to watch us dance.

"During this very important week of events, many of the chiefs and leaders of the Sioux Nation will meet to talk about the state of the Indian Nation. As chief of the Sioux Nation, it is my responsibility and duty to attend this meeting and to lead the discussion wisely and peacefully. However, as I've said before, I am too old to make this trip alone." Then he turned to the medicine man, and said seriously, beseechingly, "I need your help, Starfire! You must pray to Wakan Tanka on my behalf and ask him to give me spirit and courage." Then he spoke more sorrowfully, "For I am prepared to receive my death dream."

"Death dream," echoed Corporal Buccanon.

"I am ready," said Chief Long Wolf, sadly, mournfully.

Cole and Corporal Buccanon realized just what the chief was actually asking the medicine man, the shaman, to do: He wanted Starfire to help him prepare for his death.

"Some warriors will want to fight for the honor of being appointed the next chief of the Sioux Nation," said Starfire.

Chief Long Wolf knitted his brow and shook his head violently. "No! I will not have them fighting like wild savages in the wilderness. This will be settled reasonably, peacefully or I shall personally have them locked up."

"But you may not be able to stop them," Starfire said, his eyes narrowing suspiciously. Cole thought they reminded him of the screaming eagles and the burning flames of hell decorating his Softail.

"Don't tell me your people still act like warriors and Indian chiefs?" Corporal Buccanon said, his voice betraying a state of amazement and incredulity.

"Yes, Corporal Buccanon," said Starfire angrily. "We still have warriors who pride themselves on their hunting, fishing, and fighting skills. You would be surprised to learn that many of the military societies of old that many people had thought we had abandoned have actually survived and still exist today—the Cheyenne Wolf, the Elk, the Bowstring, and the most fierce and savage of them all: the Dog Soldiers."

"You don't say?" Corporal Buccanon said.

"They are capable of anything, and I'm afraid of what they might do under these shifting and changing circumstances," said Chief Long Wolf, sadly. "Nevertheless, I shall select a chief to replace me, and there must not be any fighting amongst the warriors and braves." Suddenly, Chief Long Wolf looked exhausted. "I do not know what to do." He paused momentarily to think, and then he said more calmly, "I shall pray to Wakan Tanka. I shall pray for guidance, strength and peace—mostly peace."

Then Starfire said, "Chief Long Wolf, you seek your death song and that is a matter between you and Wakan Tanka, the Great Spirit. You know what has to be done. My heart is sad and heavy, and my counsel to you, great chief and old friend, is to go to the Sacred Hills. You must go there to pray and fast until you have successfully communicated with the underworld and with the Great Spirit, Wakan Tanka, and have received from him your vision and death song that you so greatly desire."

Chief Long Wolf nodded sadly, and Cole and Corporal Buccanon looked on in amazement.

While Morningstar packed the motorcar with provisions and equipment for Starfire's own period of seclusion and watched for the appearance of Lame Horse, Starfire began chanting, again. He shook the rattle over the head of the chief, and then he went outside the tepee and started beating the drum.

Chief Long Wolf closed his eyes and meditated as Starfire performed a wild and ceremonious dance around the tepee. Watching the spectacle, Cole had the idea that Corporal Buccanon was indeed enjoying himself and had been captivated by the power and charm of the shaman. Cole, on the other hand, sat pensively, gloomily as though the whole thing—the vision, the quest for a death song, and the Sun Dance ceremony—was an imbroglio that would trap him in some unforeseeable and horrible destiny.

This went on for a long time, and then Chief Long Wolf slowly opened his dark, piercing eyes, leaned toward Cole and said, "Captain, will you accompany this old chief and his granddaughter to the Sun Dance celebration?"

Overwhelmed by a feeling of despair and gloom, Cole didn't know what to think, so he frowned with a sigh of resignation.

Part V—The badlands of South Dakota

Chapter 27 - Journey to the badlands

After visiting the gravesides of Black Hawk, White Cloud, and Running Deer, and after seeking the counsel of Starfire, the Oglala medicine man and shaman, Chief Long Wolf and Little Flower prepared for their journey to the Sun Dance celebration in the Badlands.

Corporal Buccanon checked over his Harley while Cole threw their luggage in the back of the pickup truck and assisted Chief Long Wolf who struggled to climb into the front passenger seat. Little Flower sat in the middle, between Cole and her grandfather, and was very excited about the trip.

Corporal Buccanon led the way on his Road King. As they pulled out of the driveway and onto the road, Chief Long Wolf turned around in his seat as if to take one last look at the dilapidated house. He had the idea that this might be the last time he would ever see the old homestead again. This was where he had made love to Running Deer and where they had raised their son, Black Hawk, who would have become the next chief of the Sioux Nation had he not been senselessly murdered by the poachers who were hunting for fur. Before leaving, he went into every room of the ranch house and stood for a long time just gazing at the walls and chanting and praying.

"What are you looking at, grandfather? Did you forget something?" asked Little Flower. She turned and looked up into her grandfather's face.

"No, Little Flower. I didn't forget anything," Chief Long Wolf said sadly, and then he looked down at Little Flower, smiled tenderly and lovingly. "I have everything I need right here with me now." He wrapped his thin arm around Little Flower's small shoulders and hugged her.

Immediately after turning west on Highway 90, Cole and Corporal Buccanon were overtaken by a group of twenty or thirty bikers straddling Harley-Davidson motorcycles. They were apparently on their way to the gathering at Sturgis. Corporal Buccanon accelerated the Road King, and for a while had kept up with them, riding side by side. But, eventually he fell back, waving at many of the riders as they passed him, making the sign of peace, and shouting something inaudible over the roar of the Harleys.

In the meantime, Chief Long Wolf was staring out the window, preoccupied with thoughts of the abyss, the eternal darkness, and his death song. In his mind, he saw a horrible sequence of images – images of a cradle rocking, and then splintering and breaking apart before his very eyes. To calm his nerves and to rest his mind, the chief meditated and chanted aloud, while Little Flower talked to Cole about her love for the Sun Dance. As they approached the Badlands, it seemed to Chief Long Wolf that the cradle was rocking much harder than usual and with a viciousness and fierceness that frightened him.

Chapter 28 – Skull and bones

They had just passed Presho and were ten miles outside of Murdo when another biker pulled up behind them.

As Little Flower glanced out the window, she suddenly saw a Low Rider pull up alongside the pickup truck. A young man of about twenty-five, dressed in a black leather jacket, black jeans and boots, was driving the bike, and behind him sat a young woman, his fiancée or perhaps his wife. She had her arms wrapped tightly around his waist and appeared to be holding on for dear life. At first, Little Flower thought the couple riding alongside them were merely on their way to Sturgis or the Sun Dance ceremony. She smiled at them. But then, she remembered the green great horned owl that was perched in the tree outside her grandfather's house, and suddenly she felt something was wrong.

"Look!" shouted Little Flower excitedly, raising her eyebrows in horror and nodding her head toward the window.

Cole's eyes were fixed on the road ahead of him. Nevertheless, he quickly turned his head to glance out his window. He saw the biker and his female companion and his eyes widened when he saw their grotesquely convoluted faces staring back at him. He saw their lips moving frantically. They were trying to say something, but Cole couldn't make it out. It appeared to Cole as if they were beckoning him onward and forward. For a moment, he thought they were trying to warn him about something. He concentrated on their lips again and it appeared as if they were saying, 'Keep going!' or 'Don't look back!'

Cole felt the strain in his body. His face was suddenly haggard and drawn, and his hands gripped the steering wheel of the pickup truck so hard that his knuckles had turned ghastly white. Twice, he almost drove off the road and into a ditch. Little Flower stared wide-eyed at the aberration, wringing her hands and cringing back in her seat, and leaning against her grandfather. The old chief sat quietly and calmly, chanting and praying peacefully, as if nothing out of the ordinary was happening. This wasn't exactly a Sunday drive in the country, Cole thought anxiously.

The motorcyclist and the woman continued to motion wildly, convulsively with their arms and to shout incoherently.

"They're trying to tell us something," Little Flower shouted. "What is it? What are they trying to tell us?"

"I don't know. I can't make it out," Cole said, glancing at Little Flower and Chief Long Wolf.

"Why don't they stop? Why don't they stop?" Little Flower cried hysterically.

"I don't know," said Cole uneasily. "It looks like he wants us to follow him or something."

Cole saw the couple looking back over their shoulders, repeatedly, as though they were being chased. Cole looked into his rearview mirror and saw nothing. And then, finally, the frightened couple on the Harley made one last effort to communicate their warning to Cole before feverishly racing ahead of the truck. They quickly passed Corporal Buccanon on his Road King, disappearing around a bend in the road.

Shortly afterwards, Cole heard the roar of another motorcycle approaching from behind them. Looking into his rearview mirror, he saw the Fat Boy approaching fast. Cole knew that his truck was traveling at a moderate speed and the cyclist could easily overtake it. When the motorcycle finally caught up with the truck, Cole thought it was odd that the biker had reduced his speed and merely cruised behind them.

Cole glanced through his rearview mirror, but was unable to see the face of the driver, only his long black robe, hood, and long sleeves flapping wildly, furiously in the wind.

The biker on the Fat Boy had followed the truck for approximately a mile before accelerating and pulling up alongside the truck. Cole turned to get a glimpse of the rider, and when he did he saw something evil and wicked. Beneath the rider's black hood, Cole saw a grinning skull staring back at him. It was grotesque and horrible. And, it reminded him of Shakespeare's Yorick, the king's jester—a white sculptured form devoid of flesh and sinew. Its eyes were nothing more than hollow sockets, and its crooked teeth sparkled in the sunlight. They were long and sharp like the teeth of a wolf.

The next thing Cole realized was that Little Flower was screaming, and he was slammed on the brakes, bringing the truck to a screeching and swerving halt, burning rubber in the middle of the road. The Fat Boy, however, carrying the demon with the grotesquely, grinning and fleshless skull, never stopped but raced along the highway and quickly disappeared over the next ridge.

Chapter 29 – buffalo Horse and Rider

"Did you see that?" asked Cole, incredulously. "I had to be hallucinating. I thought I saw . . ." Visibly shaken and annoyed, he turned to Chief Long Wolf and said irritably, "Will you stop that infernal chanting? We were almost killed just now."

"You were not hallucinating, Captain Cole. You saw it with your own eyes; you saw the demon, the Beast, transformed into a deadly human figure. He came to me in a dream last night and he told me that he has escaped from the abyss and he's roaming the earth looking for dead and living souls. He wants to possess and dominate them."

"Oh, grandfather, I'm afraid," Little Flower sobbed, quietly.

Suddenly, Chief Long Wolf became stern and firm with Little Flower. "Do you, Little Flower, have faith in your ancestral gods— the gods of the Sioux—Wakan Tanka, the Great Spirit, and the gods of Wind, Rain, Sky and Earth? Do you?"

"Yes, grandfather, I do." Little Flower was crying and trembling now, and it nearly broke Cole's heart to see the young girl in such distress.

"Then, you have nothing to fear from the Beast, my child," Chief Long Wolf said firmly. "He is powerless! Even a field mouse of little faith is mightier and stronger than him!"

"You must be mad, chief, if you believe that," said Cole. "What you're saying is impossible and defies all logic and reason. Will you explain to me how you could just sit there so calmly, as if nothing had happened? Look at me! I can't even stop myself from shaking."

"I can sit here calmly, Captain, because I have learned what it means to live as one with nature. I have trained myself to recognize what is true and what is false and to accept the harmony of all things in nature and in this world and in the next. I'm sure you would have to agree that there is no point in hitting one's head against a wall or against a rock, is there? We know who will win that contest, right? The wall or the rock will win. The Sioux believe that life and death are one and the same thing. So, why struggle, Captain, against the inevitable? Accept your destiny! Wakan Tanka, the Great Spirit, and the gods of the Earth and the Sky, and the Wind and the Rain, are powerful, supernatural entities—we cannot go against their will."

"I don't believe that," said Cole, and he felt that it was useless to remonstrate or argue logically with anyone who was so entrenched in superstitious beliefs.

"Grandfather, what does the demon want with us? Why was he following us?" said Little Flower nervously, her body trembling.

"The demon has come for me; he wanted to let me know that he was going ahead of me to a place where he will wait for my arrival."

"And then what will happen, grandfather?" asked Little Flower.

"He will kill me and take my spirit into the abyss where there is nothing but eternal darkness."

"No, grandfather! No!" Little Flower cried tearfully.

"Dry your eyes, Little Flower. Do not cry. When I fall from the cradle headlong into the darkness of the abyss, Wakan Tanka, the Great Spirit, who watches over all of us, will send a mighty buffalo horse and rider to rescue me."

"What do you mean?" asked Cole.

Chief Long Wolf looked up at the sky and continued. "I shall know the buffalo horse and rider, my savior, when I see them. I've already seen them in my dreams, so I know what they look like. He will come riding a buffalo horse and his arms and legs will have the claws or talons of an eagle. His buffalo horse will have two curved horns sprouting from its head. Its eyes will glow, a striking yellow and red. And, its nostrils will grow large, while sucking in air and moisture.

"The buffalo horse and rider will courageously enter the abyss and with his sharp talons, the rider will catch my falling spirit. He will guide the buffalo and its mighty wings and he will raise my humble spirit from out of the eternal darkness and chaos of the abyss and into the light. And then, he will deliver me to a dwelling place high atop the mountain of Everlasting Happiness where the Serpent and the Beast will never reach me.

"From the safety of an eagle's nest, dear child, I shall look down upon the world and behold everything in it. I shall delight in its beauty and harmony. I shall watch you, Little Flower, as you grow into a beautiful, well-educated young lady and a woman. Eventually, you shall take your rightful place in the world among your people as a princess of the Sioux Nation. When the time is right, you shall lead our people, and your son shall become the new chief."

Cole felt envious of Chief Long Wolf as he spoke patiently and steadily to Little Flower, reassuring her that everything was going to be all right and that nothing, nothing in this world could hurt her now—not the Demon or the Serpent or the Dragon or the Beast. And Cole felt even more envious of Little Flower because she actually believed it.

When Corporal Buccanon realized that the pickup truck was no longer following him and had come to a stop in the middle of the road, he swung his Road King around and drove back to see what had happened. By then, Little Flower had stopped crying and was sitting quietly next to her grandfather.

As he approached the truck he shouted loudly, "What happened? Is there anything wrong? Why didn't you beep the horn or something, Captain, to let me know you were going to stop? I'll be damned! Did you see the couple on the Low Rider a few minutes ago? They were burning up the road as if the Beast was after them. And how about the rider with the hood on his head! He was driving the Fat Boy! What the hell was that all about? It looked as if he was trying to catch up to them or something. Damn fools!" Corporal Buccanon looked at Cole, Little Flower, and Chief Long Wolf. He thought their faces looked eerily strange and calm, but he sensed that something had happened, something was wrong, something had frightened them. Then, he thought about what he had said—about the Beast and the hooded rider – and suddenly he turned pale.

Chapter 30 - The badlands National Park

by early evening Cole and Corporal Buccanon had turned off the main highway and entered the Badlands National Park, near the towns of Wall and Philip. But instead of heading south toward the parking lots and campsites, and the level grounds and fields where the Sun Dance would be performed, they headed north into the Sacred Black Hills.

They drove north until the road came to an end. Leaving the pickup truck and the Road King, they started out on foot, carrying seven or eight travois poles, deer and buffalo skins, and several packages of food and supplies. Later, they would use the travois poles to build their tepees.

Although Chief Long Wolf had wanted to ascend the Sacred Black Hills alone and select a secluded spot to build his camp and then wait for Wakan Tanka, the Great Spirit, Cole wouldn't have anything to do with it. He scoffed at the idea when the chief said he would rather wait alone for the arrival of Wakan Tanka, the Great Spirit, and that from it, he would receive the words and vision of his death song. Tenaciously, Cole argued with the chief until he finally agreed to let them accompany him to his chosen spot on the Sacred Black Hills.

Slowly and deliberately, like an old Indian scout tracking enemy soldiers through a forest or across the Great Plains, Chief Long Wolf led the way. He led them before towering pines, along flowing streams and dried up gullies. He ascended the hills, climbing rocks and boulders, squeezing through narrow passages. Finally, after little more than an hour, they came to a precipice and a plateau. It was an old campsite atop a desolate sacred hill. From where they stood, they saw, stretching out before them in a view of panoramic majesty, the Sacred Black Hills—a landscape of hills and valleys, red rocks, stones, boulders of granite, and towering Ponderosa Pine trees. These were the same Sacred Black Hills of the ancients, the same Sacred Black Hills that had been stolen from the Sioux Nation years ago.

The tepees went up quickly—two of them: one for Chief Long Wolf and the other for Cole, Corporal Buccanon and Little Flower. While Cole and Corporal Buccanon laid out the travois poles and fastened them with twine and cords, Little Flower unraveled the deer and buffalo skins and stretched them over the poles. She fastened them with a stitch of twine. Then, Cole, Corporal Buccanon, and Little Flower laboriously heaved the poles into an upright position and fanned out the legs until each tepee looked like an upside down ice-cream cone. When everything was completed, Chief Long Wolf entered his tepee and waited . . . and waited . . . and waited.

Chapter 31 – The Prayers and Fasting of an Old Man in the Sacred black Hills

For three days, Chief Long Wolf sat before his tepee and watched the sun rising triumphantly in the morning and setting heart-wrenchingly in the evening. In his solitude, he thought about many things. He thought about his life and his love for the earth, the sky, Grandfather Rock, Wakan Tanka, the Great Spirit, and how they had never diminished in intensity even during the lean and rough years when his life was a boiling cauldron of frustration, desperation, and hardship.

He thought sadly, morosely about Wounded Knee, December 29, 1890, when three hundred and fifty Sioux were massacred by the troops under the command of Colonel James Forsyth. He could see the four Hotchkiss canons opening up and cutting down, indiscriminately, men, women and children. He saw the battlefield, cold and white, under a cloudy, gray sky. He saw the dead—men, women and children—frozen under a blanket of snow; he saw Big Foot, sick with pneumonia, and now long dead; he saw skeletons of tepees standing forlornly in a bleak, haunting landscape of death and destruction.

He thought about the siege of 1973, when members and supporters of the American Indian Movement occupied the Pine Ridge Agency, and how the incident had escalated into a state of siege. He remembered how the dissidents had held out for seventy-one days before two Indians, Frank Clearwater and Buddy Lamont, had been killed, and a federal marshal wounded.

He thought about Running Deer who was now waiting patiently for him on the other side, and Black Hawk and White Cloud, who were so young and had so much to live for but, nevertheless, had died at the hands of poachers.

He thought about Little Flower, his granddaughter—a fragile little girl—who had become the hope and dream of the Sioux Nation. And, finally, he thought about Cole and Corporal Buccanon—how their lives had been forged together as one, all heading down the same path, all heading down the same road to an abyss, to Golgotha, to the tomb. Chief Long Wolf spent the remainder of his time fasting, chanting, meditating, beating the war drum, shaking the rattle, and praying to Wakan Tanka, the Great Spirit, for strength and courage and his death song.

By the late afternoon of the second day of prayers and fasting, Cole got worried when he and Little Flower went to Chief Long Wolf and saw him lying prostrate across the threshold. Cole wanted to run to the old man and give him succor, but Corporal Buccanon held up his hand and said sternly, "No, Captain Cole! Remember what Chief Long Wolf told us! We should not go near him, or talk to him. If we should disturb him now, he might never have another chance to receive his death song."

"I don't care about his death song, he's an old man and he needs our help. We can't just leave him lying there, he may be dying," said Cole fretfully, nervously.

"But that's exactly what we have to do, Captain," said Corporal Buccanon.

"This is absurd! This is madness! I must've been out of my mind when I agreed to this," Cole fretted, and then he added, commandingly, "We've got to do something, now!"

Trembling imperceptibly, Little Flower wedged herself between Cole and Corporal Buccanon as they came around and stood face to face. She was worried about them. She knew that they had been confined together for two long days and nights and could do nothing but sit and wait for Chief Long Wolf to receive his long-awaited vision. She thought that Cole and Corporal Buccanon were like animals that had been locked in a cage and were now getting ready to attack one another. There was no doubt in her young mind that the stress they were feeling was getting to them and was eating away at their nerve-endings, and that wasn't good.

Cole continued reasonably, "The chief is an old man, he shouldn't be fasting—it's foolish and dangerous."

"Starfire said that it wouldn't do him any harm." Corporal Buccanon argued sternly, his dark, cruel eyes boring mercilessly into Cole.

"Starfire!" Cole said incredulously. "Hah! I don't believe Starfire. And besides, who the hell is Starfire? He's nothing but a shaman, a medicine man—a quack!"

"This is the way of the Sioux, Captain. It's their culture, their way of life. You have no right to interfere," Corporal Buccanon said, now more hotly.

"He could be communicating with Wakan Tanka," said Little Flower quietly.

"Look, honey," Cole said softly, tenderly as he knelt down and turned to Little Flower. "Your grandfather is not communicating with Wakan Tanka, but he might be trying to communicate with us—just maybe he's trying to tell us that he needs medical attention." Then, he stood and faced Corporal Buccanon again. "Stay here with them. I'm going back to call the rescue squad." Cole turned and started walking toward the trail when suddenly Corporal Buccanon came up from behind, grabbed him by his shoulder, and spun him around like a top.

"No!" said Corporal Buccanon vehemently, scornfully. "I won't let you destroy this old man's dream. You've destroyed too many dreams already in your life."

Cole turned away again, but before he could take another step, Corporal Buccanon was all over him. They struggled violently, each desperately attempting to overpower the other with brute force. Little Flower tried unsuccessfully to push them apart, crying, "Please stop fighting! Please stop fighting, Captain Cole! Please stop fighting, Corporal Buccanon! Please! Please!"

They all fell to the ground in one big heap of flailing arms, legs and elbows. They rolled across the grassy field, kicking and yelling wildly.

Somehow they managed to scramble to their feet, and Little Flower frantically followed Cole and Corporal Buccanon as they struck and pummeled one another mercilessly. Fists were flying in every direction. Once after Corporal Buccanon fell to the ground, Cole grabbed him by his collar, pulled him to his feet, and threw him bodily, violently, toward the tepee, where he landed against one of the travois poles, nearly collapsing the frail structure. Wiping the blood and sweat from his face, Cole advanced swiftly, like a leopard, toward Corporal Buccanon, who had been momentarily dazed. He wrapped one hand around the corporal's bloodstained collar, and the other he clenched into a fist and raised it high into the air and held it there like a hammer that was about to deliver a crushing blow.

He was prepared to strike the bloody face again when Little Flower stepped in between them and, looking up at Cole with her tear-filled eyes, pleaded in a sweet, angelic voice, "Please, Captain Cole! Please don't hit him again! Please! Please!" And then suddenly, Cole stopped. He loosened his grip and lowering his hand. He looked at Corporal Buccanon scornfully. Once released, Corporal Buccanon fell back against the travois pole and collapsed to the ground like a raggedy scarecrow.

Little Flower ran into the tepee and came out a moment later with a canteen of water and a handkerchief, which she dampened and applied to Corporal Buccanon's battered and bloody face. "You ought to be ashamed of yourselves—two grown men, fighting like schoolboys." And then turning to Cole, "You could have killed him!"

"He doesn't deserve your pity, Little Flower. He's just a miserable, angry person who doesn't know how to move on with his life. He doesn't know how to let go of the past, how to forget, and more importantly, how to forgive. I've had it with him. Once we get help for your grandfather, I'm--." Cole realized that Little Flower was no longer listening to him. She was staring at something, and whatever it was, it changed her face into a radiant light. When he turned to witness what had caught her attention, he saw old chief standing before his tepee, with his arms outstretched and raised toward heaven in supplication. The chief uttered a few words—a chant—and then entered his tepee, again.

The next moment, Little Flower was shouting gleefully at the sight of her grandfather, as Corporal Buccanon staggered to his feet. In the meantime, Cole marched defiantly into Chief Long

Wolf's tepee, disregarding the myths and beliefs of the ancient Sioux, the Cheyenne, and the Arapaho, and saw him sitting comfortably on a buffalo skin and praying to the Great Spirit, Wakan Tanka.

Cole was shocked when he saw the chief's face. It was drawn and weary with pain. He knew the chief was under a great deal of emotional and physical strain, and he was worried that the stress would eventually kill him. Inwardly, Cole was revolted by the idea of the death song, the self-imposed fasting, the Sun Dance, the self-torture, the war dance, and the ghost dance. To Cole it was nothing more than rigmarole and old pagan rites that should have been forgotten and buried long ago. He said firmly, "I think it's time we pack up and go home, Chief—"

"The cradle rocks above an abyss and common sense tells us that our existence is but a brief crack of light between two eternities of darkness," Chief Long Wolf said strangely, eerily. "Thank you, Captain Cole, for being a true friend and for being concerned about the welfare of an old man, but you've heard Starfire, the medicine man. I must communicate with the Great Spirit and receive a vision of my death song." He said this calmly and softly.

Cole frowned and said angrily, "Starfire is not a medicine man. There are no more medicine men. Starfire is a man like you and me, except that he has knowledge of herbs and home remedies. If you continue your fast, old man, you could die. You're too old." And then solemnly, tearfully, "I don't want to see you die, old man. Think about Little Flower and what it will do to her."

Chief Long Wolf smiled at the mention of Little Flower's name. Looking at Cole, he said, "Little Flower is my granddaughter, Captain, and she could fill a home with laughter, warmth, love and tenderness." Then, he paused as if to let these words sink into Cole's head and memory. "She is all I have left in this world, Captain. She is a wonderful little child, a princess, the hope and future of the Sioux Nation. When I am dead and my warrior spirit has entered the great abyss to do battle with the Beast, I shall think fondly of the princess, Captain Cole. And, I shall also be grateful to you and Corporal Buccanon for protecting and guarding her here on earth."

"This is madness. You don't know what you're saying," Cole said sharply.

"I only ask one thing of you, Captain Cole," Chief Long Wolf said firmly, steadily, "that you love her and teach her the culture and ways of the Sioux." And then, more tearfully, "She must never forget who she is or where she came from. She is a Sioux from South Dakota. She comes from the land of Wounded Knee, the land of the magnificent Sacred Black Hills, of Pine Ridge and Rosebud. Teach her about the places and history of her people— Cheyenne River, Standing Rock, Lower Brule, Wolf Creek, Crow Creek, Wovoka, the Indian Messiah, the Sun Dance, the ghost dance, the war dance, and the snake dance. Remind her of Sitting Bull, Kicking Bear, American Horse, Red Cloud, Two Strike, Crow Dog, High Hawk, Plenty Horse, Short Bull, Young-Man-Afraid-of-His-Horse, Big Foot, Yellow Bird, and Starfire. Remind her about Black Hawk, White Cloud, and Running Deer—how much they loved her, and how they would have showered her with love and riches from the gods and from the spirits of the earth and sky, from the Great Spirit, Wakan Tanka, if only they had lived. Tell her that she is not alone, that the spirits of the dead are watching, and that they are happy and some day we shall all be together again."

"These are things that you should tell her," Cole said softly to the chief.

"I have spoken to Little Flower about all these things and much more," Chief Long Wolf said, reassuringly. "But I know that if she were in your care, she would grow up to love and respect life and the world. She would remember her father and mother, and perhaps even her old grandfather chief." Then he raised his voice and said, "I would like you to adopt the child, Captain Cole! Take her to Nashville, and send her to the finest schools and universities. She is very intelligent for her age. She needs a mother and a father, a family, a home, and love - most of all love. Your reward, Captain, will be great." He paused and after a while, he said, "I know Black Hawk would have wanted it that way."

Cole sat back in despair and sadly examined Chief Long Wolf's face and thought that the chief was finally hallucinating, that the want of food and water had gone to his head and that was why he didn't realize what he was saying. Then he said, "Chief, we have to go! Immediately! I have to get you to a doctor before it's too late. I'm sorry, Chief—we have to go!"

"I promise you, Captain Cole, I shall go with you tomorrow. I shall not resist and I shall even visit a doctor if it will make you happy. But I must insist that I remain here this evening for one more moon," Chief Long Wolf said sternly. "I am tired now. Please go. We shall talk again tomorrow." And then with a wave of his hand, he concluded their conversation, dismissed Cole, and having lain down, fell into a deep, sound sleep.

During the night and throughout the next day, Chief Long Wolf tossed and turned in his sleep, as he fell in and out consciousness. So preoccupied was he with his fits, thoughts, and dreams that he heard nothing of the howling wind that had suddenly descended them from the northwest and swept mercilessly, turbulently, through the Sacred Black Hills of South Dakota.

Cole, Corporal Buccanon, and Little Flower rarely ventured out into the windstorm, except to check on the condition of Chief Long Wolf. However, when they saw the chief the next morning, and to what extent his health had deteriorated during the previous night, they had cast aside the Sioux traditions - the vision quest and the death song - and tried to make the old chief eat something so he might regain his strength. Corporal Buccanon was astonished when he heard Cole spouting a stream of curses as he watched Chief Long Wolf lying unconscious and helpless on the buffalo skin while Little Flower attempted, unsuccessfully, to spoon feed her grandfather corn meal.

Cole blamed himself for the chief's weak and life-threatening condition because he had procrastinated when he should've acted. If he had gone for help, as he originally had intended, then Chief Long Wolf might not have fallen so seriously ill. Corporal Buccanon was right, he thought. First, I failed my men on the battlefield in South Vietnam when I led them into an ambush and nearly got everyone killed, and now by acting indecisively, I've jeopardized the life of Chief Long Wolf.

As evening approached, the windstorm howled and screeched furiously like a banshee. Little Flower and Cole did their best to ignore the howling wind, and to concentrate on Chief Long Wolf and his comfort. Every hour or two, the chief would open his weary eyes and search the tepee. When he found Little Flower, sitting next to him, he would smile warmly, and then slowly lower his head and pass out again. Shortly after sunset, Chief Long Wolf suddenly woke up and for a moment he imagined he heard the sound of a beating drum. He wasn't alone—Cole, Corporal Buccanon, and Little Flower had heard it, too. They looked at one another as the eerie sound of the drum intensified.

As it grew louder and louder, Cole envisioned a drummer boy marching toward the tepee, moving closer and closer. With preternatural strength, Chief Long Wolf stirred, pulled himself up to his feet, and tottered to the portal of the tepee. Then, he tossed aside the buffalo skin, exposing the interior of the tepee to the windy elements.

Little Flower shrieked and ran to the side of her grandfather, who had collapsed against a travois pole, and was now staring out into the darkness. Cole and Corporal Buccanon went to the portal and fought desperately against the gale force of the wind to recover the buffalo skin as it flapped furiously. Before they could pull the flap in place over the portal and fasten it to one of the travois poles, Little Flower suddenly shrieked again. Cole looked up and saw three strange figures emerging mysteriously out of the darkness of the night and moving in their direction.

Chapter 32 - Three Ghostly Figures and the Death Song of black Hawk

Chief Long Wolf immediately recognized the three ghostly figures. Black Hawk was standing in the center, wearing a breechcloth, a red bandanna, moccasins, and quill feathers. His eyes were glaringly red and matched his red and black face, which had been painted for war. He was beating a war drum that hung from a strap and which produced a dirgelike rhythm that reminded Cole of a death march. Standing a few steps behind him was his mother, Running Deer, and his wife, White Cloud. His mother was dressed in a radiantly white shawl and his wife was wearing deerskin decorated with a string of beads, quill feathers, and shells.

Over the rhythmic pounding of the war drum and the incessant howling of the wind, Running Deer stepped forward, and wailed a song of lamentation. She cried loudly:

Long Wolf! Take me with you,

Along shimmering roads under the sweltering sun,

Rising like waves in the morning light,

Into the blasting furnace we step,

The door of the abyss has been left open.

A lizard scampers across a rock to some cooling shade,

Look! A Vulture circles overhead among white cumulus clouds,

A prairie dog is running loose,

A grasshopper leaps to safety,

A pocket gopher is burrowing in the sand.

With parched lips I seek water in the dry gully,
And in the valley of death.
Oh, merciful God!
Oh, merciful Wakan Tanka!
Onshimala ye—pity me!

Open flatlands of salt and dust,
Of tumble weed and sagebrush,
With cacti fingers rising in the sun,
And thirst rising in thy throat.

In plunging canyon gorge we rode,
Red, steep, sculptured cliffs and buttes,
Beneath rocks and boulders overhanging,
And the streams and creeks boiling.
A grim and lifeless valley,
Surrendering reluctantly to a sunbaked earth
And storms of sand and dust,
And headstones of settlers and cavalrymen long dead,
And ghost towns and trading posts long forgotten.
Amid the desolation of wasteland,
Beyond Austin and Fort Churchill,
Stood a row of withered yellow wildflowers
Called Rosebud and Pine Ridge and Cheyenne.
Oh, Long Wolf!
Oh, Great Spirit!
Oh, Wakan Tanka!
Where are the tepees and the fine buckskins?
The moccasin leggings and buffalo robes?
The headdresses and war bonnets of thy people?

And then, addressing Black Hawk, Little Flower, and the Sioux nation, White Cloud spoke her song of lamentation, tearfully, mournfully:

Oh Sacred Black Hills—I leave you now, I leave you now my husband—too soon, too soon.

I leave you now my old warrior,
Hunting in the steppe of the Great Plains,

In the valley of the red Grand Canyon,
Riding across the Enchanted Mesa,
Roaming the Sacred Black Hills.

I leave you now my daughter—sweet princess of the Sioux,
Amid the howling wolves and green horn owls,
Oh Wakan Tanka! Have pity on her.
Lead her to the Sacred Black Hills.
I leave you now my nation—Sioux ancient and young,
A warrior princess to strengthen you,
To fight and die for you,
And who shall bear your children.
Oh Wakan Tanka! Have pity on them.
Lead them to the Sacred Black Hills of the Sioux.

And finally, Black Hawk recited his death song, which Chief Long Wolf sadly heard for the first time:
The wind blows strongly,
Over the four points of the earth,
Like the breath of the Great Spirit, Wakan Tanka.
But, I am but a grain of sand,
A teardrop in the ocean of the universe,
Riding the wind.
I am gone, Father.
Swept and washed away - now and forever.
A memory—soon forgotten—even by you.
Who is Black Hawk? Where is thy Son?
Now I am with Grandfather Rock—Eternal Rock of All Ages,
On the Mountain of Everlastingness Happiness I dwell,
On the Mountain of Everlasting Happiness—I am happy and glad.
After the spirits and phantoms of the night had delivered their songs of death and lamentation, they shimmered away, disappearing slowly, like a mirage. A moment later, the beating of the drum ceased, the wailing stopped, and the only sound that could be heard was the banshee of the wind howling furiously, triumphantly in the night. Little Flower was crying quietly and cowering beside her grandfather, who had fallen into another deep sleep.

Cole pulled the buffalo skin back over the portal and held it firmly in place while Corporal Buccanon fastened its ends to the travois pole. It was happening again, he thought—the visions, the appearance of spirits and phantoms, like the Beast and the funeral procession. He desperately wanted to believe that his mind was playing a trick on him, that the things he saw were not real. But when the others had confirmed that they, too, saw the vision, he grew angry with himself because he had no reasonable explanation for the appearance of Black Hawk, White Cloud, and Running Deer. In his mind, he knew the reality of the situation—Black Hawk was dead, yet he saw him standing no more than ten feet away, and he heard the beating of the drum and the chanting of his death song—yes, his death song, not Chief Long Wolf's. Reluctantly, Cole knew that, at this very moment, he could not even trust himself to discern between what was real and what was imaginary.

Cole turned to Corporal Buccanon. "Give me a hand moving the chief." Then, taking the chief by the arms—each taking one side—Cole and Corporal Bucannon dragged his slumbering body gently into the center of the tepee where it was drier and warmer. They covered the chief with a buffalo skin, and then they kept a vigil, alternating the watch every four hours. Cole observed the chief as he slept tumultuously, tossing and turning most of the night.

Later that evening, Cole imagined he saw someone, the Great Spirit, Wakan Tanka, enter the tepee, quietly and surreptitiously, kneel down beside the chief, and whisper something into his ear—perhaps, it was his death song. Then, suddenly, Chief Long Wolf fell into a deep, peaceful sleep. It was as if he knew that Wakan Tanka was near and had whispered in his ear. It was as though he knew instinctively that the deed was done, the lot cast, the ransom paid, and the spell or trance of the Beast had been broken.

Chapter 33 - The Council of Chiefs

The campsites and parking lots were already overflowing with cars, motorcycles, campers, and recreational vehicles by the time Cole, Corporal Buccanon, Chief Long Wolf, and Little Flower arrived at the Sun Dance ceremony. Thousands of visitors and Native American Indians from various tribes were milling about the campgrounds.

As soon as they saw Chief Long Wolf and Little Flower, a crowd gathered around the pickup truck. Chief Long Wolf climbed out of the truck clumsily and shook hands with his many admirers. Chief Joseph, a spokesman for the Council of Chiefs, pushed his way through the crowd and officially, ceremoniously greeted Chief Long Wolf. He advised the chief that he and Little Flower were to spend the night in the comfort of the council's designated headquarters, which turned out to be a large recreational vehicle.

Since many of the chiefs and leaders of the Sioux had arrived the week before the Sun Dance ceremony to get everything ready for the celebration, they were more than a little anxious to get the show on the road. They knew their beloved Chief Long Wolf, who had led their nation for more than fifty years, was old and nearing the end of his path. In fact, they believed that he was tottering on the edge of a precipice and was about to fall into the eternal darkness of an abyss. This was almost certain to happen, of course, unless Wakan Tanka sends the buffalo horse and rider to rescue his spirit. They knew that this might be their last opportunity to see the old chief on this side of the river, and more importantly, they also knew that with the death of Black Hawk, the natural line of succession—determined by blood—would temporarily be broken. The chief would have to select a successor from the ranks of the minor chiefs to follow in his footsteps until Little Flower was of the age to select a husband of her own. He would then become the next chief, and through her their son would continue the bloodline.

Shortly after their arrival, the Council of Chiefs formally greeted and welcomed Chief Long Wolf and Little Flower. After the annunciation and formal salutations had been completed, as prescribed by protocol, Chief Long Wolf strolled through the campsite, surrounded by his council. There was Chief Joseph, a tall, distinguished man of the Oglala tribe, Chief Whirlwind of the Brule tribe, Chief Lazy Bull of the Hunkpapas, Chief Wild Dog of the Miniconjous, Chief Little Cloud of the Sans Arcs, Chief Black Crow of the Two Kettles, and Chief Eagle of the Blackfoots. They walked to an adjacent field where several young braves had pitched a large white tent. They entered the tent and sat in a circle and talked about the activities of the Sun Dance ceremony.

In the meantime, Cole and Corporal Buccanon drove around searching for a spot where they might set up their camp. They came to an area—a clearing in the woods—where the landscape was covered with tepees.

"I guess, this is the place," Corporal Buccanon said cheerfully as the Road King came to a stop alongside the pickup truck.

Cole looked at Corporal Buccanon and suddenly, he found himself struggling to suppress an urge to knock him off his bike and pummel him all over again. He realized that if Little Flower hadn't stopped him when she did, from knocking some sense into Corporal Buccanon's thick head back in the Sacred Black Hills, he would have killed the bastard, and then how would he have explained that to Susan?

They found a spot, unpacked their supplies and pitched their tepees.

On the eve of the Sun Dance ceremony and throughout the long night, Chief Long Wolf met with his chiefs and talked about the future of the Sioux Nation, discussing such issues as land fraud, corruption, exploitation, oppression, extortion, embezzlement, fixing tribal elections, and crime. Then, he met individually with each chief to discuss his own personal vision for the advancement of the Sioux Nation.

Emerging from their discussions with a sense of excitement and anticipation, Chief Long Wolf and the Council of Chiefs left the white tent. They strolled solemnly along a path until they came to a large field where many of the tribes had gathered and had been waiting patiently for their arrival. There in the open field, under the moon and the stars, the chief and his council watched young braves as they performed a version of the Snake Dance. When that was over, the hawks and warriors with painted faces took the center of the field and performed the traditional War Dance.

Chapter 34 – Indian War Dances

A crowd of considerable size had gathered in the clearing to watch the military societies of the Sioux Nation perform their war dances. Cole, Corporal Buccanon, and Little Flower pushed their way to the front of the crowd and in an open field, they saw three dog soldiers from the Cheyenne tribe. They were dancing. Two of the dog soldiers were dressed skimpily, wearing nothing but a breechcloth, a bandanna, and quill feathers. The chief dog soldier was dressed regally, wearing a feathery war bonnet, leggings, a fringed shirt, and moccasins. Their faces had been painted red and black, and they were carrying tomahawks.

As Cole watched the War Dance, he thought he was watching a beautifully choreographed stage show or ballet—the kind of show one might have seen on Broadway with Gina Anderson. The warriors were dancing surreptitiously and cunningly around the campfire that was burning in the middle of the field. A chiaroscuro of light and dark colors flickered across their painted faces. Cole thought the reenactment was hauntingly familiar, especially the scenes depicting the stalking, scalping, and killing of the enemy. He watched with wide eyes as the dog soldiers leaped across the fire and shouted wildly. Despite the pounding of the war drums and the shrieking of the warriors, it seemed to Cole there was something magical and yet horrible about the performance. Suddenly, he realized what it was. The dance was nothing more than a dance of death. When stripped of its integument and choreographed movements, Cole saw its cruelty and brutality. He had never realized it, until that very moment, just how preoccupied the Native American Indians were with death. Death was their constant companion—always standing at their side or shadowing them during the hunt for buffaloes, when raiding a fort, plundering a settlement or a homestead along the frontier or a wagon train heading west or fighting soldiers on the Great Plains. If they had any fear of death, thought Cole, they were hard pressed to show it in their outward appearance. Why, even old Chief Long Wolf had courageously defied and flirted with Death in the Sacred Black Hills—fasting until he eventually received his death song.

When the dance had ended, the crowd clapped furiously and enthusiastically. Six more dances were performed, and after the show, the crowd slowly dispersed and vanished into the darkness of the evening, returning to their tepees, tents, and recreational vehicles. Chief Long Wolf turned to the Council of Chiefs and graciously declined the use of their recreational vehicle. Instead, he returned with Little Flower to his own tepee where he spent the rest of the night meditating and chanting.

Chapter 35 – The Return of the Stranger

Restless and unable to sleep, Cole had quietly returned to the field where the war dance was graphically reenacted earlier in the evening. He wove his way through the pines and stopped abruptly when he noticed a camper was sitting under a tree. The camper was a young man, and when he looked up, Cole felt his heart pound and his pulse begin to race. He recognized the young man as the stranger he had met on the road just outside of Independence, Missouri. What was he doing here? How did he get here? The young man was leaning against the trunk of the tree and reading the Good Book.

When the stranger saw Cole, he raised his voice subtly and read aloud the following passage:

Then I saw an angel come down from heaven, holding in his hand the key to the abyss and a heavy chain. He seized the dragon, the ancient serpent, which is the Devil or Satan, and tied it up for a thousand years and threw it into the abyss, which he locked over it and sealed so that it could no longer lead the nations astray until the thousand years are completed. After this, it is to be released for a short time.

When he had finished, he looked up at Cole and said, "Are you ready to face the dragon, John? Are you prepared for the coming battle as I have warned you? Please, sit down with me for awhile, so I might have a word with you." Cole stepped closer but remained standing, suddenly feeling angry.

"What in the world are you gibbering about? And how did you know my name? I don't know you, and I never saw you before except for that one time on the road in Missouri," Cole said, visibly shaken and surprised.

"Actually, I've known you for ages, my son. Even before the beginning of time."

"Who are you? What exactly do you want from me? And why are you here?" Cole asked suspiciously, thinking that the young man might be nothing more than a hallucination, a mirage, a phantom. Or, it might just be the Beast, playing a bloody, rotten trick on him. He wanted to turn away and run, but he found that he couldn't take his eyes from the stranger, whose voice was calm and soothing.

"'I am the Alpha and the Omega, the beginning and the end.' I am here, John, for the same reason you're here—because you honor the memory of Black Hawk, a friend who saved your life in Vietnam, and because of your love for Little Flower and Chief Long Wolf. As you might have figured out by now, you are inexplicably tied to them. For years now they have been a part of your life and you a part of theirs, though all of you never knew it until now—now that you have answered the call. The Father asked, 'Who should I send? And you answered His call.'"

"I did?" asked Cole. His anger was turning to fury.

"Yes, you answered His call. And like the Lamb that was sacrificed for the sins of man and now sits at the right hand of the Father, you must sacrifice yourself, John."

"I must?" Cole frowned and looked at the stranger who continued speaking with a low, steady voice.

"If you wish to find redemption and salvation in this world and in the next, you must give freely of yourself to those who have been lost to the Beast. Do you want to be saved, my son?"

"From what?" demanded Cole, furiously.

"From the fires of hell," said the stranger.

Cole said nothing.

"You must face the Dragon—the Beast! You've already met him on the road. Of course, he was only playing with you then, trying to scare you. He would like nothing better than for you to turn around and go back to Nashville or New York. He is testing your faith. The next time you should meet with him, however, he'll not be playing with you. He wants something from you John. Two things to be exact. Two things that you currently possess and which he hungers for. Do you know what they might be?"

Cole shook his head. He had several ideas but he wasn't sure.

"Your body and your soul," said the stranger. The young man paused momentarily and with his soft, radiantly blue eyes searched Cole's face. "Of course, the outcome of your struggle with the Beast will depend entirely on you. And, that's how it should be. Moreover, it will be final or eternal."

Cole's face suddenly turned pale and sickly, and the stranger smiled and reflected genuine commiseration.

"But, do not be afraid, Captain Cole, because I believe you are ready for the battle."

"Yeah! I'm ready for the battle! Sure! Like I was ready in Vietnam?" Cole asked sarcastically. "And what about Chief Long Wolf and Little Flower? What will happen to them?"

"Chief Long Wolf has led the Sioux Nation for many years, for more than half a century. He is a good man, one who sacrificed much for his family and his people, working against oppression, hatred, and exploitation. Now, a shepherd will come to lead him home. He will be led to the gloriously promised land of plenty, where the Great Plains are vast, where the buffalo herds are large, where the streams are clean and fresh, and where the harvest of wheat and corn is bountiful."

Cole shivered uncontrollably and the young man smiled and laughed triumphantly, as though he was laughing in the face of death and despair. Then, he rejoiced and said, "The time is close at hand when he will meet all the Sioux chiefs. And I assure you, before this day is through, he will dance the Dance of Peace in the land that had been promised to his ancestors." He smiled and Cole suddenly felt sick and weak. Then the young man said with authority, "Go now and prepare yourself for the battle! The Beast, the Serpent, the Dragon is waiting for you. You're path is set, John. There is nothing you can do to alter your destiny. You have no other choice but to fight and to win the battle and to come home gloriously and triumphantly like a hero. There's much to be done. Many people depend upon you, especially one little girl in particular—a little princess. But, in fact, the future of the entire Sioux Nation depends on you, and on her as well." He sighed and for a moment Cole thought that he sounded like a mere mortal—

one who was extremely tired and exhausted. Finally, he said to Cole, "God Bless you and peace be with you."

Frightened nearly out of his mind, Cole said anxiously, "I am not one of your faithful follower. I've seen too much and heard too much in my short lifetime to think that anything good could come of this." He stepped closer, and sat down opposite the stranger. "It's as though I'm back in the jungles of South Vietnam all over again. We were lost then, you know, frightfully lost, and we couldn't find our way out, we couldn't even get in touch with our commanding officers. We had no artillery or air support. We had nothing! The enemy slaughtered us, mercilessly. Believe me when I tell you, we were lost all right! Damn lost! And that's how I feel right now."

"I know," said the young stranger, and then he smiled.

And, for a moment, Cole felt as if nothing else in the world mattered. All he knew was that the stranger's smile and soft words were like a narcotic, numbing his frayed-nerve endings and alleviating his pain and suffering.

Chapter 36 - Captain Cole's Dream

When Cole left the stranger, he returned to the tepee where Chief Long Wolf and Little Flower were sleeping soundly and deeply, and he watched them for a long time. He thought about Chief Long Wolf and his long, hard life, the death of Black Hawk, and White Cloud, and Running Deer. He thought about Little Flower, who was just beginning her life and has so much to look forward to. Suddenly, he felt distressed and forlorn, and he wished he had never answered Corporal Buccanon's phone call or read Black Hawk's letter—or rather Chief Long Wolf's letter. He felt as if he should have remained in New York City with Gina Anderson, where his life had been mapped out and well defined, and where his emotions for the most part were suppressed and locked away in a special place deep inside of him. Now, as he gazed down at Chief Long Wolf and Little Flower, he felt as though someone had violated that special place where he kept a tight rein on his emotions and had blown the door wide open – right off its hinges.

Then he wept. When he had finished, he returned to the tepee he was sharing with Corporal Buccanon and went to sleep. He dreamed he saw images of Sioux warriors performing a War Dance and American soldiers fighting in the jungles of South Vietnam. Black Hawk was the connecting figure, the common thread, appearing first as a warrior with red and black face, dancing around a campfire, screaming and howling, and then as an American soldier dressed in khaki brown fatigues, carrying Captain Cole to safety and taking a bullet in the back. In a third image, he saw the funeral procession moving slowly along the road in Omaha, Nebraska. Then, the procession stopped, and Black Hawk and Corporal Buccanon appeared, leading three Sioux warriors and three American soldiers to the rear of the hearse. Slowly and ceremoniously, they pulled the casket from the hearse and carried it to a funeral scaffold that had been prepared along the side of the road and was customarily used as a crematorium for Sioux chiefs and warriors. As they placed the casket on the scaffold, Cole could hear the soft voice of the young man from Independence, Missouri, reading from the Bible. He said joyfully, triumphantly, "I am the resurrection and the life, whoever believes in me, even if he dies, will live, and everyone who lives and believes in me, will never die." Then, the funeral scaffold was set afire, and Cole saw himself burning and falling, perpetually falling, deeper and deeper into an abyss. Then there was total darkness.

While Little Flower and Corporal Buccanon were sleeping peacefully, Cole woke up in a river of sweat. He got up, pushed aside the buffalo skin draped across the entrance of the tepee, and watched the sunrise in the east. In the distance, he saw the majestic mountains and watched a bald eagle soaring high in the sky, until it had disappeared behind a ridge of tall pine trees. Then, Cole closed his eyes and prayed earnestly for the strength, courage, and faith to get him through this nightmare.

Chapter 37 - The Sun Dance

by six o'clock in the morning, the Badlands came alive with thousands of Indians and tourists. In one of the great open fields, merchants had erected wooden booths and begun selling their wares, including strings of beads, colorful Indian headdresses, war bonnets in full flower, and tepee coverings bearing pictures of buffalo, elk, antelope, and bear. Several of the booths had been carefully decorated with Sioux shields, buckskin shirts, and Arapaho bead pouches with porcupine quill, buffalo robes, fur hats, necklaces, and calumets. Another merchant was selling Hopi Kachina dolls, the He-e-e Kachina dolls, doeskin paintings, colorful blankets, and paintings of former chiefs of the Sioux Nation. There was Red Cloud, head chief of the Oglala Sioux; Rain-in-the-Face, a famous chief of the Hunkpapa Sioux; War Eagle, a Yankton Sioux. One of the more popular paintings was a portrait of Sitting Bull, the famous Oglala chief, who fought against General George Custer at the Battle of Little Bighorn. And there was Crow, the Sioux chief who started it all with a battle cry and when it was over, the Seventh Cavalry had been wiped out. Graphic battle scenes of both The Battle of Little Bighorn and The Battle of Wounded Knee, where thousands of Indians—men, women and children—had been slaughtered, were also on display. Indians and tourists strolled about the fairgrounds, tasting food and trying on clothes. The smell of sweet cake and corn bread filled the air.

Chief Long Wolf emerged from his tepee in midmorning. He saw the Council of Chiefs patiently waiting for him outside. When he greeted them, the entire entourage surrounded him. Slowly, they made their way to a large tent pitched in the north end of the great field. Beneath the huge white tent, Chief Long Wolf sat down with the chiefs and members of the Sioux tribes. A breakfast of sweet cakes and corn bread and coffee was prepared and served. Cole, Corporal Buccanon, and Little Flower were escorted to the tent and were seated in a prominent location next to the members of the Cheyenne and Arapaho tribes. Cole saw Chief Long Wolf sitting in the middle of the large white table. To his left, he saw Chief Lazy Bull and to his right, Chief Joseph. Chief Joseph was grinning and chatting lively with members from his tribe.

"Look!" said Little Flower, "Chief Joseph is sitting on grandpa's right."

Corporal Buccanon, totally confused, asked, "What does that mean?"

"That means when grandpa dies, Chief Joseph will become the next chief of the Sioux Nation. He will lead our people for many, many years," Little Flower said, wiping tears from her eyes.

"Don't you worry, Little Flower. Grandpa's not going anywhere, not for a long time," said Corporal Buccanon, trying desperately to cheer her up.

After breakfast, Chief Long Wolf and Chief Joseph emerged from the large tent and walked among the crowd, frequently stopping to chat with merchants, tourists, and bikers from Sturgis. When they reached the south end of the field, Chief Long Wolf took a seat on a wooden platform that had been built especially for the ceremony.

Thousands of Indians and tourists had gathered in the field and formed a large circle. They watched in awe and excitement as the Mandans performed the Bull Dance, and then the famous Buffalo Dance. The Choctaws performed the Eagle Dance; the Apaches—The Fire Dance; the Hopis—the Snake Dance; and the Sioux—the traditional War Dance, and finally the celebrated Sun Dance.

The Sun Dance, of course, was the main attraction of the afternoon and would be repeated daily for eight consecutive days. Each of the seven tribes comprising the Sioux Nation would have an opportunity to participate and perform the Sun Dance. When everything was ready, twelve warriors had stepped forward and circled the sacred tree in the middle of the field. Attached to the top of the sacred tree were twelve long cords woven from the tail of horses. As the warriors gracefully approached the sacred tree, each tethered themselves to it by grabbing hold of one of the cords and looming it through slits that had been cut into their shirt. The end of the cord was then tied into a knot.

Suddenly, the sound of music—beating drums and chanting voices—filled the air, and the warriors began to dance and wave their arms, but never moving very far away from they stood. In fact, it appeared to Cole as if they were dancing in place. As they danced, they tugged at the cords connecting them to the sacred tree and scattered feathers into the air. When the cloth of the shirt had had enough, it split open like the flesh of ancient times, but without the blood and gore. Released from the sacred tree, the warriors collapsed to the ground, counterfeiting a trance or a vision. When the last of the warriors sank elegantly, gracefully to mother earth and father rock, the crowd burst into applause, and then everyone joined in the singing and dancing.

Even Cole was swept away by the music, the sound of the beating drums, the chanting voices. He danced wildly, joyfully with Little Flower and Corporal Buccanon, and for a while he lowered the barriers of self-defense that often acts as an inhibitor of civilized men. For a moment, he thought he was truly free—free like the eagle, like the wind and the wild animals. Everything around him contributed to his feeling of freedom, and he rejoiced in it. He loved the feeling of being connected to the earth, of being a part of nature, being a part of this whole mysterious universe and cosmos—and he rejoiced in it and thanked God that he was alive.

Chapter 38 - The Capture of Lame Horse

The following morning, Chief Long Wolf emerged from his tepee and greeted Chief Joseph and his old friend Thunderbird, a Miniconjou medicine man and shaman. Thunderbird was a short man with long, black hair, a large, angular nose, high cheekbones, and piercing black eyes. He greeted Chief Long Wolf anxiously.

"Chief Long Wolf, old friend, Wakan Tanka has blessed you—you are still alive and kicking, and look as though you have the strength of ten horses."

"Ah!" Chief Long Wolf said, pleasantly, cordially, as you would speak to an old friend. "I am old and tired. Soon I will cross the river and Little Flower, my granddaughter, will see to everything."

"Yes," said Thunderbird, nodding to Little Flower. "She is certainly beautiful, and wise like her grandfather." Then he frowned and said, "Chief, I've been hearing things, terrible things about Starfire."

"What about Starfire?" asked Chief Long Wolf.

"I've heard nothing definite, only rumors, you understand."

"What about Starfire?" Chief Long Wolf repeated, firmly.

"I've heard that Lame Horse caught up with Starfire in the Sacred Black Hills, and killed him," Thunderbird whispered, gravely.

Chief Long Wolf sighed sadly and thought about his last meeting with the shaman, and then he said calmly, stolidly to Chief Joseph, "Notify the authorities, and then organize a search party and scour the Sacred Black Hills until you find Starfire and Lame Horse."

Chief Joseph immediately called the Council of Chiefs together, organized a search party and commissioned them to find Starfire and Lame Horse. Later that morning, approximately thirty Indian scouts and hunters dispersed and started combing the sacred hills.

Cole and Corporal Buccanon pondered the situation and decided to return to their earlier campsite and to begin their search from there. As they trudged through the hills, climbing boulders, passing through red canyons, and dense areas of pines and cottonwoods, Corporal Buccanon remarked harshly, "I thought I was through with search missions when I left South Vietnam."

They searched for hours and it was midafternoon when Cole and Corporal Buccanon came upon a small clearing on a plateau and saw Morningstar. She was praying, and chanting mournfully. Lying motionless on the ground before her was Starfire, the medicine man and shaman of the Oglala tribe. He was obviously dead and had been covered up to his neck with a buffalo robe. His face was smeared with paint and blood, yet, Cole thought that Starfire looked as if he was sleeping and hadn't been stabbed seventeen times in the back by Lame Horse.

Morningstar's face and arms were also covered with a red pigment. It was a pigment derived not from some plants found in the forest or from Starfire's wounds, but from her own blood that had gushed forth from self-imposed cuts as she slashed her face and arms with a hunting knife as a sign of mourning.

Cole and Corporal Buccanon approached Starfire and Morningstar nervously, cautiously, and hadn't realized they were in any danger until they saw Lame Horse stepping out from behind one of the pine trees. Lame Horse reminded Cole of the warriors he had seen in the War Dance the night before. He was wearing a breechcloth and a headband with quill feathers, and in his right hand he was holding a tomahawk, which he was waving precariously over his head. He looked angry—his face contorted into a gruesome and ugly mask.

Then, without any further warning—except for the sound of a blood-curdling cry—Lame Horse attacked Cole and Corporal

bones rider he met on the highway. Now, he sank his head into his hands and rolled his head back in despair and frustration, realizing that he loved the old man, and the little girl, and that he would do whatever he had to do in order to prevent anyone or anything from hurting them.

Finally, he fell asleep, and while Corporal Buccanon dreamed about the jungles of Vietnam, and Little Flower dreamed of happier days with her grandfather, Cole returned gloomily and hauntingly to the funeral procession. The procession had stopped, as it had before, and Black Hawk and Corporal Buccanon were leading three Sioux warriors, and three American soldiers. They approached a hearse, which was waiting at the side of the road, and slowly and ceremoniously slid out a casket through its rear door and carried it to a funeral scaffold. They placed the coffin on a platform between four standing posts that had been lavishly decorated with the head and tail of Chief Long Wolf's favorite riding horse. A large group of people, dressed in leather jackets and sunglasses, obviously the HOGs from Sturgis, had gathered behind the young man from Missouri and were listening to him as he read a passage from the apostle John. Then someone with a torch set afire the funeral scaffold.

Cole saw himself and Chief Long Wolf burning and falling freely into the eternal darkness of an abyss. But as he was falling, it seemed to Cole that something was terribly different this time. They were not alone. Cole felt another presence in the abyss as if someone or something was with them. Suddenly, he saw it in all its shapes and forms. First, it appeared as a huge red dragon "with seven heads and ten horns, and on its head were seven diadems." Then, it had become an ancient serpent, moving surreptitiously through the darkness, its huge body coiled like a spring, its tail rattling, its head raised, poised, ready to strike, its tongue slithering in and out of its mouth, and its sharp fangs dripping venom and death. Finally, the Beast appeared "with seven horns and ten heads."

Cole wanted to scream. He wanted to fight the battle, because he thought he was ready, he was prepared, and most of all, he was willing to sacrifice himself if necessary. The one thing he wanted to avoid was another ambush like the one in Vietnam. He was determined this time to be triumphant in battle or to die trying. He struggled to open his mouth, forming the words, but not a sound was heard. Then, he saw a flash of white light and what appeared to be the shape and imagine of a buffalo horse with horns curving and spiraling out from its head and a rider with the claws of an eagle. With clenched teeth, yellow eyes, and flaring red nostrils, the rider and buffalo horse swooped down swiftly, miraculously, like an F-16 fighter. Within an instant, it had captured the spirit of Chief Long Wolf and carried it out from the abyss. With its precious cargo in hand, the rider and buffalo horse flew high above the pine trees and into the light of day where the sun was shining in the heavens, and finally came to rest at the top of a mountain—the Mountain of Everlasting Happiness.

Then, Cole saw another vision. He saw himself running ahead of another and coming to an empty tomb that was carved out of a rock. The boulder, which sat before the tomb, had been pushed aside. Then the other one arrived. It was the apostle Peter. "He bent down and saw the burial cloths there, and the cloth that had covered his head, not with the burial cloths but rolled in a separate place. Then the other disciple also went in . . . and he saw and believed."

Cole imagined that he saw Jesus in a place called Gethsemane, and he felt his sorrow and distress. He heard Jesus say, "My soul is sorrowful even to death," and, "My Father, if it is possible, let this cup pass from me." But then, something happened inside of him and he felt as if suddenly his faith had been strengthened when he heard Jesus say, "Yet, not as I will, but as you will."

Cole realized at that moment that what had saved Chief Long Wolf's spirit from the Beast and the eternal darkness of the abyss was not the buffalo horse and rider, but his faith in Wakan Tanka, the Great Spirit, and in Grandfather Rock. He felt as though he had just stepped into the tomb, saw the burial cloth rolled up and in a separate place, and realized that Jesus had risen from the dead and that death and the Beast no longer had any power over him. He felt his heart fill with the burning news of this rediscovered knowledge, and he wanted to run and spread the word to all he met along the countryside and in villages, towns, and cities.

It seemed to Cole that his faith, which centered on the light and resurrection of Jesus and which Father McFarland had preached in Nashville, had now been demonstrated poignantly, unmistakably by Chief Long Wolf, Black Hawk, and even Corporal Buccanon. And from everything else that had taken place on the road—meeting the young man from Independence, Missouri, and confronting the Beast—Cole felt that his faith was alive once again, that it had been rekindled by this strangely unfolding nightmare.

He understood wearily that like Jesus and Simon, who were pressed to carry the cross through the street of Jerusalem to Golgotha, the place of the skull, every man must carry his cross in life. No one is exempt and no one can bribe another to carry it for him. It is something from which you cannot escape. You are born into it! You must carry it alone! Some carry it quietly and meekly to their graves, while others carry it proudly, ostentatiously. There are times when the cross is invisible and you do not realize that you are carrying it. But, nevertheless, it is there on your back. Then, at other times, it shall weigh heavily upon your shoulders and the weight of it shall crush you. And, you shall trudge grudgingly through the streets until you reach Golgotha where you shall collapse to the ground. And then, when it is time, they shall strip you, lay you on the wood, and drive the nails through your hands and feet.

Golgotha is everywhere, along every highway and byway - in the valleys, along riverbeds and streams, at the top of lofty mountains, at the bottom of red canyons, and along the Mississippi River. One can find it on the banks of the Great Lakes, down in the bayou, on the Great Plains, along the coastline, in lonely hospital rooms, in crowded and noisy emergency rooms and nursing homes—where there is life, there is a place called Golgotha.

Cole was convinced, however, that if there was anything good that might come out from this dreadful experience which we call life, it was the idea that there was someone like Jesus waiting for you at the end of the path. And, all you needed was faith and hope in Jesus to get you there.

The light of Jesus that radiated brightly from the tired eyes of Chief Long Wolf had fallen upon Cole and pierced his armor of

self-defense like an arrow passing through the air. It had touched
his very soul and spirit. Suddenly, Cole found himself facing the
light and he realized he was on the path of redemption and
salvation.

No one knew exactly when it happened, but at some moment
in the middle of the night, while everyone was asleep and
dreaming, Chief Long Wolf tried to sit up but had collapsed. He
had wanted to speak to Little Flower and tell her that he loved her
and that she would be all right with Captain Cole and Corporal
Buccanon, but instead, the young man from Missouri was
standing before him. He approached the chief and gently caressed
his face. In a low, inaudible voice, Chief Long Wolf whispered his
death song:

I am here, Great Spirit,
Great Wakan Tanka,
Onshimala ye—pity me,
I am alone.

I am not afraid to die.
With body and soul,
I embrace the eternal darkness.
I am in harmony with mother earth and grandfather rock.

Like the rock I shall become,
The rock that never dies,
But lasts forever.

The cradle rocks above an abyss,
And into eternal darkness,
Of an abyss,
I shall descend.

I lay upon the burning scaffold,
Falling to the Beast's abode.
All the mysteries of life will unfold,
Falling to Beast's abode.

Like warriors of old I shall fight,
With painted face gruesome and bright,

be all right, that no matter what happens here on earth in this life, in the end everything would work out fine.

"And then I saw a young man in a long white robe. A crowd of people had gathered around him and he was writing something with his finger in dirt. When he looked up, I saw his face and recognized him. It was the young man from Independence, Missouri. It was the stranger! By God! It was the stranger, again! Several villagers came up to him and pointed to a woman who had been standing alone and opposite the crowd and who apparently had sinned. They wanted to stone her because she was a prostitute. The elders and religious of the village told the young man that she had to be stoned to death—that that was the law. And as he continued to trace in the dirt, he said simply, 'Let he who is without sin cast the first stone.' And then slowly the crowd dispersed one by one. Now left alone, the young man turned to the woman and said, 'See, where are all your accusers? There is no one here to condemn you and I do not condemn you either. Go and sin no more.'

"And that's when everything I had believed and thought was true for so many years simply fell apart for me—right at that moment. And all the bitter feelings I had about the war in Nam, how it turned out, the wasted lives—all of the hatred bottled up inside of me—was swept away. There was nothing left. And I thought, 'What a damn fool I've been for all these years.'"

Then he wept remorsefully and afterwards he said, "I'm sorry Captain. I knew in my heart that you did your best in Nam. I had known for a long time that there was nothing you could have done to prevent the ambush from happening. It's just unfortunate so many fine young marines had to die," and then after pausing thoughtfully, "You know, Captain, when I get back east, I'm going to the Wall – the Vietnam Veterans Memorial Wall - in Washington, DC. I've never been there. I've never been to the Wall—after all these years. But I'm going now, I want to see the Wall and run my fingers across their names."

"We'll go together," said Cole.

"Yes, we'll go together, Captain." He said this with renewed pride and friendship in his voice.

And as they sat together in the tepee, quietly gazing at the corpse of Chief Long Wolf and waiting for the arrival of Chief

Joseph, they both realized that they had finally made peace with one another.

Chapter 41 - The Return of Moose Mulligan and the HOGS

When Little Flower returned to her grandfather's tepee with Chief Joseph and the Council of Chiefs, a crowd had gathered outside. Moose Mulligan and his wife, Barbara, who had come to the Sacred Black Hills to witness the Sun Dance, saw the crowd and casually sauntered over to see what might be the cause of all the excitement.

"I say, Barbara, aren't they the young men we saw outside of Tekaman—the ones who had an accident and were stranded on the side of the road?" asked Moose as he waved to Cole and Corporal Buccanon.

"Yes, I do believe they are," said Barbara Mulligan.

Moose wove his way through the crowd until he came up to Cole and slapped him on the back, warmly, firmly. Informed that Chief Long Wolf had died during the night, Moose entered the tepee and examined the chief's body. A few minutes later, he reappeared, shaking his head mournfully. He said, "He died in his sleep, very naturally it seems. His heart probably just gave up. I'm sorry."

Little Flower ran into the tepee, clung to the corpse of her grandfather, and wept grievously, loudly because her grandfather meant everything to her. She could not imagine living alone without him. He was the chief of the Sioux Nation and he was always there for her. Now, Wakan Tanka had taken him away. He had fallen into the eternal darkness of the abyss, and she prayed earnestly that the buffalo horse and rider with eagle claws had been there to carry his spirit to the Mountain of Everlasting

Happiness. A long time passed before Little Flower could smile or laugh again. Although Cole and Corporal Buccanon tried to lift her spirits, they knew that only time would heal her broken heart.

Before returning for the final run of the Harley-Davidson races at Sturgis, Moose turned to Cole. He said quietly so no one but Cole might hear him, "Captain, last night, while Barbara and I were camping out in the field just south of here, we ran into a few of our friends. Although they had been drinking, they had their wits about them. Well, anyway, they said they saw Chief Long Wolf walking through the woods late last night with a young man. They said that they looked rather ghostly, like a mirage, something transparent—if you know what I mean. They said there was some kind of strange bird - it might have been an eagle - following them. They heard the sound of its wings fluttering in the air and when they looked up into the dark sky, they saw it soaring overhead. My friends cried out to the chief, but he never turned around. He just kept on walking. And then, the chief and his walking companion disappeared into the darkness."

Part VI—Wolf Creek, South Dakota

Chapter 42 - A Farewell to Chief Long Wolf

Cole and Corporal Buccanon made arrangements to transport the body of Chief Long Wolf back to Wolf Creek, where the people of the town witnessed a funeral like no other in the town's history. First, when the news of Chief Long Wolf's death and funeral arrangements had been posted in the newspapers and made public, thousands of Indians and visitors throughout the Great Plains, the Southwest, and the Northwest converged on the sleepy little town. Nearly every motel room and popular bed-and-breakfast establishments was sold out. Everyone that was still living and whom had come to know, love, and revere the chief, flocked to his funeral. Old Ben Hancock and his sons, Theodore and Charlie, of Hancock and Sons Funeral Home worked feverishly to accommodate the unexpected crowds, renting additional folding chairs and printing at least a thousand extra prayer cards. Secondly, the people of Wolf Creek felt extremely honored and pleased that Chief Joseph and the entire Council of Chiefs had come to visit their town and pay homage to their beloved Chief Long Wolf.

As Cole occupied himself with details of the funeral, Little Flower sat languidly staring into space, as though the stuffing of life had been kicked out of her. Her wet, moist, soft eyes never strayed from the visage of her grandfather as he lay in his coffin. He was dressed splendidly in full regalia, and whenever she looked away, it was only for a moment to lower her head and dab at the corner of her red, bloodshot eyes with Cole's handkerchief.

Friends and acquaintances approached the coffin, kneeled, recited a few prayers inaudibly, and then went to Little Flower, who sat stolidly in the front row. They said, "Poor child. Wakan Tanka, the Great Spirit, is with you. Chief Long Wolf is like grandfather rock now. He has crossed the river . . . he is on the other side . . . the buffalo horse and rider with eagle claws has rescued his spirit from the eternal darkness of the abyss. His spirit now lives on the Mountain of Everlasting Happiness. Cheer up! Cheer up, child! All is not lost!"

Early the next morning, Chief Joseph, the Council of Chiefs and a small group of acquaintances met at the funeral home to pay their last respects. After a brief ceremony and a few prayers, everyone rushed to their cars while Ben Hancock and his sons went to work closing and sealing the coffin and wheeling it out to the hearse waiting out front. At the church, Father Good-Horse-Trader waited patiently for the funeral procession. When it finally arrived, the pallbearers quickly wheeled the coffin into the small church where the priest and the friends and family of Chief Long Wolf celebrated a mass. Walking behind the coffin down the center aisle of the church, Little Flower trembled, pitiably. And although Cole and Corporal Buccanon never left her side—not even for a moment—Little Flower hardly noticed them.

The wind was blowing gently across the land and through the cemetery in late August as Father Good-Horse-Trader said a closing prayer, made the sign of the cross over the coffin containing Chief Long Wolf's body, and then reluctantly ended the service. The small group dispersed slowly, returning to their cars. Several of the mourners had stopped to chat with one another and, looking back at Little Flower, who was still standing at the foot of her grandfather's grave, shook their heads sadly, and whispered among themselves. Satisfied that there was nothing more to see or do, they slowly slid into their cars and drove back to town.

Little Flower was now left alone with Cole and Corporal Buccanon, and silently, forlornly, they watched the groundskeepers struggling laboriously to lower the coffin into the ground. Finally, Cole turned to Little Flower and said softly, "I think it's time we should be going, dear." And then Little Flower withdrew quietly, calmly and went back to Wolf Creek with Cole and Corporal Buccanon.

In the ensuing weeks and months, Cole's legal mind was put to work transferring the land, the deed of the house, and the accounts of small monetary value, representing the bulk of Chief Long Wolf and Running Deer's estate, to Little Flower. Of course, everything would go into a trust until Little Flower turned eighteen.

After it was all over, Cole thought for a long time about his life and realized that it was nothing more than an empty shell. A shell that he had flaunted with his fame as the lead prosecutor in the state of New York. If he dared to let anyone get close enough, he was afraid they would see through his shell and uncover his charade. Gina Anderson and her father were part of that charade. With knowledge of the law, and with Gina clutching his arm and her father opening political doors, there was no stopping him if he wanted such a life. And for a long time he had deceived himself into believing that he did want that kind of life. That is, until now. When Corporal Buccanon had phoned him several weeks ago and told him about Black Hawk, he knew innately that his life was about to change forever. Returning home to his ancestral farm in Tennessee, seeing his mother and father, and Susan and Corporal Buccanon, and even Father McFarland, after an absence of fifteen or more years, was a shock that made him wonder about the life he had left behind when he went to New York. He thought about his Harley, racing along the highway with Corporal Buccanon, and the funeral procession where he saw spectral ghosts of his Aunt Lucille, Mr. DeForest, his high school English teacher, his buddies Donald and Danny Wu, Bobby Canary, and Benny Saltzman. They were all there along with Jake Snow and his mother and father. He tried to visualize in his mind the driver of the hearse and Mr. Johnson before he had turned into the Beast. And, then there was the stranger who was sitting under the tree and was watching Cole and Corporal Buccanon, as they fought with one another in the dirt like schoolboys. He remembered Corporal Buccanon's tale about the raven that had attacked him in the cornfield. There was Chief Long Wolf who deceived him by writing a letter to Cole and Corporal Buccanon and signing it with his son's name. His son who was dead – killed by poachers. He remembered how Black Hawk and Corporal Buccanon had saved his life during the war. He would never be able to pay them back in full. There was White Cloud and Running Deer who meant so much to Black Hawk and Chief Long Wolf. He knew now that Chief Long Wolf was indeed the chief of the Sioux Nation and he was a brave chief and a good man. He had come to love this old man. And, then there was Little Flower. It occurred to Cole that everything that had happened in his life thus far had one purpose and one purpose only and that was to bring him to Little Flower. He realized that his life was intertwined with Little Flower's and that everything that had occurred had happened so that he might fulfill his destiny with her. And, he asked himself what was that destiny? She was after all, the daughter of Black Hawk and White Cloud, the granddaughter of Chief Long Wolf and Running Deer. She was a genuine princess by blood and one day she shall lead the entire Sioux Nation – her and her husband, and her child, the future chief by blood of the entire Sioux Nation.

It was with this line of reasoning that Cole had finally decided that Little Flower should return with him and Corporal Buccanon to Nashville. Back in Nashville, she could start a new life, make new friends, and meet many new people. And besides, Theresa, William, Jake, and Susan would be there. He knew instinctively that they would love her and would look after her when he wasn't around. And he made a promise to himself that that won't be for long, because he was already thinking about giving up his law practice in New York, and returning permanently to Nashville.

Little Flower, of course, adamantly refused to leave her grandfather's house, and for days she argued and cried bitterly with Cole and Corporal Buccanon. Then, after several weeks, she finally agreed to go—but only after Cole had promised that every summer, she could return to Wolf Creek, South Dakota, to visit her grandfather's home, which she had inherited. Also, she would visit his graveside and the gravesides of her grandmother, Running Deer, her father, Black Hawk, and her mother, White Cloud, and attend the annual Sun Dance ceremony in the Sacred Black Hills.

And after many years had passed, when she was much older and had a family of her own, she frequently thought about those bittersweet days in South Dakota. She never forgot the spirit of her grandfather, Chief Long Wolf, chief of the Sioux Nation, and how she had climbed onto Cole's Softail wrapping her arms tightly around his waist and pressing her face against his strong back as he drove away with Corporal Buccanon. She had looked back to see the great Sacred Black Hills—she saw the Mountain of Everlasting Happiness and what appeared to be the specter of the spirit of her grandfather. She waved good-bye, her eyes filled with tears, and then she looked up and saw an eagle soaring high overhead. It had followed them for some distance before disappearing behind some tall pine trees, and the wind had blown through her long, black, glistening hair, like a comb, pushing it back, back, back toward the land of the Sioux.

THE END

About the Author

Anthony A. Policastro has a dual degree in Business Administration/Economics and English from Rutgers - The State University of New Jersey.

In 1999, he received The Ruth Fryer Memorial Award for academic excellence in creative writing from Rutgers University – University College Newark.